# TROUBLE
# ON THE
# ICE

K Patteson

# Other works by K. Patteson

*Ross and Jack Series*
Trouble On The Water

*Individual Books*
Ghost Island

To Ben.
You are my Jack.  Quiet and steady, there when I need you.
If I ever fall, I know you will be there to catch me.


Also to Amy.
My Sam.  The one who can talk me into doing
stupid stuff I have never regretted. If I live to a hundred,
as long as I have you, I will never feel older than fourteen.

# 1

Pedro sat calmly on the bare floor next to the window with his long legs stretched out in front of him, hands calmly folded in his lap. Not a stick of furniture was present in the barren room. No sound but the ticking of his watch and some noises from the street below. It was a tranquil scene except for the long rifle mounted on a tripod next to him. It faced out the window to the apartment next door. Anyone who dared to look would have seen it, but Pedro wasn't worried about that. He had been trained to hide in plain sight. He knew how infrequently people looked up.

With his large brown eyes and deceptive smile, you would be fooled into thinking Pedro had nothing to do with the gun. That somehow he and the gun were in the same room by accident. In truth, Pedro and the gun were almost one. While trained in several methods of killing, Pedro was an exceptional sniper. So, sitting alone in a room or on a rooftop and picking his victim off while they walked down a crowded street was rather the norm for him. He wasn't sure why he wasn't better at killing up close (though he could get the job done). It always ended up a little sloppy. Long distance killings though, he could shoot the person clean through the eye and be in the next town before the police figured out the angle of the bullet.

Looking casually out the window, he took note of the sun's descent in the sky. Pedro's eyes fell to the window across the alley. He had set up the rifle where it needed to be, now all he had to do was wait for his victim to appear. The client had insisted he be in position well in advance. They wanted this done cleanly. No rushing. Pedro couldn't blame them for wanting it done well. It was their father after all, and while he had no such parental attachments, over the years he had gotten the impression people felt strongly about parents. Normal people that was. Not Spartans.

While Pedro looked all the world like a human, he lacked what made humans so...*human*. Emotions. He felt no fear, no love, no sadness, no joy, and little pain. All of these had been great qualities when he and the other Spartans were military machines. Designed for war and raised in a laboratory, they were intended to replace regular soldiers. The soldiers with families, who were affected by the deaths of their comrades in arms would be given administrative duties. Spartans would do the fighting, the killing and the dying. It was literally what they had been designed for. Purchased from their maker by the US military, they had been deployed and then returned.

Pedro probably shouldn't have been surprised that they were returned. It was clear that they made the regular soldiers uncomfortable. A lot of Spartans had a hard time reading human emotions. Pedro had started out that way, but was rather good at it now. He had known something was up by the way everyone had reacted when he had shot that prisoner pointblank as the man pleaded for his life. They had been in the middle of the desert with few supplies to spare and the man was injured. Taking a prisoner would have jeopardized the unit. There had been talk of a court marshall, but the commanding officer, who was the only other person in the unit who knew Spartans had been mixed in with the regular soldiers, had covered it up. Now, the Spartans were expired military equipment who had found a way to make a living by taking advantage of their unique skills. Murder for hire.

He checked the scope one more time to make sure it was aimed correctly before leaning back again. These were his hunting grounds. Being darker skinned, he had been able to move around the Middle East with ease. Once the world discovered Spartans existed, there had been more work than he could handle. He had brought a few of the other darker skinned Spartans back with him to meet demand, but attention had been too hot. The more civilized nations were looking for them, and the reward for catching a Spartan made it too dangerous to operate, so they had ultimately decided to go underground. It had been a year since Ikan Hui though, and things seemed to have settled down enough for them to go back to work. So here he sat. Waiting for his kill to sit down to dinner.

There were not many Spartans left. As you would imagine, given their lifestyle, a few had been lost along the way. After their "parent company" Genetix was dismantled, there wouldn't be any future generations of Spartans either. Pedro and the others had watched for the first few weeks after Ikan Hui while Genetix was torn to shreds. Mother had taken the easy way out and killed herself, Father had not been so lucky. While Pedro thought Father had carried himself with as much dignity as he could have managed, and while most of the evidence pointed to Mother as the main architect, Father had been the only one left to carry the blame. His career over, all his scientific work ruined, Pedro heard Father had reached out to one of the other Spartans to kill him. Father didn't want to know when or where it was going to happen. Pedro wasn't sure who he had approached, but he would have done it and given father a discount. Father had always treated them with respect. Mother had not.

There was movement in the apartment across the alley, and Pedro slowly sat up. The target today was the patriarch of the family. It was the daughter who had approached Pedro. The old man was a millionaire several times over. Unfortunately for him, he had decided to make his children fend for themselves and make their own way in the world until they inherited at his death. They had decided to expedite things a little. Pedro watched as there was general movement from the apartment across the street. He looked at his watch, dinner was supposed to kick off at seven, it was five til.

Pedro checked the scope. They were supposed to put the old man at the head of the table, which would put the old man's back to Pedro and give Pedro a perfect shot. A woman passed the window and acted as if she were going to sit down before the daughter grabbed her arm and moved her down a chair.

Pedro laid on his stomach and got himself ready. He settled the butt of the rifle on his shoulder, found the crosshairs, and patiently waited for his target to appear. The daughter said she wanted it to be a surprise, "Maybe wait until they are halfway through dinner. I want my reaction to be genuine."

Pedro was pretty sure it was going to be a surprise to the old man no matter when he did it.

The daughter smiled and pulled out the chair for her father. An older man with white beard came into view and smiled at his daughter and the person across from him, then sat down in the chair in front of the window. Pedro tried to take aim, but the man's head was moving around as he greeted and talked to the people around him. This didn't upset Pedro, Spartans didn't get upset. Pedro would simply wait until the old man sat still for a second.

Eventually, the food arrived, and everyone settled

down. Pedro took a deep breath. The old man took a bite of food and held still. Pedro got the spot he wanted in the crosshairs and pulled the trigger. Almost immediately, blood splattered on the now cracked window. He waited a moment and checked to make sure the old man was down. Pedro would not leave until he was sure the old man was dead. Spartan training. The old man was laying face first on the table, a steady stream of blood leaking across the white tablecloth. There had been a split second of silence and then prolific screaming.

The calmness with which he moved belied the chaos taking place in the apartment across the street. While women screamed and checked in vain to see if the old man was still alive, Pedro packed up his gun. Without another glance at his victim, he dismantled the gun into four pieces. Unscrewing one piece from the other. Broken down, he placed the rifle in a soft sided case. The case went over his shoulders like a backpack. He then donned his Thawb (traditional robes) and his red and white head scarf. The long robes easily hid the gun case. Only two minutes had passed since the lethal shot was fired. It would not occur to anyone to look and see where the bullet had come from for another minute and a half.

As calm as if he was going out for evening prayer, Pedro left the apartment and calmly descended the stairs into the street. The wailing from the women in the apartment where his victim lay could be heard on the street below. People on the street had stopped and were looking up to see what the noise was about. Pedro stopped and looked with the others for a moment. It may be noticed if he didn't, and part of the Spartan training was to blend into their surroundings. After seeming to give the right amount of curiosity, Pedro continued on his way back to Spartan base camp. As he turned the corner from the side alley between buildings and onto the main road, Pedro heard the sirens of the emergency vehicles starting to make their way through the streets. Hitting the main road, Pedro soon became invisible in the crowd of the other people walking the street, most of whom looked exactly like him. In an instant, Pedro blended in with the other bearded men busily making their way home. His phone rang.

"Marhaban sadiqi." *Hello my friend.* Pedro answered.

"Are you on your way back?"

"Yes."

"We have a job offer.  A big one."

"I'll be right there."

# 2

Lillian got off the bus at the end of the high street and turned left down Little Park Drive. She was smartly dressed in designer slacks, her Burberry raincoat cinched tightly around her small waist. Her Dolce and Gabbana handbag was filled with papers from work slung over her shoulder. Once off the high street, it was a short walk to her house with its bright blue front gate. The gate had been blue when she bought the house and in no way matched her personality, but she had liked it nonetheless and hadn't the heart to paint it another, more reasonable, color. Her stomach was growling, and she had spent most of the bus ride from the university taking a mental inventory of her fridge in an attempt to figure out what to have for dinner. The blue gate made a welcoming squeak as it opened. It was better than a guard dog, nothing got past the squeaking gate. Taking the last few steps from her blue gate to her front door, Lillain dug out her house keys and unlocked the door. It was a small house, but it suited her. She had only bought the house in Cambridgeshire two years ago after working at the university for ten years.

As was her habit, Lillian took her purse off and hung it on the hook in the hall. One arm was out of her raincoat when she smelled it. Prima cigarettes, a Russian brand she recognized because her grandfather had smoked them. For a moment she was confused. Had she entered the wrong house? Lillian looked around her. This was her front door, her hall tree.

"Please, come in." A low voice said from her sitting room. The voice spoke Russian, a language she had refused to speak since she left. Lillian didn't move, did not reply. She thought about grabbing her purse and running, but she didn't. If she ran, she could never come back. A knot formed in her stomach as cold chilled her veins. They had found her. Slowly taking her coat off the rest of the way, Lillian carefully hung it up and followed the trail of cigarette smoke into the sitting room.

Even knowing he was there, it was still a shock to see

him.  His tall frame folded in half in the lounge chair she had bought because it reminded her of the one her grandmother had in her sitting room.  He had helped himself to her scotch, the glass hanging loosely between his thumb and finger.  The other hand held the cigarette that had given his presence away.  This annoyed her. She didn't smoke, didn't  like the smell of smoke, and now that lingering smell would be a constant reminder that she could not outrun her past. Without being obvious, Lillian looked around for clues as to how the bastard got in.

"I hope you don't mind, I let myself in."  He said in his low, slow voice.  He made it sound like he was there for dinner with a relative.  It annoyed Lillian even more than the smoking.  The bloody arrogance.

"What do you want?"  She answered in Russian.  She had not heard herself speak Russian in so long, it sounded strange.  Lillian knew who he was. He was well known in Russia for causing  people to run off the roofs of tall buildings.  The name Alexi Stanovich was synonymous with death, and with good reason. As far as she knew, he never did the deed himself, but death was never far behind him. To top it all off, he looked the part.  Tall and thin with a long face that showed little to no emotion. Give him a black cloak, and he was the living embodiment of the grim reaper.

They had met before. It was possible he was there to finally punish her for leaving Russia, but she knew as well as he did that there were ways of killing her that didn't leave fingerprints on her scotch glasses and the smell of Russian cigarettes in her curtains.

"Your government needs your help." He did not look at her, just stared out the window.

"I didn't realize you were working for the British government now." She said with more courage than she felt. He took a drag on the cigarette and one side of his mouth curled into a half smile.

"Pretend all you like, but Russian blood flows through you." They always did this. To love Russia was to love the ones who ruled her. To deny the ones in charge was to turn your back on Mother Russia.

"Why are you here?" Lillian sounded annoyed.

"I need information." Lillian slowly collapsed onto the arm of her couch. So he wasn't here to kill her. He needed something.

"What kind of information?"

"You are going on a research trip this summer, yes?"

"Yes."

"I would like to know what the research is about, who else is going, and any details about the ship you can provide." It was too simple.

"What possible interest could this trip be to you?"

"It is of interest. The rest does not concern you." Lillian knew what the object of the trip was, and she suspected she knew why this particular research trip was of interest. Ocean that had been covered in ice and never before available to humans, were now melting. Leaving minerals and oil resources available for the first time in man's history. The Russian government had made a game of getting into these areas and removing what resources they could before anyone had a chance to regulate them. They had been showing interest in the shipping lanes opened in the Arctic since it was clear the ice was melting. It was even rumored they had put flags on the ocean floor to claim the area for themselves. Lillian was a little surprised and disappointed they even knew the trip was happening.

"I'm afraid I can not help you. I did not go through the great pains and personal sacrifice of leaving Russia just to be forced into this kind of work again. Please leave." The tall man lifted an eyebrow and finished his drink.

"That is, of course, your right." Lillian sat on her hands to keep them from shaking. Tonight might be the night she died. In theory, she was okay with this. Better to die than do what they asked. At least she would die with her dignity. In truth, she was petrified. He slowly and carefully folded away the travel ashtray that had been sitting on his knee. Standing, he placed it in his pocket. "I can not say that we are not disappointed in your answer, but it is understandable." There was no way it was going to be this easy. There was no way that she would refuse him and he would just leave. There was no way they sent a top official all the way here when they knew there was a good chance she was going to refuse. Lillian sat waiting for the hammer to fall.

"It is a shame really, if you had been able to do this for us, we were willing to lift the bounty on you. You would have been able to return to Russia without fear." He slowly and carefully buttoned his overcoat and came to stand in front of her, so that she had to tilt her head as far back as it would go to meet his eyes. He pulled gloves out of his pocket and started putting them on. "As it is, I will not be able to lift that bounty, and you will not be able to attend your parents'

15

funerals." Cold ran through Lillian.

"My parents aren't dead."

"Oh, but they will be. By the time I reach my dinner reservation this evening. Such a shame to lose them both at once. May I be the first to give you my condolences." Lillian wasn't sure she was understanding him. The smile on his face did not match what he was saying.

"They aren't dead yet?"

"No my dear. But unless I send word," he paused to look at his watch, "and soon. They will be." Lillian couldn't think. It was one thing to kill her, but her parents? Lillian pictured her parents. In her mind's eye her mother was always in the kitchen. An apron covering her small frame. The woman seemed to cook constantly but never sat down to enjoy the food she made. Despite having very little when she was growing up, they never went hungry.

Then she thought of her father. When Lillian thought of him, he was in one of two places. Sitting in his chair, as tired and worn out as the man himself, reading his paper. Or he would be in the garden. More than once they had gotten by on the food he had miraculously grown in their small back garden. They would have no idea that their lives were in danger. That somewhere near their house right now was someone who was going to harm them. Hell, her mother would probably invite them in. Offer them tea. Would it be quick? A bullet to the head? Poison? Or would they have an unfortunate accident like so many who opposed the government? Would they try to get Lillian to change her mind by torturing them? Lillian knew better than most that these were real possibilities. Looking back at Stanovich, she thought about asking but knew it would make no difference. Lillian felt her lip quiver. She couldn't do it. She couldn't let it happen.

She whispered "I'll do it." His mouth curled into a smile again.

"Excellent. Is there anything I can pass along that would make us feel more secure in your cooperation?"

"I honestly don't know a lot about it. As far as I know, there are a handful of researchers coming, but I don't know who they are yet. I was contacted by Dr. Nils Ryeng about it a few months ago. He's concerned about the ice melting that far north, so he wants to get an idea of the environmental impacts. But I'm sure you know all that or you wouldn't be here."

"Thank you. That wasn't so hard now, was it?"

"Are my parents safe?"

"They will be monitored. Should your courage falter, should we find out you have taken steps to keep the trip from happening, we will take measures."

"Why not just kill me?"

"Tsk, tsk, my dear. Then you wouldn't have learned your lesson. Here is my card if you discover any other information. I will also remind you that it would be foolish to contact the local authorities." Shoving one hand in the pocket of his overcoat, he saw himself out. Lillian got up from the couch and watched him go safely from the living room window. He paused at the blue gate at the end of her garden and lit another cigarette before opening it, the squeak announcing his departure. Lillian watched from her window as the man's lanky frame turned left and walked out of sight. No longer able to see him, Lillian's legs gave up what strength they had, and she slid to the floor. Her heart rate fluttered, her vision was blurry. They had found her. They had not only found her, they had found a way to get what they wanted from her.

Not normally a crier, Lillian cupped her hand over her mouth to suppress a sob. It had all been for nothing after all. The secrecy, the hiding, the loneliness had all been for nothing. It hadn't mattered where she went or how safe she thought she was.

' *I could have gotten us all out.'* Lillian thought to herself. After her brother  died, Lillian had begged her parents to leave. She had papers ready for them all, but they had refused. After waiting a few months, she had fled on her own.  Not able to say a proper good-bye, Lillian had been somewhat comforted that her parents had at least known she was alive.

Half crawling to the kitchen, Lillian grabbed a bottle of wine from the fridge and poured herself a glass. She took a long deep swallow and felt some calm return. It wasn't too late, Lillian could still get them out.  It would be harder right now, but if she played along, she might be able to do it. Oddly, that made her feel better about the situation. Finishing her glass, she went to her dining room table and opened her laptop. With hands shaking, she thought about who could help her.  There weren't many left anymore.  Reaching out to some old contacts, she made what arrangements she could over email. Lillian then shot off an email to Nils Ryeng as well, asking questions about the trip. Feeling like an ass for doing it, she knew if the tables were turned, Nils would do the same thing and not think twice about it.

Having done all she could for the moment, Lillian filled her wine glass again and allowed herself a few tears. She looked around the house, her house. Her safe place for the past years. Now it smelled like a Russian assassin. Would there ever be a time in her life when she wouldn't have to worry about them? A smile crossed her face. She had been a nobody in Russia, her family were not the poorest of the poor, but they were close to it. Her brother had gotten into a little trouble for some anti-government rallies he had attended, but they were still a family of no consequence. Until Lillian had been tested in school. The family, and certainly Lillian herself, had known she had above average intelligence, but when she had been in high school, the offers started rolling in. All Lillian had wanted was to go to university, to learn everything there was to know. Her government wanted her to come work for them. Now they had found her again. If she did this for them, what else would they ask of her? All that trouble just to end up where she had started as a seventeen year old girl.

"For fuck's sake." She said, putting her head in her hands.

# 3

Lillian was still looking at her computer an hour later. It had been forty-five minutes since she had sent her last email. Staring at the screen saver, she thought back on the events of her life that had led her to this moment. Reliving that dark night, hiding in the trunk of someone's car, driving to parts unknown. The smell of the car's exhaust, the roughness of the carpet, and the complete lack of suspension.

When the phone rang, she jumped back into the present. Lillian thought about not answering it. Her hands began to shake again as she stared at the phone, jumping again on the second ring. Venturing to look to see who was calling, she let out a breath and answered it.

"Nils?"

"Lil, how the hell are you?" He sounded cheerful as

always.

"What's going on Nils?" Lillian tried for a light tone.

"I'm in London for a few days if you can believe it. Meeting with some people about the trip. I thought I would call and see if you wanted to go out for dinner?"

"What? Dinner? Did you get my email?"

"What email?" Lillian's foggy mind was finding it hard to believe that Nils was calling for any other reason than the email she sent.

"I sent you an email about the trip."

"I haven't checked my mail all day. Come on Lil, it'll be great to see you again."

"I'm not sure that's a good idea." Lillian wasn't sure she wanted to see anyone at the moment. Especially Nils.

"You are going to turn me down? I know it's short notice Lil, but how long has it been?" He was smiling into the phone, she could tell. Nils was always like this, always seemingly happy. It was what had annoyed her the most about him. Lillian knew a good spy would accept the offer, take him somewhere where the drinks were strong, and get every ounce of information out of him. But she wasn't a good spy. She didn't want anyone near her. She was dangerous. Anyone who came near her would be watched. Nils was already on their radar for his conservation work.

"I'm just not sure I can." Lillian answered. His voice grew serious.

"Everything okay? You sound stressed. Tell you what, I'll grab a curry and some wine and come over. Are you still at the same place?"

"Yes." Lillian answered before she could think of a plausible excuse.

"Great, I'll be there in about an hour." He hung up the phone. *'Damn it.'* She thought to herself. This is what Nils was like. Adorable, likable, and impossible to say no to. Hanging up the phone, Lillian went upstairs to splash water on her face and tried to make it look like a government agent had not been sitting in her living room making threats. Her hands had still not stopped shaking when Nils knocked on her door. Already? His warm smile greeted her when she opened the door. He held up the carrier bags of the take out food and pushed his way past Lillian into the house.

"I didn't realize until I got there that I completely forgot to ask you what you wanted. I got what you used to get, I hope you still like it." Nils headed for the kitchen table with great familiarity. Lillian bit her lip and followed him.

"That should be fine. You didn't forget the poppadoms did you?" Going for an air of levity.

"Of course not, what do you think I am?" He was placing the takeout containers on the table. With steadier hands, she poured the wine. It was so familiar that she almost forgot what had happened earlier, but the faint smell of cigarette smoke kept reminding her.

"Aren't you going to ask me what I am doing in London?"

"I assume something for the trip."

"Yeah, okay, probably not a huge mystery. I am getting more money than I thought. How many times does a scientist get to say that?" Nils raised a glass to her and took a deep swig. "I am going to be able to get a boat with icebreakers on the front which means we can cruise a little farther north than planned ." Lillian smiled, trying to take an interest in what he was saying. It really was good to see him. His positive energy was contagious. "You're still coming aren't you?" He asked, still looking concerned at how silent and reserved she was.

"Of course, I wouldn't miss it." He filled his plate with food and sat down across from her. Lifting his glass, he said, "To science."

"To science." She replied. He used a poppadom to scoop food, and she took a sip of her wine to see if she could stop her hands shaking.

"Lil, you okay?"

"Fine, why do you keep asking?"

"No offense, but you don't look well." Lillian looked for something to say, something that would be believable to tell him so that he would leave it alone. Let him talk about whatever nonsense he wanted to talk about, and go home. Lillian made the mistake of grabbing her fork, which rattled against the plate. She dropped it quickly, but he had seen it. "Lillian? Speak to me." He reached across and held her wrist. "Is it something back home? Are your parents okay?"

"I can't tell you Nils, that's the problem. I can't speak to you."

"Why not, what have I done?" She took another shakey drink of her wine, a bigger one this time. The cat was out of the bag, no reason to hide anything now. Her nerves relaxed just enough to keep her from crying again.

"It isn't what you have done Nils, it's what I've done." He dropped his food. Coming around the table, he knelt down next to her, taking her hands in his. Lillian looked away from him. His deep green eyes weren't going to help keep her quiet.

"Tell me, what could you have done that was so bad?" She shook her head and buried it in her hands. Nils put a hand on her back and rubbed soothingly. "Tell me Lillian, please. Whatever it is, we will get through it together."

"We are all in danger, Nils. I've put everyone in danger." She let it out. It didn't matter, Alexi was going to do whatever he was going to do. Lillian let the shame wash over her. She had agreed to do it, and then she hadn't even been able to keep it to herself. Some spy she was turning out to be, some wine and a good looking Norwegian and she was telling him everything.

"Who's in danger?"

"Everyone on the trip. You." He took Lillian's hand into his.

"You better start from the beginning." Taking a deep breath, she told him about Stanovich with the cigarette. About her parents back in Russia who were being watched in case she refused or backed out.

"If I don't do it, they are dead." Concern was clear in his eyes. The happiness and confidence were gone.

"What are they going to do to the ship? To the researchers?" He asked. Nils knew enough of her past to not be surprised that she had been approached. The government had known about Lillian before she left Russia. She had been warned while they were in school together that she should not go home.

"I don't know. He didn't mention a whole lot about it. He wanted to know any information I could give them about the trip. Who was going, what they're researching, that sort of thing. If I had to guess, they don't want us finding whatever it is we are going to find." Her head was throbbing. She took another sip of wine. Nils sat quietly next to her.

"Why go through all this trouble? They could just discredit the research." He finally said.

"I don't know. Maybe to discourage other research trips."

"Mugging a bunch of scientists would do it."

"I am so sorry, Nils. I didn't want to say yes, but my parents." He rubbed her back again. "Don't worry, Lil. We will get through this. They aren't going to stop us." Determination was back in his voice. Lillian looked at him.

"What?"

"We are the only ones who can stop them. We can prove what they are up to. We can prove that it is causing damage to the environment. Someone is drilling up there. There has already been a small amount of evidence that something is going on. I'd bet my back teeth it's them. We have to do this Lillian, we have to stop them." She had seen this look on his face before when they were students that had protested a lot together. This was his protest face.

"Nils, what about the others?"

"Don't worry about the others. They will be fine."

Nils went back to his dinner, but his mood had changed.

"If they are after the data, we will let them have it." Nils then proceeded to outline how the data the trip produced could be saved. "I will need your help, Lil. We can't tell the others because they won't come if they know what is going to happen, and we need them."

"That doesn't seem like fair play." Lillian was beginning to regret telling him again.

"If they find out and back out of the trip, what will happen to your parents?" Nils asked. Lillian considered what Nils had in mind, but she was not convinced it would work. Nils should know better than anyone that the Russians didn't like being outsmarted, and the lives of her parents were on the line. They had finished their dinner and moved over to the couch in the living room.

"I never thought I would be a double agent." Lillian smiled, sitting down heavily. They had finished off two bottles of wine, and she was happy to report that Nils was even looking a little tipsy.

"Who would have thought science would be so risky?" Nils answered as he nuzzled her neck. "You would make a very convincing Bond girl, you know that? You even have the right accent." This counted as teasing Lillian. She had worked very hard to get rid of her Russian accent when she had arrived in England.

"What would that make you? Bond?"

"Unfortunately not, I'm not nearly good enough at all that running and fighting stuff. No, I'd be the helpful scientist who tells him all the vital information and then gets out of there before it gets messy. There is one thing Bond and I are rather good at though." He turned Lillian's head with his hand and pulled her in for a long, deep kiss.

"Nils." He took this as encouragement and pulled her closer.

# 4

"Jack, I can't." Ross was pacing the floor in her apartment.

"You could Ross. I could meet you halfway. We would fly the rest of the way together. Hell, we could stay wherever halfway is."

" Do they have nice hotels in Chad?"

"Chad?"

"Africa, it's the halfway point between Boston and Indonesia. I looked it up."

"It's an option Ross. If you want me to meet you in bloody Chad, I will."

" You don't understand. I can't."

"You're right, I don't understand. I understood when you were afraid to travel, but now you are heading off to the Arctic, instead of coming out here to see me."

"Jack, you are there. You are where it all happened."

"So, you are going to avoid this entire part of the planet?"

"To be honest, I went thirty years without being near that part of the planet, so I'm sure I'll survive another thirty without seeing it again."

"But I'm here Ross, this is where I am. I can't always come and see you, Love. I just can't afford it." Ross hung her head. He had a point and she knew it. He had come at Christmas to see her. To see Sam and meet Ross's parents. Ross had promised to come and see him in the summer. Now it was summer and the thought of boarding a flight for Jakarta was enough to make her start twirling her hair. She was breaking a promise, and he had every right to be mad at her.

Si leaned against the control panel and watched his son pace back and forth in front of him. The sun was setting on day three of this argument. Lord knew what their phone bills were going to be. What was worse than the daily calls was dealing with his son's mood afterwards. It was a decent sized boat for two men. Made somewhat smaller when one of them was in a tizzy, which Si knew Jack would be. "I'll gladly give you the money, son. Go see the lass." He had said it more than once.

"That's not the point. She said she was going to come here. She's never going to get over this fear until she comes out here and sees that nothing is going to happen." Jack would say, pointing his finger to make his point.

"Many relationships have died because of a 'point' son. Be careful." Si did not give out relationship advice. That had been Bev's department. Jack's mother. Now that she was gone, he still trusted her to make things right for Jack. So far, she hadn't done such a good job. Jack's marriage had ended years ago, resulting in the decline of he and Si's shark diving business, which is why they had taken the job at the resort Ikan Hui a year ago. That venture had literally almost killed them. They had met Ross and Sam, which had been the only good thing about it. Si quickly played through the events of that terrible afternoon in his head. That's all it had been, one afternoon. Yet they were lucky to still be alive. He especially. If it hadn't been for Jack, he would have been a goner.

She was a fantastic woman, Ross. Very intelligent and not afraid to show it, which Si liked. Sam was also amazing. Small, but full of sass. If he was half a century younger and not still committed to Beverly,

Sam would have been in trouble. However, both women, as wonderful as they were, lived halfway around the world.

"I'll come out after this research trip, okay?" Ross pleaded not for the first time. "Let me just get my feet wet and then I'm sure I'll be able to do it. Plus, I'll have the money."

"You don't need money Ross, I have everything you need here on the boat." What they both knew, but Jack was too stubborn to admit, was that he wanted her first flight after Ikan Hui to be to him, not some science trip in the arctic north.

"It's an expensive flight, Jack, you know that. Please honey, don't be mad at me. I feel like I need to do this to get back to normal. I know you want me to come out there, but I think this is better. Sam agrees with me." Ross had, in fact, almost declined the offer of the research trip. After what had happened the last time she traveled, she had vowed to never travel again. But Dr. Nils Ryeng was a persuasive person when he wanted to be. Plus, there was science involved. In the end, she hadn't been able to pass up the opportunity of making a new discovery.

"Of course she does." Jack sighed, and Ross could

picture him running his hands through his hair, his jaw clenched with tension. "Call me when you get there, okay?"

"I will. Give Si a kiss for me."

"Get out here and give it to him yourself." Jack said sternly and hung up. Ross stood there staring at her phone for a while. Why was this so hard? They'd been having the same conversation for days, yet nothing had changed, not her fears, and certainly not Jack's stubbornness. Ross jumped at the doorbell. Putting her phone down on the counter, she went to the door and looked through the peephole to see Sam standing there. Ross had to assume it was Sam because all she could see was a bottle of margarita mix being held up to the door.

"I thought we said we weren't going to drink tonight." Ross said as a way of a greeting.

"Correction. You said you weren't going to drink. This momma is out of the house without a husband or child for the first time in a year. She is going to drink big girl juice and get silly." Sam said, while pushing past Ross and heading for the kitchen.

"Who's watching Ruby?" Ross had to admit she was a little sad that Ruby wasn't there. The baby's chubby thighs and cheeks always cheered Ross up. She had wanted to see her before leaving, but Ruby was five months old now, and Sam had not had a night off from motherhood since she had been born. Sam had earned a night out. With familiarity, Sam went around Ross's kitchen pulling out what she needed to make the margaritas.

"Phillip. She's eaten, and I changed her diaper before I left. He should be good for a few hours with no trouble. I swear Ross, I don't know what happened to me. I used to just leave the house. Ya know, pick up my purse and go. I have been making lists of instructions for him since two this afternoon. Not because he asked me to, but because I was that worried about leaving the two of them alone without me." Sam took a sip of her freshly made margarita, closed her eyes, and sighed deeply . "Holy Mary, mother of God! That's good!" Sam said.

"How long has it been since you had a drink?" Ross asked. Sam tilted her head back and thought about it.

"Nine months pregnant. She'll be five months next week…over a year. Here's yours."

"I'm not drinking, I have to fly tomorrow."

"Shut up and drink. You can't make me drink alone."

How many hangovers had started with those exact words over their long history together?

The plan for the night was simple. Ross was packing for her trip. Sam wanted a night away from the family and really, any excuse would do, so she was going to help Ross pack. They both knew that very little packing was actually going to happen, and the event was a very thin excuse to have a girl's night. Sam had not ignored the phone still sitting warm on the kitchen counter, or her friend's mellow mood.

"Heard from Jack recently?" Knowing perfectly well she had.

"Just now, actually." Ross took a small sip of her drink. She could tell Sam had been off the sauce for a while because this was a very weak margarita .

"And...?"

"About the same. I can't make him understand Sam, and if I'm honest, I'm getting tired of trying." Sam was walking towards Ross's bedroom where her suitcase was open and the items she had already packed were on display.

"Ross, you have to do what you are comfortable with. Jack is going to have to deal with it." Sam said over her shoulder. She picked up a packed t-shirt with her thumb and finger and flung it into the corner.

"It's what's going to happen if he can't get over it that is worrying me." Sam turned to look at Ross.

"You think this is game-ending?"

"We don't seem to be able to get past it." Sam made a pouty face.

"Aw, you guys are having your first fight."

"Sam, this is a little more serious than that I think. It may be our first and our last." Sam turned her attention back to the clothes.

"New couples always think that. It's because you've never fought with him before, so you don't know how it works."

"You are talking out of your ass." Ross said. Just because Sam had been a serial dater before finally marrying Philip didn't mean she knew what was going on with Jack and her.

"No, it's true. I went to school with this chick who became a marriage counselor. She said most of what she does is teach people how to fight...you know, with words." Sam had apparently chugged her first margarita because her speech was already getting a little slow. "You have to learn how to argue your points with the other person and not hurt their feelings."

"Too late for that. He's already hurt because I'm not going there instead."

"Yeah, that's a tough one. If he's going to have a chance with you, he is going to have to understand that science is, and always will be, your first love."

"In a way, I wish I could make myself go out there with him but I get short of breath at just the thought."

"Ross, what is this?"

"It's a pair of waterproof bibs."

"What in Christ do you need those for? They are horrible."

"I am going to be on a boat, on the water, in a cold part of the world. I thought they might help keep me warm and dry." Sam tossed them aside, apparently offended by them. Ross would put them back later.

"Didn't you say that Nils guy was on this trip?"

"Yeah." Ross knew where she was going with this. Sam thought Nils was hot. In all honesty, he was. Nils was also very aware of how women reacted to his looks and his Nordic accent. Ross had never found arrogance particularly attractive.

"If you take these, you have to promise he will never see you in them." Sam held up a pair of Ross's underwear affectionately referred to as granny panties.

Ross snatched them from her.

"Sam, you are trying to help me save my relationship with Jack. Remember?" Sam shrugged.

"Always good to have a back up plan." Ross rolled her eyes. "Oh, I almost forgot. I got you a present." Sam shuffled out to the living room and rooted around in her giant 'mom bag,' finally pulling out a small bag.

"You didn't have to get me anything."

"Don't be silly, it's nothing big. You are going on a trip for the first time since the resort. It's just a little something." Ross opened the bag and pulled out a pink knitted hat with a very furry, oversized Pom Pom on the crown. She grabbed it just in case it really was a small creature that had been sewn to the hat. "Isn't it cute? Keep your head warm out there." Ross couldn't help but smile. It was a perfect Sam gift. Functional and adorable with just the right amount of color.

"It will certainly keep my ears warm and help them find me if a thick fog rolls in. A bird might attack me though, thinking this is a squirrel or something." Ross said, indicating the fury ball on the top of the hat.

"Shut up." Sam grabbed the hat back and pulled it down on Ross's head. "See, you look great." Ross doubted it, but she would wear it anyway.

# 5

On the other side of the world, Jack was stewing. He rubbed his hands through his hair and rested them on his neck. He wanted his girl here, and to be fair, when he had left her after Christmas, she had said she would come. Now she was backing out, and not only that, going on this work trip to the frigid north. Jack couldn't help but feel a little cheated. Not for the first time, he wondered if Ross really did feel the same way about him as he did her. Having been in a one sided relationship before, Jack had no interest in entering into one again. The night was dark and cool. He realized he was still pacing up and down. Tired of pacing, he stormed into the cabin and plopped himself down in one of the chairs. Si couldn't help but notice Jack's entrance, but said nothing. He looked from his son out to the ocean in front of him.

"Shut up." Jack said. Si lifted an eyebrow.

"Did I say something?"

"I can hear your thoughts."

"Well, let's hope that's not true."

"She's not coming."

"I gathered."

"I don't get it, I just don't get it. She's traveling, she's going there, why can't she come here?"

"Did you ask her that?" Si was not cut out to be a therapist. He was from the day when you went to the bar and drank until you couldn't remember what you were upset about. He walked over to the fridge and pulled out two beers, and popping the tops, he handed one to Jack who took it as if by reflex.

"Says it's because we are where it happened." Jack took a long sip of the beer. Si hoped they had enough in stock for this, the boy was really feeling it.

"She isn't wrong." Si pointed out, taking his captain seat back. Jack winced. That is what it was, what was getting at him so hard. Ross wasn't wrong and neither was he. It was driving him crazy. How could they both be right? Coming back to the place where it all happened was no doubt going to bring up memories, and Jack bloody knew it. There just wasn't anything he could do about it.

"Absence makes the heart grow fonder and all that." Si offered as help.

"Bullshit. All it's done is piss everyone off. Dad, I'm not sure this is going to work." This hit Si in the stomach.

"Aw come on, son. It won't always be like this."

"Dad, if we can't ever see each other, it's going to be rather hard to maintain a relationship, isn't it? She's there and I'm here. It's bloody expensive to get to either place. It's expensive to get halfway to either place." Jack finished his beer with a long gulp and went to the fridge for another. Si felt this strange urge to do whatever was necessary to keep Ross around.

"Can you go to her, Son? I mean if that's what it takes."

"She's getting ready to leave for this job. Besides, that isn't the point. She was supposed to come here."

"Oh son, don't do that."

"Do what?" Jack popped the top on his second beer and drained half of it.

"Get all hung up on 'points'. It has killed more than one relationship. If twenty-five years of marriage taught me anything, it was that compromise and forgiveness worked a lot better." Jack lowered his beer and took a long hard look at his father. A man he considered to be one of the least compromising people and perhaps one of the more confrontational he had ever had the misfortune to deal with. That being said, he tried to remember his parents fighting. There hadn't been many. Most of them, he would have considered his mother the winner, and there had been signs of compromise.

"You and Mom were never apart for more than a few nights." Jack retorted with a fair amount of snark.

"Bollocks. You forget boy, there was a time before you. I was broke as hell when I married your mother. She was working, but we were both young and not earning much. I wanted to buy her a house. Some place where we could settle and start our family. I certainly didn't have enough money for that, so I went to work in the gold mines. Bloody hard work, and I didn't want your mother anywhere around the camps. She stayed with her parents and I went there." Jack had literally never heard this before and searched his father's face for any sign he was making it up. Si was known to not let the truth get in the way of a good story, but he had usually been drinking when this happened. While Jack was getting ready to start his third beer, Si was still nursing his first. Si looked thoughtful and a little sad, which he often did when he spoke about Jack's mother. When he was lying, you could usually tell by the glint in his eye.

"When was this?"

"Oh, we hadn't been married a year yet. You could make fast money in the mines, if you found something. I was young and dumb and thought if I worked as hard as I could, I would make our fortune. Nearly broke myself trying."

"Did you do it? Did you find enough?"

"Eventually. Certainly didn't happen the way I wanted it to, or as quickly as I wanted it to. I thought I'd find a large nugget and go home holding my head high. I was away from your mother for eight months. Found enough flakes of gold dust to fill half a jar. With that money and the money your grandparents chipped in, we had enough."

"So it worked out?" Si shrugged his shoulders.

"I came home, not feeling like a complete arse. Fifteen pounds lighter, missing my wife so bad I could hardly stand it. She picked out a house, and nine months later you were born." Si toasted Jack with his beer and drank.

"Sorry, what was the point of that story?"

Si shrugged. "I don't know. You said I was never away from your mother for more than a few nights. I was." Jack was starting to feel the three beers he had chugged. He was sitting lower in his chair and some of the fight seemed to have gone out of him.

"You'll figure it out boy. This job won't last forever, and neither will the one she's getting ready to go on. Your relationship has never been a normal one, so why should it start now?" Si was right. Theirs was not a normal relationship. It had started during a hostage situation for Christ's sake. Jack rubbed his hands over his face again. He wanted so badly to show Ross what he was doing out here. He knew she would love it once she was there, on the boat. Being on a boat and working on the sea was so much a part of who he was. If he added it up, he had probably spent more time on the water than he had on land. He didn't dare think of a future with Ross. Not long term anyway. He had never thought about moving in with her, or any of the other normal things couples do after dating for a year. Maybe they were fools to think there was anything they could do about the distance. They had told each other it wouldn't matter, and when it came to how he felt about her, it didn't. But what future was there? If there wasn't a future, they were just wasting each other's time.

Jack drained the rest of his beer, and tossed it in the trash can as he left the cabin. "I'm going for a walk." Obviously, he was limited to the boat, but Si knew to give him his space.

# 6

What Jack didn't understand, what no one understood, was that science was Ross's safe place. Her boss and co-workers thought she was a workaholic, but in reality, it was just where she felt the most comfortable. There was a purity in science that made Ross feel safe and warm. Science didn't care about feelings, what mood you were in, what religion you were, or who was president. It was either proven or not proven. Working through the series of findings that led you to other scientific findings was a world that made sense to her. Science was logical, and in its purest form, was devoid of emotions or outside influences.

That is why traveling to the arctic north to look at water samples for traces of hydrocarbons and sulfur was a lot less fearful to her right now than traveling to the Indian Ocean to see the boyfriend she hadn't seen in six months. Ross had come to terms with the fact that this made sense to no one else. Being around Jack made her feel things that remained mysterious and uncomfortable. Looking for hydrocarbons in the freezing water of the North Sea would make her feel normal, sane.

"Of course you want to go to the frozen north to look at water. Why wouldn't you when there is a perfectly attractive Australian man waiting for you with open arms in the Indian Ocean?" Her friend Sam had said when she first mentioned the trip.

"Sam…"

"Honey, I know. You are scared, and why wouldn't you be? Hell, I could have told him which trip you were gonna take, but he doesn't know you like I do. Give him some time to take a cold shower and calm down."

"I'm not afraid of Jack."

"You are a little afraid of Jack."

"What the hell are you talking about?"

"Ross, I saw how you two were with each other when he was here for Christmas. You're afraid of your feelings for him."

"That's ridiculous. I love being around Jack."

"My ass it's ridiculous. You've fallen for him Ross, which is something you don't have control over. None of us do, and it's scaring the hell out of you."

"You think I'm trying to sabotage my relationship with Jack?"

"No, I think you are keeping him at arm's length until you know exactly what is going on. What I'm telling you is, I think it is too late. You tripped and fell for him. You fell hard. You are made for that man, and that's all there is to it. Your parents love him too. I think I actually saw your mother drooling over him at Christmas dinner." Ross stood there clutching a sweater tightly. She didn't like what Sam was saying. Mostly because it seemed to be based in truth.

"She's always had a thing for men with accents." Ross thought back to Christmas. Her mother had been rather giggly, but Ross had blamed it on the extra glass of wine her mother had with dinner.

"I think I'm going to make myself a drink after all." Putting the sweater in the case, Ross headed for the kitchen.

"Must run in the family." Sam said to her as she walked out of the room. "Not that Jack doesn't have other things going for him. Just be careful Ross." Sam said louder so Ross would be sure to hear her in the kitchen. "You push him away too hard and he might actually think you don't care about him." The thought made Ross's stomach sink as she took a sip of her drink. Sam was right, of course, though Ross could not afford to let her know she agreed. Ross knew what Sam was talking about. After a few glasses of wine, Ross had come very close to telling Jack she loved him at Christmas. It depended on the day as to whether she was glad she didn't.

"It doesn't help, of course, that you are going with the dishy Nils." Sam added as Ross entered the bedroom again. Sam had met Nils briefly when Ross and Nils had gone on a research trip together in school. Sam had met her coming back and locked eyes with Nils who had turned his charm on full speed. Ross had not been impressed, Sam had.

"Jack doesn't know what Nils looks like, thank you."

"I would be jealous if my girlfriend was going on a trip with a Nordic God."

"A Nordic God who knows he looks like a Nordic God. The man's ego is almost as wide as his charismatic grin."

"I wish I was going with you."

"No, you don't. You said you were never traveling with me again, and Phillip threatened to hide your passport if you ever tried."

"Oh yeah, that's right. How is it that you have just amazingly bad vacations?"

"Luck, I guess." Ross didn't have great luck with traveling in truth. Aside from the bombing at the resort the year before, Ross and Sam had gone on a trip to Jamaica and found herself swimming in a school of jellyfish.

"Well, hopefully, this one will go better."

"Oh, it will because this isn't a vacation. This is a work trip." Ross had thought about this and had repeated it to herself multiple times. *"This was a work trip. Any resemblance to a vacation was strictly coincidental."*

The honest truth was, Ross needed this trip. She had made a major discovery about a year and a half ago that had made a huge difference in getting rid of ocean plastics. After coming back from the resort at Inkan Hui, Ross had finished up the project she had been working on and published a few papers on the subject. Since then, she hadn't done very much professionally. Ross had been unable to focus on any subject or come up with any new ideas. There was plenty of work to do, but she felt the need to publish another paper or risk losing her scientific street cred. When Nils had called and offered her this trip, she saw it as a lifeline. She had not mentioned any of this to Jack or Sam, and she wasn't entirely sure why.

# 7

Alexi Stanovich confidently strode the corridor of the historic government building, one hand tucked into the pocket of his expensively tailored suit. The other hand twirled an unsmoked cigarette in his hand. He had not been able to smoke in the building since the early two-thousands, but he could still hold one if he wanted. With his usual arrogance, he walked into the office of the Chief of Security and right past the secretary and into the inner office. Alexi enjoyed the secretary's shocked face and paid no attention to her pleas for him to stop. Instead, he turned and gave her a winning grin before barging into the inner office without so much as a knock. Knowing nothing bad would happen, Alexi entered without fear.

The Chief of Security was a fat old man who had not been in the field for over twenty years. Alexi held no more respect for him than he did his secretary, but the Chief could still have him killed. He wouldn't do it himself, but the result would be the same. The fat old man was on the phone when Alexi entered, and his face turned red at being interrupted. Alexi signaled to him to take his time and then pretended to not be listening to the conversation as he read the titles on the bookshelf. The Chief quickly wrapped up the phone call and yelled, "What the hell are you playing at?" Alexi smiled. "I hope you have a very good reason for entering this office without an invitation." Alexi pulled his hand out of his pocket and placed a business card on the desk in front of the Chief who was now purple with anger.

Almost stunned, the Chief read the card and then picked it up, the color of his face returning to normal. Alexi smiled to himself. He had guessed right that the Chief would welcome the interruption when he saw what Alexi had brought him. "Is this what I think it is?"

"Yes." Alexi sat down.

"How did you...?"

"I made some enquiries while I was away. I still have some connections in certain circles. They went underground after last year, but now they are working together as a team. The person who gave me that number said they are starting to take jobs now that things have calmed down a bit, but everything is still very secretive. No one knows where they are. You make arrangements through a third party, if the Spartans are interested in the job, then one of them contacts you."

"You have called it, this number works?"

"It does. I was thinking of using them for our little mission up north."

"We have our own people for that." The Chief pointed out. It was actually rather late in the game to throw in another team, Spartans or no. However, Alexi knew that the President had been trying to get in touch with them since the world discovered their existence last year. If they were as good as everyone said they were, they may still be able to use them.

"The President was very adamant that there be no connection back to him on this mission. This would be one more degree of separation. They promise absolute secrecy. While it will be clear that the attack was carried out by Spartans, they are able to guarantee that there will be no way to trace it back to who hired them."

"They never leave survivors. I thought you were hoping to use our informant again." The Chief said. Alexi twirled the cigarette in his fingers.

"I thought about that on the flight home. I don't think we will be able to use her again. I was hoping to ignite her patriotism, but I'm afraid she doesn't have any." Alexi didn't mention that there had never been any proof that any patriotism ever existed.

"I think she will do what we have asked her on this mission, but I would not be able to trust her in future missions." Alexi also failed to mention that he never had any intention of letting Lillian live. This had been the second time she had told him 'no'. He had planned on killing her after she said no the first time, but she had gotten out of the country very quickly. There was no reason to bore the Chief with his private vendetta, but he would enjoy reading about Lillian's death when the attack on the research vessel was reported. Almost as much as he knew the President would enjoy reading about Dr. Nils Ryeng's.

Nils' organization had recently revealed that the Russians were capturing whales and holding them to sell to foreign markets. A very profitable secret the Russian government had managed to keep for several years. Somehow Nils Ryeng and his organization had gotten pictures of the whales in their holding tanks. The press had been so bad, they had been forced to let the whales go. To make matters worse, the whales had already been purchased and were awaiting transport. The Russians had to give their patrons back their money. The President still could not talk about it without getting angry. Nils' team was now very close to discovering who was drilling the recently defrosted arctic north. While the mission had originally started as a mission to scare the researchers and steal the data so that nothing could be proven, it had very quickly turned to a mission of revenge. Alexi reveled in the efficiency of getting rid of two enemies in one mission.

The Chief was still holding the card in his hand. "It is a pity she can not be brought around. She has a brilliant mind and I'm sure would be of much use to us."

"Yes, very true. However, I fear at this point it would be a liability. I have been able to ensure that the source of the attack does not trace back to us, and while I have been able to ensure her silence during the mission, should she survive, there would be questions asked. I can not be sure that she would not intentionally or otherwise let it slip."

"If you say so, I will trust your judgment." The Chief said. "I take it their services do not come cheap?"

"That is correct." Alexi pulled another piece of paper out of his pocket and slid it across the desk. The man's eyebrows went up as soon as he saw the number.

"That is considerably more than we were looking to spend."

"Like I said, no one will be able to trace the attack back to us." The Chief nodded his head. He knew as well as anyone how badly the President wanted this done without bad PR.

"Leave it with me. I will make sure it happens." Alexi got up from his seat. "And if you ever walk into my office again uninvited I will have you shot on site." The fat man smiled at him as he said this. Alexi nodded again and turned to leave the room.

"Alexi." The Chief said, Alexi turned around.

"I know the President will be happy to have the Spartan's number and I will make sure he knows how I got it, but if any of this goes wrong, I will also make sure he knows who to blame."

"I would expect nothing less." Alexi left the office, giving the secretary another winning smile and walked quickly back to his office. Closing the door behind him, he took a deep breath. The ball was in motion, and as long as everything went well, he had just secured his future as Chief of Security. If it went wrong, though, he would probably find himself at the bottom of a tall building after an accidental fall. With his mask of calmness once more in place, Alexi carefully hung his jacket on the back of his chair and opened his computer. He reached out to the contact email he had been given by the Spartan to confirm that they were good for the mission and to ask where the money should be sent. After forwarding the account information to the Chief, Alexi leaned back in his chair. In a few days time it would all be over. If this went well, there was no doubt in his mind that the President would want to use the Spartans in future missions. Alexi's job might have gotten a lot easier.

# 8

Ross gave herself a firm talking to. Unfortunately for her Uber driver, it had been out loud. *"Come on Ross!"* She said to herself and forced herself out of the car parked precariously in the drop-off lane at the airport.

"You can do it." The Uber driver had helpfully offered in his thick accent. He was also eager to get Ross out of the car. With that boost, Ross got through check in and security. Getting on the plane was another matter. It had taken four phone calls to Sam, the last of which had ended in, "Ross, put one damn foot in front of the other and get on the damn plane!" and a Xanax, but she managed it.

*"What are you going to do for the other three connecting flights?"* Ross thought to herself. *"We'll worry about that when we get there."* Surprisingly, once on the plane, she calmed down a bit. The inflight movie and reading the

latest edition of *Chemical Science* kept her distracted. She had three layovers, and at every one, she was asked if she was really heading for the Arctic. It was fine, it segued nicely into explaining the specialized equipment she had brought with her that could not go through the airport's scanners.

At each layover, Ross thought she would have a hard time getting back on the plane, but surprisingly, the closer she got to her destination, the less anxious she was. *'See, getting started was the hard part. An object in motion stays in motion.'* Ross chanted to herself as she walked around the airports waiting for her next flight. She thought about calling Sam to brag about how well she was doing, but Ross had woken the baby twice already. Better not risk it. She texted her instead, but Sam had not texted back. In a moment of weakness, having not gotten a hold of Sam, Ross texted Jack just to let him know she was starting her journey. She had also not heard back from him. *'They both hate me right now.'* Ross thought to herself. She didn't blame them. Even for Ross, she was being complicated. "They think I'm complicated on the outside? They should see what goes on in my head!" Ross had not meant to say this last part out loud while she was trolling through

Facebook in the waiting area at her gate. The gentleman sitting next to her folded up his paper and decided to relocate to another row of chairs. "Sorry, I didn't mean to say that out loud." Ross told him, but he refused to make eye contact with her.

By the time Ross got to her final destination, she was flying in a six-seater ice plane and feeling more like herself than she had felt in a year. The adventurous spirit that she usually felt when traveling had replaced the fear, which was good because the six seater bounced around considerably more than was desirable. Ross pulled her equipment up into the seat with her instead of letting it bounce around the back of the plane. "Is this normal?" She yelled into the headphones to the pilot.

"It is a bit bouncier today than normal. Jet streams are being a bit bitchy. Barf bags are in the pocket behind the seat." The pilot did not seem to be all that concerned about the turbulence. Or that the plane would fall apart from all the sudden movement. Even yelling 'Yahooo' when the plane took a particularly low dip. Ross clung to her equipment bag and closed her eyes. Extremely glad she had taken the Xanax. "*You should be freaking out. You have every reason to be freaking* out. *Any sane person would be freaking out right now. Modern medicine is the only reason you are NOT freaking out right now. If you die, you will at least die calmly."* Ross chanted to herself trying to tune out the thuds coming from the plane with every jolt of turbulence.

Thankfully, the turbulence evened out by the time they needed to land. Ross half stumbled out of the plane and had to stand there for a moment getting her land legs back before heading out of the airport. Unfortunately, the delays she had encountered with her layovers meant Ross arrived only an hour before the ship was set to sail. Pushing down the nausea that was washing over her, Ross grabbed her bags and headed for the waiting taxi.

It was a very short trip from the airport to the docks. Ross had just enough time to check and make sure she grabbed all her luggage from the plane before they pulled up. It couldn't have been more than five minutes. *'That is the shortest trip I have taken in two days.'*

The driver got her right to the boat named *'The Hunter'*. A boat that didn't look nearly as fierce as her name implied. It looked like a decent sized research vessel, and its size made Ross feel better about being out on icy water. Seeing no one else about, Ross pulled her duffle bag out of the back of the taxi. It was summer here in the Arctic Circle, but it felt more like early spring in Boston. It was sunny, but a cold wind blew with a little bit of sea spray mixed in, which made the waterproof puffer coat necessary. On land, there was no sign of ice or snow. Ross finished pulling all the equipment out of the taxi, checking her phone one more time before heading onto the ship. She had texted Jack when she landed to say she had arrived safely, but he had not responded. Busy trying to figure out what time it was in Jack's part of the world, she didn't hear the person coming up behind her.

"Ross?" An accented voice called out. Ross jumped and turned.

"Nils, oh my God, how are you?" Ross had met Nils years ago as a student on another research trip. They were both in  school back then and eager to prove themselves. He truly was adorable. With a broad smile, a witty sense of humor, and at the moment, a cute man bun. He looked like he could still be a student.

He pulled her into a big hug. "You okay, you look a little gray?"

"Thanks Nils, it's good to see you again. No, the plane ride here was a little bumpy."

"I heard it could be. I didn't risk it. I drove up from Alberta instead . I'll give you a ride back when the trip is over."

"You had to find one of the coldest places on earth for this trip, didn't you? There wasn't anything in Hawaii that needed researching?" His smile widened.

"I would be surprised if there was anything in Hawaii that hadn't been studied at this point. Most researched waters in the word flow around Hawaii. But these waters, Ross. These waters have only recently been released from the ice. Imagine what secrets they can tell us." God, he was a charmer.

Ross's mind flashed back to the last time she had seen Nils. He had, after a few drinks, stripped down to nothing and jumped into icy water. He didn't stay in it for long and was still smiling when he walked back out of the water, explaining that in his native country, this is often done to get the blood flowing. "This is what my people have done for centuries and is why we live so long." He had explained to the group of smiling women who had gathered.

Nils put an arm around her neck as they started to walk towards the ship.

"This is summer, Ross. I'm so glad you could make

it. Don't take this the wrong way, but I was really hoping you had nothing else going on."

"No offense taken. What are you going to do with the information though? Even if I can prove there has been drilling in the channel? What are you going to do about it?" Nils' face went serious, which Ross didn't like. It seemed unnatural.

"I, along with several environmental agencies, are trying to get the waters protected at least until we have a chance to study what is here. So far, we have been told no one is using the water because it hasn't been charted and is still full of ice floes."

"But you think it is being used?"

"I know it is. Previous research groups have found evidence in the food content of animals' stomachs and changes in their health consistent with other environments where drilling has occurred." She knew it was wrong, he was a brilliant scientist with a good cause, but Ross couldn't help staring at his man bun and wondering how he got the bun so tight. She had never been able to bun her hair. His accent also had her distracted. It was so warm and inviting, she quite honestly stopped paying attention to what he was saying. Jack's Australian accent also had an effect on her. Best not to think about that right now.

"Any idea who is doing the drilling?"

"The Russians."

"How do you know?" Ross asked. Nils shrugged. "We know." Nils' attitude was beginning to make Ross wonder what she had signed on for. She had agreed to come out and test ocean water samples for any traces of hydrocarbons, a common component of gasoline. If the hydrocarbon was found to also contain sulfur and nitrogen, then this might be evidence of crude oil and that someone was drilling in the area. If we knew someone was drilling and we knew who, what was she doing here? Ross decided to change the subject.

"Are the other researchers here?"

"For the most part. I was actually out here to look for you and for Dr. Lillian Petrov. You two are the last to arrive."

"Where was she coming from? I ran into more than one delay in getting here."

"Heading over from London."

"Well, between connecting flights and no one believing that anyone would actually want to come here, she might be running late."

"Let's get you aboard and then I will come back and

look for her. The captain wants to get out of harbor before nightfall and so do I. The farther we get tonight means the earlier we can start researching." Nils grabbed her heavier bags. He was a huge flirt, but a gentleman as well. Ross rolled the case that included her research equipment behind her.

They had reached the bottom of the gangplank that would take them to their home for the next week. Ross quickly ran through a checklist in her mind of anything she could have forgotten. There would be no stopping by the store once she was aboard. The ship's name in huge letters was right in front of her.

"The ship's name is the Hunter? Seems a little aggressive for a research vessel, don't you think?"

"Agreed, but she was the only one I could find that had ice breaking ability."

"You told me this was summer here. Why do we need an icebreaker?" Ross pretended to be annoyed. Nils flashed her his winning grin.

"This is summer, and rather warm for summer at that. Usually there is still snow on the ground. One of the reasons we are here is because the ice is melting, and those ice chunks will tear a decent sized hole in a ship without an ice breaker."

They walked up the stairs and stepped onboard. Nils moved confidently on the ship, Ross let him lead her down the side to a door that led them down the stairs into the belly of the ship. They went from bright natural light to dim artificial light. Navigating a maze of narrow corridors, Nils showed Ross where she would be sleeping. "You'll be sharing with Lillian if that's all right ?"

"Fine."

"We gentlemen will be just down the hallway." Cramped living quarters were not uncommon on these trips as most of it would be taken up with scientific equipment, food, and whatever else was needed to keep the ship going for so long. The crew would also have their own accommodations. Nils had informed her there was a captain and three support crew. They would be responsible for cooking their own food. "This is not a catered cruise." He had said, with a smile.

"I'm going to head back out and see if Dr. Petrov has arrived and if the captain needs anything. We are hoping to be away in less than an hour." Nils left her alone in the tiny room. Ross flopped her bag down on the bed and looked around for where she was going to put everything.

She smiled to herself as she unpacked the incredibly utilitarian clothing she had brought. Sam would hate it. After Sam had 'helped her pack', Ross had gone back through her luggage and removed all the useless 'colorful' and 'flattering' clothing Sam had sneaked in and replaced it with warmer, more useful items. Ross was happy to report there was not one 'pop of color' in the bag. Her standard boots were the only shoes she had brought, as well as waterproof overalls to keep her legs dry when she was out working on deck in the wind and the sea spray. Ross chuckled to herself as she thought of someone else who would like her overalls. Pulling her phones out of her coat pocket, Ross checked her phone again to see if Jack had texted her back. Nothing.

```
Ross:  Can you tell Jack I made it here okay.  We are
   setting sail in about an hour.  I  don't know what
   reception will be like.
Si: Will do. Love you. Safe journey.
```

Si replied immediately. If she was honest, it broke Ross's heart a little to see his answer come back so quickly. It meant Jack had gotten her message, he just wasn't answering.

# 9

Nils got Ross settled into her room and then went back out to look for Lillian. Her late arrival had him nervous. He hadn't spoken to her in a few days, and he was worried she had changed her mind at the last minute. He stepped onto the deck just in time to see Lillian get out of her taxi, and his grin returned. Nils half ran, half skipped down the gangplank to help her get her luggage out of the car. Ross had packed almost everything in a duffle bag. Lillian was sporting designer rolling luggage and looked like she was heading for Paris, not a research trip in a barren part of the world. He wondered with a smile on his face if she was planning on wearing those heavily pleated dress pants out on deck with the wind and the sea spray. That fashionable scarf she had tied around her neck wasn't going to do much to stop the chill either.

"Whew, you had me worried. I thought maybe you had changed your mind." He said, coming up beside her. She slammed the boot of the taxi shut a little too aggressively.

"I did. Several times." Nils grabbed her by the shoulders.

"I told you, it will be fine." And folded her into an embrace.

"And as I told you, you have no basis from which to make that claim." Lillian pointed out.

"Look, we have a plan, right?"

"Right."

"They will get what they want, and we will get what we want."

"Nils, for the last time. These are not people who are just going to go away when they get what they want. That is not what they do, trust me. They use you for whatever it is they need you for and then they get rid of the witnesses."

"I have dealt with people like this before, Lil. My organization has come across them several times. Trust me, I know what I'm doing." Lillian shook her head at him. As sure as he was that he knew what he was doing, she was just as sure that he didn't. At least this way, though, they might be able to salvage the research and the trip wouldn't be a complete waste of time.

"I suppose there is no chance of convincing you to cancel the whole thing and we will fly to some reasonable country with warmer weather and a five-star spa?" She asked before stepping up to the ship. It was hard to tell with Lillian if she was joking or not. It had been what he found most interesting and challenging about her. The smile left Nils' face. He was asking a lot, he knew that, but there was no other way to protect the waters and ice they were going to be studying. If they didn't do this, in a few years, maybe even less, the place would be thick with oil rigs and mining companies destroying the Arctic.

Nils took her hand in his and gave her his most trustworthy face. "Lillian, we have a plan. I think if we stick to the plan, it will all turn out all right. I don't want anyone to get hurt. If I honestly thought that there was a chance of that happening, I would call the whole thing off." Lillian resigned at this point. She knew that no matter what happened, it wasn't going to end well for her. If Nils did take her advice and call the whole thing off, they would kill her parents, and there was a very good chance they would kill her as well. At least the other scientists would be safe though. Since this had started, since she had told Nils what had happened, Lillian had been wondering what research was important enough to justify this amount of risk? Einstein had fled Germany. Galileo had suffered for his science, and Darwin was still taking hits even though he'd been dead over a hundred years. Was this really on the same scale?

Nils seemed to think they were saving the world, but Lillian was more realistic. They were saving a part of the world for a limited amount of time. All evidence showed that the ice was melting, and it was going to continue to melt, which meant the shipping lanes were going to get wider, and it was going to get easier to drill a seabed that humans had never accessed before. At the very best, it seemed like they were delaying the inevitable. What kept her motivated wasn't just Alexi's threats. It was the discoveries that could be made. Along with making oil and minerals easily available, the melting ice was also revealing a part of the natural world that had never been seen. Though she still wasn't sure it was worth the cost, Dr. Lillian Petrov wanted to see what all that ice had been hiding for millenia.

Lillian didn't like winning through bullying. When you boiled it down, that's what it was. Bullying. They were using intimidation to get her to do something she didn't want to, and it made her mad. Lillian wanted to beat them simply to show them that she couldn't be bullied. Then she would think of her parents and lose her nerve. It was all so complicated.

"I hope you are right, Nils." It really was the only way she could see it ending in any sort of good way.

"I hope so too. Are you clear on the plan?"

"Of course, but I don't like it."

"A week, then it will all be over." Lillian looked at her phone one last time before getting on the ship. She was waiting for a message from a friend of her brother's. Not willing to trust that Alexi would keep his end of the bargain, Lillian had put a plan in place to get her parents out of the country. It was risky. There was no way for her to inform her parents of what was happening without exposing everything. No doubt Alexi's people were listening to her phone conversations with them. Her parents were being watched, she had been able to confirm that. It would be almost impossible for anyone to enter the house without Alexi and his people knowing, and they would know her brother's friends. Her brother had been part of a small group of like minded people who made a habit of causing trouble for the government.

Lillian felt a pang of guilt for the fear her parents were going to experience, but it was better than being killed in your own home by the government you trusted. If everything went to plan, by the time she stepped back off this boat, they would be safe no matter what the fallout from what she and Nils were going to do. If everything went *extremely* well, they would be spending Christmas together in Lillian's little house with the blue gate. It would be the first Christmas they had been together in over ten years.

There was no message. Lillian's hand shook as she put her phone back in her purse. Taking one more look around at land, Lillian turned and went below deck. Nils grabbed a nearby phone on the wall and called the captain. "We are all aboard." There was no turning back now. With back straight and eyes forward, Dr. Lillian Petrov boarded 'The Hunter' for what promised to be the worst research trip anyone on board could imagine. She just hoped no one realized she could have stopped it.

# 10

Pedro sat with the other Spartans at the table in their safe house, combing through their job offers. It was a meeting they had once a week to go over new jobs and plan. They all still took independent jobs. Their prices reflected how much talent was needed. It required more organization than they had before. The biggest problem was getting in touch with potential clients without leaving a digital trail of crumbs. It appeared that while the revelation of their existence had appalled certain people, others had been eagerly seeking their services. The whole thing had been incredibly good publicity for them.

"How many do we think it will take for the research vessel up north?"

"I think one could do it. One plus a pilot." Pedro said.

"Probably, but this is a government job. According to our contact, they were going to send six people for the job. I think we could charge for four plus a pilot." Dominic said. While they charged appropriately for their skilled services, it had been almost a year since they had worked and their last job had been pro-bono.

"Six people seems like a lot for four scientists and a crew of three." Pedro added.

"They aren't us." Hesa replied.

"That is why I think we can get away with charging for four. It will keep our reputation and increase the cost at the same time."

"Too bad we can't charge for documents, that would really bring the price up." The Spartans often used fake passports and other papers to get around undetected. Hesa was the expert in this. He was also very efficient at killing people, but his false papers had fooled governments the world over.

"Our job after this is a mission in South Africa. We'll need documents for that. At this rate, we should be able to get more technology and replace our weapons within six months. The plan as it stood right now was for three of them to make the attack while a fourth was in charge of transport.

"This job in South Africa, it's going to be a complicated one. We already have one person in place, would it not be best to send another person in as support?" Pedro pointed out.

"I see no reason to send you out there early just to avoid getting cold." Dominic snipped. Pedro worked in the desert. While Spartans were designed to feel less pain, Pedro felt the cold all the way to his bones. The mission was also on a boat, which meant there was a chance of getting cold and wet. An idea he liked even less. If the mission could be achieved with one less person, and he could go help the mission taking place in a warmer location, he really didn't see what the problem was.

"It's not just to avoid getting cold. I also think we have too many people."

"This is potentially a repeat client. It's a government job, and the government has suggested they would have regular work for us if this all goes well. I think we should get them used to paying for our services. You are coming." Dominic said. Pedro would have been annoyed had it been an emotion he could feel. As it was, he felt a shiver go up his back at the anticipated cold.

Dominic went into his room and came out with a black duffle bag.

"Where are you off to?" Hesa asked.

"Weekend hunting trip nearby. There's a mafia informant being hidden by the courts. The mafia knows where he is, but they can't get to him."

"Happy hunting."

"Always." Dominic answered, tucking one of his many false passports into his top pocket. They never hunted in their own backyard. That was a hard rule. "I'll be back in two days, then we leave for the Russian mission." Dominic left. Pedro looked around. There wasn't much to be done before the mission. It was going to be rather simple. Seven people on a boat in the middle of the Arctic. Even if they managed to escape the Spartans, they would freeze to death in the water. Pedro decided to go to his own room and start packing his warmer clothes. He had one sweater he thought may be of use.

While Pedro was busy trying to find ways of not freezing to death, Inspector Louis Dufort of Interpol was looking out the window of his office, smoking and trying to spot the tiny people walking on the street below him. He hated his office. If he was in his office, it meant there was nothing going on. If there was nothing going on, he was bored, and Dufort hated being bored. He had been put on the case, with several other investigators the world over, of tracking down the Spartans after their attack on the resort the previous year. He, along with others at Interpol, had been looking for a ring of organized professional hitmen for years before the existence of the Spartans had come to light. The killings they had investigated had been clean. One shot. No evidence. No motive. No witnesses. No trail.

For the last year, Dufort had been part of a group working in other countries tracking down who had hired the Spartans for the numerous assassinations that had taken place throughout Europe. Dufort had always suspected that they were dealing with an organized unit of people. Not just one hitman. Some of the murders had happened in seperate countries at almost the same time, but with no evidence to go on, it had been impossible to prove. He couldn't believe the Spartans were what they said they were. He could never have imagined that there was a team of genetically modified humans that had been designed to kill now roaming the planet. Dufort had thought they were a very well organized terrorist organization when he first learned of the Spartans. As hard as it was to believe though, all the evidence was there to show that the Spartans were exactly what they said they were. Humans made for the specific purpose of killing.

In the past year, Interpol had retroactively attributed over three hundred and thirty murders throughout North America, Europe, Asia and Africa to Spartans simply based on the cleanliness and precision of the "kill," and the total absence of any other suspects. Dufort had closed fifteen of those cases in Europe alone. While he had no idea which Spartan had committed the murders, he was able to attribute them to the Spartans based purely on how they were carried out.

Every piece of paper they had gotten from Genetix, the company that had created the Spartans, had been picked over in the smallest detail. From there they had been able to find the false identities of the Spartans and the areas they frequented. Dufort had spent nine months tracking every lead. As best they knew, there were less than twenty Spartans still in operation, but all trails had run cold. For over a year now, no one had heard of the Spartans. The killings had stopped. The Spartans were nowhere to be found. Some in his team had thought they had all gone off and killed themselves, but Dufort's gut told him otherwise.

With nothing left to investigate, Dufort had come back to the head office. There was talk of assigning him to another case. But he wasn't done hunting Spartans yet. He knew they were out there, somewhere, and he knew they would surface sooner or later. There were still several murders he would like to see them hang for. Not to mention, he also knew there were several people and governments who would like to use them. The only good thing that one could say about the Spartans was that they revealed Genetix for what they were doing. If they weren't such evil bastards, Dufort would applaud them for what they had done.

"Inspector?"

"Hmm." His assistant came into the office and dropped a file onto his desk.

"I think this is what you have been waiting for." He said.

"What?"

"One of our informants in Turkey. They are starting to hear chatter about the Spartans." Dufort turned around quickly.

"Chatter?"

"Nothing specific, but their name is being mentioned in certain circles."

"In what way?" Not wanting to point out that the inspector could read the file for himself, his assistant picked up the file and read from it.

"They are not working independently anymore. It looks like the Spartans have joined together and are for hire."

"Are they just putting it out there, or has someone hired them?"

"We don't know."

"Are they operating out of Turkey?"

"Don't know."

"How many are there?" The assistant rolled his eyes.

"We don't know. They are just rumors and rumblings."

"What the hell DO we know?" The assistant made a point of looking at the file again.

"Our informant also said he was approached by an Iranian diplomat wanting to know if he had heard anything about the Spartans. Including if they were still around and still for hire." This is what they had been afraid of. The only saving grace was they didn't come cheap, and that had been when they were working independently. Lord knows what it costs to hire all of them.

"I guess I'm going to Turkey then." Dufort smiled. Finally, he was going to get out of this bloody office.

# 11

Ross was just hiding her chocolate stash when someone else walked into the room. Turning like she had been caught at something, Ross was greeted by a slightly surprised looking woman with the blackest hair she had ever seen.

"Hello. Sorry to scare you." The woman said in an accent Ross couldn't place.

"I was so into putting my stuff away, I didn't hear you come in. Dr. Ross Halloway." Ross extended her hand.

"Dr. Lillian Petrov."

"I hope you don't mind that I took this bed. I'll be more than happy to switch with you if you like." The woman had a very stern expression on her face, and it made Ross feel as if she had done something wrong.

"No, this one is fine, I'm sure." As she tossed her

very nice hard-shelled case onto the bed. Opening it, everything had been perfectly folded and tucked away, held in place by the straps of the case. Ross had never used those straps, figuring if she packed the case tight enough, she didn't need them.

"I always worry I've forgotten something on these trips." Ross nervously said, trying to make small talk.

"I always make a list to make sure I don't. If you are missing something, let me know, I might be able to share. I find it's important to be prepared, don't you?" Ross thought this probably passed for politeness and thanked her. Making an excuse to go up on deck, Ross left Lillian to unpack in peace. She found Nils checking to make sure some of the equipment was battened down properly.

"Just met Dr. Petrov." Ross said, catching Nils' eye.

"Yeah, did you two hit it off?" His smile told her all she needed to know. They had been housed together because they were both female, not because Nils thought they would be best buds.

"I think it's warmer out here." Ross said. This got a chuckle out of him.

"She takes some getting used to, I'll admit, but she's a brilliant scientist and a good person once you get through her tough shell. She seemed pleased when she found out you were going to be here."

"Really?" Ross would like to pretend she had no ego, but she got a small jolt of pleasure whenever another scientist knew her work. "Did she say how she knew me?"

"Your work on plastics. It was a big deal, Ross. I was very proud of you." Ross blushed. So Nils had been following her career. Nice to know she hadn't disappointed. Ross had also followed his career. While he hadn't written many papers, he had certainly been mentioned in several, and on the news. Nils had no trouble jumping in front of a camera and explaining his point of view. She was the one feeling a bit like a celebrity with two people on the ship having read her paper and liking it. "It was one of the reasons I asked you to come along." Nils admitted.

"And here I thought it was because of my sparkling dinner conversation."

Ross knew that Nils' work had mainly focused on environmental issues, which she had thought curious, but you work on what interests you. Ross was beginning to think that maybe he had completely aligned himself with environmental causes as well.

Activism science. She wasn't against it so to speak, but she thought it had the potential to cloud the science itself. What would Nils do if their research here showed that there was no traffic through the area and no drilling? It would obviously affect how they went about getting the area protected. Wouldn't it be easier to show that there was traffic through the area and thereby proving that the area needed protection? Nils seemed convinced of what the result was going to be, and he may prove to be right, but science was full of surprises, and it never lied, which is why Ross loved it. Pure science, done the way it was supposed to be done, never lied. Unlike most of the men she had dated.

"Wait, wasn't she the one you were dating...?" Nils held up a hand to stop her. If she wasn't mistaken, he may have even been blushing.

"It was a few years ago."

"You invited your ex-girlfriend on a weeklong research trip?" Either Nils was willing to suffer for his science, or he was hoping to start something back up.

"We ended amicably." How many times has someone told themselves that lie? "She is the best in her field."

"Wow, I'm feeling better about being her bunkmate now."

"Why's that?"

"Girl talk is going to be more interesting than I thought." While Nils had the decency to look nervous, Dr. Lillian Petrov didn't seem like the kiss and tell type. Maybe if Ross got her good and drunk. In all honesty though, there wasn't going to be a lot of time for such things. They had one week to collect all the data they needed. The days would be spent collecting, the nights would be spent pouring over the data and making notes for the paper that would follow. They usually let off steam the last night of the trip, and if she knew Nils, there was a stash of alcohol on this ship somewhere. Maybe she could get him to jump naked into the freezing water again.

Nils went to have a last word with the captain. Ross stayed up on deck while the crew prepared to set sail. She was feeling more like her old self now. The anticipation of the adventure. Like expeditions in the early days, there were going to be discoveries made. The crew went around in their life vests very calmly doing what needed to be done to separate them from land. Ross felt the engines kick on under her, and the boat moved away from the harbor. The butterflies flapped around in her stomach, excited by the promise of unseen things.  Man had been sailing into the arctic for centuries to discover what lived there. They had all set out with a mission in mind, but it was what happened along the way that made it an adventure. This is why she liked to do these trips every once in a while.  Get out of the lab, get the wind in your hair, and do some real science.  Discover something.

Ross was glad and somewhat surprised to find she felt this way.  After her last sea voyage, she didn't think she would ever want to get back out on the water, and she had almost turned this trip down because of it.  Her last trip had certainly caused her to lose any love she had for flying.  The trip up here had been agony, but she was glad to see her love of adventure hadn't died with it.

"Ross."  Nils yelled from the doorway. "Dinner and then a meeting."  Ross took one more look around. Land was nowhere to be seen now.  The sunset was casting beautiful colors over the sky and the water.  A mixture of reds, pinks, and oranges.  Pushing her hands deeper into her pockets, she congratulated herself on making the right decision. *'Imagine what you would have missed.'* She thought to herself and then turned and headed back into the ship. For the time being, she could forget about Jack. She would take this trip, write her paper, and then take a vacation and go and see him. It was that simple. Whenever he stopped pouting and texted her back, she would tell him just that. Ross smiled to herself. They were both sleeping on the ocean tonight. Hell, it might be daytime where he was. Either way, right now they shared the ocean and the sky above and that would have to be enough for a little while longer. Wrapping her arms tight around herself, Ross turned and went back below deck.

Nils was standing at the stove, oven mitts on his hands and a smile on his face. The rest of the party were sitting around the circular table. Lillian was still looking stern, her severe black hair tied back in a ponytail. Ross made a promise to herself to try and get to know her better. Dr. Joshua Lebedev was pleasing the party with a bottle of amber liquid. Ross's glass sat untouched on the table next to Lillian who Ross thought looked relieved to see her.

"What's for dinner?" Ross asked as she passed Nils.

"My gift to you from my neighbors in Sweden. Swedish Meatballs." And he placed a tray of meatballs smothered in lovely looking brown gravy bubbling in front of them.

"This looks wonderful Nils, is it a family recipe?" Lillian asked, and once again, Ross tried to figure out what accent she had.

"Yes. They are from my Grandmother Sternburg' s side of the family." And flashed her his winning smile which Lillian tried to return.

"To our first night." Dr. Lebedev toasted, holding up the glass of amber liquid. If Ross had to guess, he had started toasting as soon as he got on the ship. The rest of them raised their glasses and toasted. Whiskey. The amber liquid was whiskey. Dr. Lebedev filled their glasses again.

"May we all find what we are looking for and write brilliant papers." They all heartily raised a glass to that. Thankfully, the Dr. did not fill his or anyone else's glass again, and they all went about eating. Silence fell around the table.

"While I have you all here," Nils said after taking a few bites of meatballs, "I wanted to bring up one or two things. Space has been made available for your independent lab stations, but as I'm sure you are all aware, we have limited space and materials, so if you could all share that would be appreciated. The captain has also asked that we not go out on the deck after dark and please do not go into the engine room or the staff rooms. Tomorrow will be our first full day at sea. Breakfast will be at seven and will be whatever you want to make for yourself. For dinner, I have put up a rotation list so see when it is your turn to cook. Dinner was early tonight. Usually, we will eat around six."

Ross went on eating while she listened to the standard safety information. Where the life vests and lifeboats were located, etc. She was already thinking about her experiments for tomorrow if she was perfectly honest. When she got back to the room, she would have to make sure her computer was fully charged and locate her notebook. She couldn't remember unpacking it. Ross sneaked a look at her phone to see if Jack had answered her text yet. Stubborn bastard. Well, at least she knew she had done everything she could to tell him she was safe.

"Ross." Nils' voice cut through her thoughts. "Tell the others a little bit about yourself."

*'Oh God, not this.'* Ross thought to herself. *'I hate this.'* But they were all sitting there staring at her expectantly. "I'm Dr. Ross Halloway, and I'm here to look for traces of hydrocarbons, nitrogen, and sulfur in the water column which would tell us if there was gasoline from

a ship or if hydrocarbon mixed with sulfur or nitrogen would indicate crude oil and that drilling was going on in the area." They all nodded their heads at her.

"And what work have you done previously?" Dr. Lebedev asked. He was an older gentleman, well at least older than the rest of them, and he spoke with a faded Ukrainian accent.

"My most recent work was on a project that looked at using naturally occurring algae to break down plastic. The main use for this being against ocean plastic." Nils was nodding his head in an exaggerated way.

"Amazing work. Ground-breaking." He said to the group. She wanted to tell him the original discovery had been made by accident. The algae had formed naturally in the tanks with the plastic completely unintentionally. It was later discovered that the weight of the plastic had gone down in the tank with the most algae. They had called Ross's team in to confirm the findings and then find a way of making the algae work on a much larger scale. Her natural inclination was to downplay her work, but it had been a big deal even if the discovery had been made by accident. Penicillin had been discovered by accident too.

"Dr. Petrov?" Nils said, looking at Lillian.

"I am sorry to follow Dr. Halloway. I'm afraid I have not written a paper in a few years now. I have been teaching at Cambridge in their Bio-Chemical Lab. Most of my students are working on a way to absorb carbon emissions from the environment. Dr. Halloway's paper impressed them greatly. My degree is in Biochemistry, but I have been working with insects for several years. I will be collecting samples of small invertebrates found in the area and examining them for traces of exposure to crude oil. Oftentimes, it is the smallest creatures that are affected first by such things, invertebrates and the like. They are then consumed by the larger animals and the effects can be found further up the food chain as time goes on. If we find that the insect community is heavily affected, it would open up further research to examine the larger species and see how it is affecting them." Nils nodded his head to this as well and looked at Dr. Lebedev. "Do you know what species of algae it was, Dr. Halloway, that formed in the tanks?" Dr. Lebedev asked.

"It was a marine microalgae. *Phaeodactylum tricornutum.*" Ross said. She had the distinct impression Dr. Lebedev had been trying to trip her up.

"I am Dr. Joseph Lebedev. My research is related to

both of yours. I am currently working on measuring the amount of phytoplankton in our oceans both in the water column and also in the stomachs of the crustaceans that eat them. By doing this, we can discover how much light and heat is making its way through the water column now that the ice is thinning and melting, and how this is affecting the species that rely on phytoplankton for food and on up the food chain. I will also be looking for any other oceanic plant life that thrives with increased amounts of light and heat to help judge how the environment is changing as the waters get warmer. Like with most environments, we are seeing some species dying out with the warmer water, but it is opening up new areas for those that like a warmer environment."

"I was surprised to hear that there was significant plant life this far north." Ross said.

"There is plant life everywhere, but in a climate like this, it tends to be on the microscopic level." The Dr. answered. He was a professor looking type if ever there was one. A receding hairline that only left a thin strip of hair around the edge of his head. Wide, almost bulging eyes, though they may have looked bulging simply because of the thick glasses he wore. It gave him a constant surprised look.

"And I, of course, am Dr. Nils Ryeng." Nils said, bringing the conversation full circle. "I specialize in minerals. My job here will be to see if there are any traces of minerals present that would be of interest to mining companies, especially earth minerals. I am probably the only one here who is hoping to not find anything." Ross remembered now. He had gotten into minerals as a way of getting rich. There was a lot of money to be made finding the minerals used in cell phones, lithium batteries and other areas of industry. Nils had even interned for a mining company. It was how they stripped the land that had turned him. Watching waterways polluted with runoff, forests cleared, Nils had gone to the other side. Using his ability to find minerals ahead of the mining companies so that protections and regulations could be put in place to control how the mining was done.

They went on that way for the rest of the evening. Discussing each other's work. Several different disciplines, all trying to show if there was human interference in the waters above Canada opened up by the melting glaciers. The party broke up around ten, and they went to their rooms. Ross plugged in her laptop and slid it under the bed, and finding her notepad and pen, placed it next to the bed. Lillian came back from the bathroom in pajamas and a robe which seemed a little formal considering the occasion. Ross thought she looked a bit green. This was confirmed when Lillian sat down heavily on her bed and placed her head in both of her hands.

"Sea sickness?"

"I didn't think I got sea-sick. Maybe it was the meatballs." Ross rummaged in her backpack and pulled out a pill bottle and tossed it on the bed next to Lillian.

"Take two of those. You'll get the best night's sleep you've ever had, and you won't vomit." Lillian took them dry.

"Why don't you feel sick?"

"I'm wearing these." And Ross showed her the seasick bands she was wearing on each wrist.

"Thank you." And Lillian tossed Ross her pill bottle back.

"Sure." Ross went to get ready for bed. When she got back, Lillian was asleep. Ross's eye was caught by her laptop, which she thought had been pushed fully under her bed when she had left. Now it was sticking out a bit. She looked at it and back at Lillian. *I'll have to be more careful about that.'* Ross thought to herself. Pushing the laptop back under the bed, Ross laid down. Pulling her phone out one more time. Still nothing from Jack. Or Sam for that matter. Her mother had texted her weather conditions for the arctic north for the next five days. Ross hooked her phone up to the charger and got into bed. There was no one to say goodnight to. At home there was only her cat Carbon to say goodnight to, but it still counted. Picking her phone back up, Ross texted Jack one more time. 'Good night.' She knew it probably wasn't night time there, but it didn't matter since he wasn't checking his messages anyway.

Jack's phone buzzed in his pocket, and he looked at it. A mixture of emotions as he saw Ross's name come up on the screen. "Good Night." It said. He should answer her. His fingers hovered over the keypad, but he didn't type anything. It's not that he didn't want to talk to her, he just didn't know how to say what obviously needed to be said. Jack felt like exchanging pleasantries right now would be the same as lying. After their last phone conversation, he had come to a decision. It was over. There was no way they were going to be able to make it work. The distance was just too great. He felt like he should end it sooner rather than later to avoid hurting the both of them any more. *'Not like this mate, you can't text her.'* He thought to himself. *'Not like I'm going to be able to tell her face to face, though, is it?'* He answered out loud. "Goodnight love." He said, but he put the phone back in his pocket without answering. The thought had occurred to him to throw his phone in the ocean. That way he wouldn't have to feel so guilty about not answering Ross, but he didn't. He took another drink of his beer and continued to look out on the water.

# 12

In the wee hours of the morning, Ross got up to go to the bathroom and couldn't get back to sleep. She laid in her bunk, eyes wide open, listening to the ship and the water. Giving up, she quietly grabbed her coat and left the room. Grabbing a cup of tea from the canteen, she headed up to the deck. Nils had said they weren't supposed to be up here, but she figured if she stayed out of sight of the control room, no one would know. The wind hit her hair, and the cold wind did more to wake her up than to put her to sleep. She leaned against the railing and sipped her tea. It was creepy with there still being light in the sky. The sound of the water moving past the ship was soothing .

"Can't sleep either?" Ross did not have to turn around to know it was Nils behind her.

"Start of cruise jitters." She answered. Nils came up

beside her, his own cup in his hand.

"I always love the start of a trip. It's not that I think I'll make any groundbreaking discovery, but you always find something that you didn't know before, don't you?" Nils said, leaning over the railing next to her.

"It's like there is something in the air. It's what connects us to the scientists of the past. I bet it's the same feeling scientists have been feeling since man first set out to see what they could see." Ross said. Such voyages were not done anymore. These days, funding had to be sought and secured in advance, and for some reason, people didn't want to pay for you to just sail about finding what you could find. " wonder if Darwin or Cook had to file endless grant applications? Sort of takes all the romance out of it, doesn't it?" Asked Ross.

"What do you think of our ship mates?"

"A bit early to say, really. Lillian seems nice enough, a bit stern. Dr. Lebedev is interesting." Ross shrugged her shoulders.

"I think I am going to hide Dr. Lebedev's liquor stash." Nils said, giving her a knowing look.

"Bit of a drinker?"

"Hmmm...he is supposed to be taking a leave of absence from his university. Apparently, he had one too many at the Christmas party and was called out for smacking the bum of the department head."

"Oh my."

"Mmmm....he made it worse by telling her he didn't know she was the departmental head. You know, her being a woman and all."

"Wow!" There was a moment of silence between them.

"Ross, can I be honest with you?"

"I hope so, Nilly. What's up?"

"I need to prove there is something going on out here. If we can't find evidence that the wildlife is being affected, then we won't have a leg to stand on when it comes to protecting it. It's not just the oil they are after. They are lining up to mine for gold, nickel, copper, gallium, and indium. They are all hungry for it, they are all looking for another source for it. The mining companies are just waiting for it to warm enough to where their machines will run here year long. The only thing holding them back is the cold. Their machines freeze easily. Thankfully, the parts for such machines are not cheap." Ross watched his face. He was impassioned. Almost mad. "Imagine there being some undiscovered species out there, and it will be gone from the planet before we even knew it was there." Ross took a sip of her tea. She remembered Nils and how intense he could get. It had been attractive when she was younger, but now she thought it sounded like he wanted her to find something whether it was there or not. Ross was all for protecting the place, and she would sign whatever he wanted advocating for it, but she wouldn't falsify her results.

"If there is something there Nils, we'll find it." She smiled over her teacup.

"Oh, it is here, I know it is."

"Then there won't be a problem, will there? What makes you so sure they are drilling anyway? I assume you had to have some evidence to get the funding."

"There have been sounds of drilling in the area."

"Sounds of drilling?"

"Other ships' radios have picked it up in the background. Drilling through the seafloor makes a lot of noise, Ross. Other groups have tried to track them down, catch them in the act, but so far they haven't managed. We think they are drilling from ships. Once the ship is full of crude, they leave. Thankfully, the

Russians haven't made too many friends of late, and the idea of them getting their hands on the oil before anyone else has made this one of the easiest trips I have ever had to find funding for."

"You would think it would be hard to hide something like that."

"This is still new territory. A lot of people still think this water is impassible. If the water isn't frozen, then there are ice floes that can wreck a ship. They think if they can't get through here, no one can, but ice is nothing new to the Russians, and you will be hard pressed to find another government willing to bend all the rules to get what they want."

"Well, if you are that sure that there is drilling going on, there is no reason to worry. We will find the proof."

"I'm really glad you are here." Nils said, placing his hand over hers.

"You invited me Nils."

"I know. I am glad you are here as a scientist. I know you will do good work. But I am also glad that *you* are here. You were always so mysterious." He was looking at her the same way he used to when they were younger. Like he was trying to figure her out.

"I'm not mysterious." Ross laughed to herself. She

used to melt like butter when he looked at her all those years ago. Nils had always been a flirt. Ross knew that. She had just been flattered he was flirting with HER. Watching it now made Ross laugh. Did he really think this act was going to work on her now? Did it work on anyone at this age?

"I always thought so. You weren't silly like the other girls. I thought you were so smart that I used to try and find interesting things to say to impress you." She laughed out loud at this.

"Did you really?" Ross hated to tell him, but she could not remember one interesting thing he had said to her back then. "The other women on the trip seemed to think you were interesting enough."

"It worked on them, but it never worked on you." Ross shrugged. That was true.

"I was there for work, Nils. It's not that I didn't notice, I just couldn't get bogged down in all that stuff. There was work to be done and I wanted to do it right." He grinned at her. He had a dangerous grin that made you wonder what he was really thinking.

"And that is why I invited you on this trip. I know no matter what happens, no matter what storms are ahead, you will do the job you came to do." Nils gave her a kiss on the cheek and said, "Get some sleep, you have discoveries to make."

"What storms? I thought all the storms were in the winter up here?" Ross said. She had checked the forecast. Her mother had continued to check the forecast. There was supposed to be clear skies the whole week.

"Oh Ross, always so literal." Nils turned and went back down below decks.

# 13

The alarm clock went off at 6:00 a.m. Ross should have been exhausted. But she wasn't. It was the first day. Getting dressed, she put on her unflattering overalls and grabbed the bag she had packed the night before and made her way to the canteen where Nils was already serving coffee and breakfast sandwiches. He gave Ross a wink when she walked into the room, Lillian right behind her. Dr. Lebedev stumbled in looking like he had a hard night and did not speak to anyone until he had a sip of coffee.

Ross didn't stick around to make conversation; she went up to the deck to set up her station. The bright sun hit her in the face as she came out on deck. She set up a table for herself at the front of the ship and carefully laid out the equipment. Most of the equipment was meant to be transported, but it was still sensitive. Taking the spectrometer out of the case, Ross calibrated it. She then took a sample of water she had gotten from the canteen and ran it through the machine. This was always an alarming exercise as she always found all kinds of things in the drinking water. Since the clean water was being held in tanks, it was not surprising to find iron oxide in the water. Rust. Ross regretted not bringing a water purifier but at least the machine was working.

By the time she had finished this and was ready for her first sample, a few hours had passed. Ross looked around and the deck was getting crowded now. All her colleagues were at their own work stations doing whatever it was they needed to do for their own experiments. The wind was strong at times and definitely cold enough to make her eyes water. If this was the summer, she was glad to miss winter. Taking her sample cups, Ross took water samples from the different water columns, carefully marking down where the ship was when the samples were taken, at what depth the cups had been lowered, and what the current conditions were. Leaning over the side of the boat, Ross pushed a button that opened all the sample cups at the same time. Giving it a minute, she then released the button and closed the cups. Bringing them back up to the surface, Ross returned to her station to run them through the spectrometer. The sample size was not huge considering the size of the body of water they were currently in. From the sample she took, Ross used a pipette to place the sample in a tube that would then be spun down. Depending on how much artifact was in the water, Ross would be able to tell if there was drilling going on. To make sure she wasn't picking up run off from the ship, her station was at the front of the ship. It seemed simple enough, but the devil was in the details. Ross had to make sure everything was recorded in such a way as to make the tests repeatable, should anyone want to.

"How are things going?" Nils asked over her shoulder. She was poised, sample tube in hand, ready to add it to the spectrometer.

"Nothing so far Nils, but the day is young. What are you up to?"

"Helping where needed. We are too far out from anything for me to do much. Tomorrow we are going to get closer to land. I'll be getting my samples then. Let me know if you find anything." Nils went off to check on the others.

Ross looked over her shoulder. Lillian was setting up special lights that would attract any passing flying insect. She was on top of the bridge and looked like a sudden gust of wind would blow her backwards. Dr. Lebodev was leaning over the side of the ship. At first Ross wasn't sure if he was working or being sick, then he came up with a water sample.

The day went on that way. At regular intervals, Ross would lower her sample cups and get samples from the different water columns. She would make her notes as to where the ship was, the current, and how far down the samples were collected, and then she would carefully run them. The spectrometer gave a print out of each sample, which Ross carefully placed in her notebook with time, date and location.

It was tedious, but that was how it was done. The fact that there were no significant levels in the water today did not discourage her. This would be her control group. By the end of the day, her back hurt from bending over the table. The wind picked up as the day went on. By dinner time they were all glad to find the shelter of the kitchen. Lillian cooked that night, and they had hearty beef stew which hit the spot after spending so much time in the cold wind.

"I normally serve it with my homemade bread, but I didn't think customs would let me through with  my rising yeast." Lillian said.

*'Of course she does.'* Ross thought to herself. *'Probably makes her own yeast as well.'*

The scientists all sat down to eat in silence. After a while, Ross turned to Lillian and asked, "Did you catch anything?"

"Not a lot today, no.  I'm hoping my bug catcher will be full tomorrow morning when I check it.  It will most likely all be mosquitos.  Though I am holding out hope for an Arctic Wooly Bear Moth. It wouldn't be for my research, I've just never seen one before and they have been found in this climate."  Lillian genuinely pleased at the idea of finding one.

"Wooly Bear Moth?"  Ross had a mental image of a grizzly bear with wings.

"Very interesting species, actually.  They were thought to be extinct until recently.  They are the fluffiest looking things. Just adorable." Ross was going to have to rethink Lillian's stern persona if she continued to go to bits about cute insects. "Nils and I are going to land tomorrow hopefully.  I'm hoping to get a wider variety of insects there.  Maybe some pseudoscorpions."

"Sorry. Did you say scorpions?" This had Ross's attention. This was the Arctic. Ross thought you just had to worry about Polar Bears and freezing to death. "There are scorpions this far north?"

"Pseudoscorpions. They look like scorpions, but they are a subspecies. They are as common as house spiders up here. Don't worry, humans aren't affected by the venom in their pincers."

'Jesus.' Ross thought to herself. There was no way she was getting into bed tonight without checking for those little bastards. She also stopped talking to Lillian before she found out what else was in the environment here.

"What about you, Dr. Lebedev, did you have a fruitful day?" The older man had been sitting in silence for most of the meal.

"I did. Lots of phytoplankton in the water column. I shall collect some more tomorrow and then start examining their stomach contents." Ross nodded her head and smiled, but after finding out that there were scorpions around, she wasn't about to ask how you examined the stomach contents of a phytoplankton.

"I caught a couple of Tardigrades, Dr. Petrov, if you

are interested." Dr. Lebedev offered.

"Oh, yes please. I find water bears incredibly fascinating."

"Water bears?" What the hell was a water bear? She was almost afraid to ask. It sounded like a fun way to describe a polar bear, but surely she would have noticed that being pulled aboard.

"Tardigrades." Lillian answered, as if this completely explained what they were.

"Sorry, I'm a chemist." Ross explained.

"They are small water-dwelling creatures with eight legs. Micro animals. They are also called moss piglets. I think piglets describe them better than bears, really. They can live in almost any environment. Your country sent them to space. They did rather well up there. I believe some were left by Isreali astronauts on the moon. They are still there." Lillian answered her.

"Moss piglets." Ross answered back.

"I'll see if I can't get one on the microscope for you later. They are really fascinating creatures." Ross wasn't sure she wanted to know what a Moss Piglet looked like, but she was fascinated to know that all these living creatures were in the water around them.

"Fascinating." Ross said.

"It is, isn't it? And to think it has been here all the time. We just didn't know it." Nils said.

This was what Ross had come for. This is what she loved about these trips. The sharing of information. Learning new things from other scientists. It was like a salve for Ross's soul. She could feel the old Ross coming back to life. For the first time in a long time, she felt like she had before Ikan Hui. Ross patted herself on the back for knowing what she needed and fighting for it. Jack would see. He would see it the next time they saw each other. She would be like she was before.

Ross was also starting to share some of Nils' desires to protect the place. These creatures had been up here for a very long time, with no one to bother them. She didn't like the idea of the poor Wooly Bear Moth and this Moss Piglet being killed off just so she could have a thinner iphone with a half a centimeter wider screen. Looking up, she locked eyes with Nils and he smiled.

"The Moss Piglet must be protected." He said through his smile.

"You should have put that on a t-shirt."

"I might just do that."

"You should. Obviously, you would have to explain

what they are first. Could be a great way to raise money."

# 14

Ross was doing the clearing up after dinner. Nils was making more coffee when, "I have to say, these research trips have gotten a lot more interesting since more women got into the sciences. Haven't they Nils?" Dr. Lebedev interrupted her thoughts. His bottle of whiskey had been sitting on the table since the start of dinner. Looking considerably lighter now, Dr. Lebedrv was looking heavier. As soon as the bowls were cleared away, they had all gone about analyzing the day's data.

Lillian had pulled out her laptop and started working. So had Dr. Lebedev. Unfortunately, he had also been drinking and getting more opinionated to the point where almost all conversation had stopped. Ross had become so uncomfortable, she had offered to do the dishes, and Nils had offered to make coffee. Dr. Lebedev's new topic injected a new level of awkwardness. Ross and Nils exchanged glances. It wasn't so much what he said that made the others look at each other, but the predatory way that he said it.

"I don't know Joseph. I always thought these trips were interesting." Nils said, sliding the bottle farther away from him and replacing it with a cup of black coffee.

"You are too young, you probably don't remember the early days when it was just men. It was the eighties before I remember there being a woman around. Some of the crew refused to sail, saying she was 'bad luck.' They may have been right. God, she had been so uptight, she didn't make it easy for herself." Dr. Lebedev's eyes scanned Lillian when he said this, which made her visibly bristle. Ross was starting to get her back up as well. Reading the room, Nils said, "Was it as bad as they said it was on the H.M.S. Endurance?"

Referring to a famously doomed arctic research trip made in the early nineteen hundreds. Dr. Lebedev did not seem to pay attention, instead staring at Lillian in an uncomfortable way. His gaze went from accusatory to predatory quickly.

"The attractiveness of the female scientist has gotten better though. Back when I was starting out, it was

always the short, fat ones with bad skin. Now look."
He raised an eyebrow at Lillian and licked his lips
before taking another drink. Nils had never seen
Lillian with any sort of weapon. She didn't really need
one. More than one person (usually a man) had
underestimated her and left carrying his shattered ego
in his hands. Some had never been repaired. "Mind
you, it has come at a cost. It has made it harder for us
men. Hasn't it Nils."

"Please leave me out of this." Nils said, not wishing
to be painted with the same brush. Dr. Lebedev didn't
hear him though.

"I mean if the promotion in the department comes up
and it's down to me, looking like this, and a woman
looking like that." He said, indicating Lillian. "There is
no question as to who is going to get it. Is there?"

At this Ross cleared her throat. She felt the blood
rushing to her face. It was rude to get into it with a
colleague on the second night of a trip and almost
guaranteed that there would be tension for the rest of
the journey, but she was finding it hard to keep her
mouth shut at this point. Since Nils had invited them
all, it was up to him really to sort it out, but if he didn't
do it soon, Ross was willing to take a crack at it.

"Joe, that isn't the reason you didn't get the job. I think it's time for you to head to bed." Nils said, in a final attempt to save the man before the women tore him to shreds. Dr. Lebedev looked at all of them like they were fools and grabbed his bottle back. "I'm not a child, Nils. I was heading departments when you were still in diapers." Ross was opening her mouth when Lilian cut her off.

"Dr. Lebedev, I think what Nils is saying is, it's time for you to go to bed before someone tells you the truth and embarrasses you."

"And what would the truth be?" Nils closed his eyes. The man was beyond help now. Either Lebedev was too drunk to see the trap he had just walked into or he was bucking for a fight. Either way, Lillian was about to pounce. A friendly smile spread across Lillian's face. Nils knew this for what it was, and he turned away so he wouldn't have to witness the carnage.

"You aren't the head of your department because you are surrounded by attractive female scientists, Dr. Lebedev." Lillian's voice was soft and smooth. Almost like she agreed with him. "You aren't the head of your department because you have a famous reputation for drinking too much and harassing your female students and co-workers. Speaking as one of those women who *is* head of her department. Possibly, because she is more attractive than her male counterparts. Something that isn't difficult since a lot of them are overweight, have incredibly bad breath and all the social graces of a slug. Though I haven't known you for a long time, judging from your professionalism and the fact you are either drunk or hungover to the point where you wouldn't know a scientific breakthrough if it hid itself at the bottom of a bottle. You are a liability and an embarrassment to any establishment you would work for. I mean, they could hardly brag about you to potential donors could they? Not many rich parents want to open their checkbooks with Dr. Drunk and Creepy leering at their wife or daughter." Lillian stood up and leaned across the table. "Is it just possible, Dr. Lebodev, that the reason you feel yourself sinking into obscurity is because that is exactly where you belong?" She picked up the bottle and poured him another drink. "Now, how about another drink and let's see if you can make a complete ass of yourself." Dr. Lebedev's face was so flushed he looked almost purple. Slamming his hands down on the table, he got up and stormed out of the canteen. A big sigh was let out by the rest.

"I'm sorry about that ladies. That isn't what he thinks of you when he's sober."

"Oh, I think it might be." Ross said, not willing to give the man an excuse.

"I better go check on him." And Nils left the canteen, correctly assuming that the women would rather be alone. The two women looked at each other and shrugged their shoulders. Lillian picked up the bottle of whiskey left behind by Dr. Lebedev and poured herself a splash and then offered Ross some. Ross accepted. Why the hell not? Dr. Lebedev certainly didn't need it anymore.

"Thank you for doing that. The man needed to be shut down. I was going to do it, but I think you did a better job of it. I bet they really do want him to retire. I can't imagine anyone wanting a man like that around their school." Ross asked.

"Oh, it's a fact. I happen to know the head of his department. We were at a conference for women in science a few years ago. She didn't mention him by name, of course. You, I had heard of. I had obviously heard of Nils, but I had not heard of Lebedev. Turns out, there was a good reason for it. She told me he was a sexist pig of an age gone by and a bum pincher. " She said, responding to Ross's questioning look.

"You knew about me?" Ross asked.

"Of course. What I didn't know I Googled."

"What did Google have to say about me?"

"You know perfectly well what it said." Lillian sounded stern again. "It was impressive." Ross had to smile. She did know what it said, and she knew it was impressive.

"Yours wasn't bad either." Ross said, pouring Lilian a drink this time.

"So you Googled as well?"

"I had only heard of Nils. We were on a research trip like this one when we were in grad school."

"I'm somewhat disappointed you hadn't heard of me, but I'm glad you agree that I'm impressive." Lillian said, draining her glass. A smile was on the woman's face, and Ross thought it changed everything about her. She no longer looked hard and calculating. "What made you get into science, Ross?"

"I loved chemistry. I was good at it. It made sense to me. I found it fascinating that chemistry had a part in just about every facet of our lives. When I got to college, I wanted to know more about it. I really liked knowing what was going on, what was being studied and what the practical application of the discoveries would be. I wanted to be a part of that too. What about you? What got a good looking young lady like yourself into science?" They 'clinked' glasses and downed another drink before Lillian answered.

"Same, for the most part. I liked how biology explained the natural world, but I was also interested in chemistry. I couldn't really choose, so I went with both. I went to school and college in Russia. I managed to get a visa to study abroad in England then I never left. It opened a whole new world for me. There was no limit on what you could learn." There was something in Lillian's eyes when she mentioned Russia. Lillian poured them another glass. "When was the first time you realized you weren't really wanted in the science world?" Lillian asked. It was so blunt, it took Ross by surprise.

Ross had talked to other female scientists about it before, the hardship of being a female in the hard sciences. They never called it being 'unwanted', but that's what it was for some. Like Dr. Lebedev. It wasn't that he could deny women contributed, he just didn't want women as equals.

"High school." Ross said without having to think about it. The first time you find your natural ability is seen as a threat by some is hard to forget. "Not only did I find out that boys didn't like smart girls, I found out that intelligent women were viewed differently by their teachers as well. Which was disappointing." Lillian nodded agreement. "I made the mistake of correcting my high school chemistry teacher, very innocently, that he had done an equation wrong. I mistakenly thought he would want to know. How wrong I was." Ross took a sip of her drink. It still stung to think about it. He had called her out in the middle of the class. It had been so embarrassing.

"He did not take it well?" Lillian went to pour Ross another drink and Ross covered her glass. Lillian shrugged and poured another for herself. Ross had heard the Russians could drink.

"He did not. Like Dr. Lebedev, he seemed to think I had done it simply to make him look like a fool in front of his class. No matter how hard I pleaded that I had simply wanted to correct the mistake, he didn't believe me. It was the only time I was ever given detention, not that I went. When I told my mother what had happened, she called the principal. Gave him an ear full. Not that it helped. The teacher didn't like that I hadn't had to pay for my insubordination either. It was the first time I found out how fragile the male ego was. I went from being teacher's pet to 'knowing too much for my own good' quickly. What about you?"

"Grade school I think was the earliest I can remember."

"As early as that?"

"Mmmm. Like yourself, I realized the adults around me who were supposed to know everything perhaps did not know as much as they thought. My parents wanted to send me to a school for gifted children. I would have been one of the few female students. My mother was actually told by the principal of the school that doing so would be tantamount to sentencing me to a lifetime of isolation. No man was going to want a 'genius' wife. Why set me up for a life of disappointment. Better to tell me there was nothing special about my abilities."

"Wow." Ross said. Genuinely shocked.

"We were from a very traditional town. Thankfully, my mother thought it was a sin to deny my god given talent. The next time I remember was in college. By that time I knew how good I was. I was smarter than half the staff and already had my sights set on studying abroad where more advances were being made. I got a worse grade on a test than I deserved. When I went to ask my professor about it, he grinned at me. You know the grin I'm talking about. The one that means there is something else they want. I told him I had double checked my math and there was no other answer. With that grin on his face, he informed me that the answer he *said* was right, *was* the right answer."

"Really!"

"That if I wanted to change his mind, I could hang my clothes on the hook behind the door and lay down on the couch."

"Jesus."

"I applied for Cambridge that evening."

"Did he change the grade?" Ross couldn't help but ask. Lillian looked her squarely over the rim of her glass.

"I left with the grade I walked in with."

"Good. What a bastard. It's strange though, isn't it. I never really think about how me just being who I am affects the men around me. The fact that I am doing my work and not worrying about what they think of me drives them crazy." Ross decided she could afford one more drink. "Sometimes I don't think they will ever get used to us."

"They will. They will have no choice." Lillian said, pouring herself the last bit of the bottle. Her Russian accent was much stronger now. Ross smiled. She sounded like a Bond villain.

"Oh yeah." Ross said. She wasn't so sure, or at least that she would see it in her time. Lillian's eyelids were heavy now. Ross was somewhat relieved to see the whiskey having some effect. "How can you be so sure?"

"Because we will not go away. In fact, there will be more of us. With every generation, there will be more of us. Dr. Lebedev and his kind will die (early of liver failure most likely) and in his place a woman will take over. In the meantime, we will do great work and make great discoveries." Lillian raised her glass. Ross raised her own, more than willing to toast such a world.

# 15

The next morning there was no mention of Dr. Lebedev's behavior. They each went to the canteen in their own time and got their coffee and what breakfast they wanted before going about their business. Ross caught a glimpse of Dr. Lebedev going to his work station and was pleased at least to see the man appeared to have a serious hangover. An apology would have been nice, but she wasn't expecting one.

They were now in deeper water away from any harbors or ports. If she found hydrocarbons and sulfur here, it might indicate that someone had been drilling. She went about her work with more interest. The readings she had gotten the day before would be good baselines. After doing her calibrations, she took her first reading. To her surprise, the numbers were up in every part of the water column. Ross did not get excited. She never got excited over one set of numbers. When lunch time hit and she was still getting elevated numbers, then she started to get a little excited. The numbers were still small, but it was enough to keep looking.

"Nils." She called out as the rest were heading down for their lunch. "I think I might have some good news for you."

"Really?" Relief and pleasure crossed his face.

"The numbers are higher today than they were yesterday. With us being farther out, I would have thought they would be down, but they aren't. It's been that way all morning."

"Is there anything I can do to help?" He looked like he would run across the water if she asked.

"I would love to find out how far away from land we are. If we are in a deeper channel, I might try and get a deeper reading."

"I'll speak with the captain. I don't think that will be an issue. This is great Ross, really great."

"Don't get too excited Nils, I might come back from lunch and they are back to normal, but right now it looks like someone has been digging up crude oil." Nils went up the stairs to speak with the captain. Ross looked around her and noticed Lillian still on deck talking animatedly on her phone. She was speaking Russian, but it was clear that she was not enjoying it. Ross thought about asking her if everything was alright but then decided she wouldn't interrupt, going below deck to grab a sandwich.

Nils got Ross readings from the captain that showed he was taking them through the deepest water.

"They are going to drop Lillian and me off on land so I can get some samples. I should be back by dinner. I want to know what you find. This is big Ross." Nils was vibrating with excitement. Ross watched from her work station as Nils and Lillian loaded themselves into a small dingy and headed off for land. Nils was buzzing. With new energy, Ross went back to her measurements while Nils and Lillian buzzed away to get their own samples on land.

There was no discussion between Nils and Lillian on the way to land. It was too noisy and Lillian didn't want to risk speaking in front of the crew member who had brought them. Having landed, Nils and Lillian split up. The area of their research had been predetermined. Lillian had taken off with her bug nets looking for grassy areas. Nils had found a patch of land that looked promising with less grass and more rock. He put his backpack down on the ground and pulled out his instruments. Taking a handheld core sampler, he plunged it into the ground and took a core sample. Examining the contents, he didn't see anything that looked particularly interesting and put it into a baggy which he labeled. Nils took random samples from the area, taking map readings as he went with a handheld GPS. Each sample went into a plastic bag that was then labeled with its exact location. He was not only looking for precious metals, but the soil commonly found along with precious metals. For the first hour, there wasn't much of anything and he felt hopeful. He may be able to report that there was nothing of interest in the land.

Moving to another location, he shoved his sampler into the ground again. He at first came up with nothing much, but then the sampler brought up Tourmaline. "Shit." Nils said out loud. Tourmaline was a common mineral found in the same mines as gold. Nils rolled it around in his hand looking at the inky blackness of the stone, chipping away at it with the handle of the sampler. There was a chance Nils was wrong, so he would double check all the samples when he got back to the ship. But he wasn't wrong. He had seen it enough to spot it in the field. Nils took more samples, Tourmaline was in all of them to various degrees. "Shit, shit, shit." He had one more location in mind for taking samples, but he almost didn't want to check it.

The presence of Tourmaline didn't guarantee that there was gold in the bedrock or the sea floor around it. Its presence was enough to get the mining companies' attention though. A consistent amount of Tourmaline would be enough for them to dig everything up until they were sure there was no gold. Putting the sample in the baggy and labeling, Nils planned on reaching out to his organization tonight and letting them know what they were finding. They would need the papers from everyone before officially applying for protection, but they could start getting their ducks in a row now. He wondered how Ross was doing with her samples. Hopefully, the numbers were still elevated. *I wonder how soon she thinks her paper will be ready to publish.'* Nils moved to his third and final location, the sun hanging low in the sky. Nils was further disappointed to find a lithium rich Tourmaline. He was half way through his last sampling when Lillian came walking towards him. She was wearing a beige jumpsuit and a mosquito net over her head. Somehow she managed to make it still look fashionable. Maybe it was the neatly tied scarf around her neck.

"Happy hunting?" He yelled at her.

"Mostly bloody mosquitoes, but I caught a few other things. How about you?"

"There is Tourmaline, for better or worse."

"Speak English please, my mineral isn't so good." She brought out her Russian accent for the joke.

"It's commonly found in the same area as gold." Her eyebrows raised.

"You aren't sure that is good news?"

"It means the land needs protecting against the mining companies. The mining companies are going to want to make damn sure there isn't gold buried deeper and they have deep pockets. Our mission just got a lot harder."

"Your mission, Nils. My mission is to get out of this alive." Lillian sat down. They were close to the spot where they were going to be picked up. Lillian carefully sat the bag housing her specimens on the ground. Nils looked at his watch. They had about fifteen minutes before their pick up was scheduled.

"Nils, I think we should tell them." Lillian said point

blank.

"We can't." Nils sounded exhausted. He had thought of nothing else since the ship left land.

"It doesn't seem fair, them not knowing. I wouldn't mind really if Dr. Lebedev got his ass kicked a little. But I like Ross, and so do you. I feel like an asshole getting friendly with her and all the time not letting her know what is going to happen. It just doesn't seem fair." Nils sat down next to her. He knew what she was talking about and the thought had crossed his mind as well. "Lillian, we can't and you know that."

"Do I? Why can't we tell them? We might even be able to put up some kind of a fight."

"Lillian, if they think that you told the rest of us, if it appears that we were prepared for what is going to happen in any way, what will happen to your parents? If Dr. Lebedev calls home and tells them that we are expecting a problem, what will happen to your parents?" Lillian clenched her jaw; they both knew the answer to that question.

"I don't like it. Ross is a good person. I feel like I am betraying her."

"Ross is a strong woman. She has survived worse than this before. You are betraying her, but it's nothing she can't handle."

"The whole thing is so unbelievable. I've been wondering if it is worth the life of my parents." Lillian had not said this out loud before, and she wasn't sure she should have now. Nils looked at her slowly.

"What do you mean?"

"Look at what we are doing here. We have some of the best minds working on saving this place. Our research is going to lead to more great minds coming out here and making more discoveries. With that information, we could protect this entire area. Other scientists could explore it. Who knows what has been lying frozen up here for all these millions of years. Is the life of two old people in Russia really worth all that?" A tear ran down Lillian's cheek. A rare thing, Nils knew.

"I cannot and will not put a price on any human being's heads, Lil. I am hoping with the plan that we came up with, we can manage both things. It will take some sacrifice, and our colleagues will have to sacrifice as well , but I think we can do it."

"I hope you are right, Nils. I really hope you are right." They waited in silence to be picked up. Both wondered how bad this was going to be and when exactly it was going to happen.

# 16

"Can I help you Sir?" The clerk approached.

"I'm heading up north. I need something to keep me warm without restricting my movements." Pedro said. He had flown into Canada a day ahead of the others so he could get some decent cold weather gear. Something that was incredibly hard to find in the middle east.

"What are you heading up there for?"

"Hunting."

"Oh yeah, what's in season this time of year?"

"I don't know, but whatever is in season we are hunting. What about these? I don't want my hands to be so cold my trigger finger doesn't work." Pedro waved a pair of gloves.

"Those are nice, they are waterproof, but if you are going to be out in the cold for an extended period of time the cold will creep in. Let me show you these." The store clerk went to walk over to a display when a small child ran up to him and stopped, looking up at him. The small child just stared at them, bundled head to toe. The mother soon caught up with it and said, "Can we use your bathroom?"

"Yes ma'am, through there." The clerk directed. The mother smiled at both of them, locked eyes with Pedro and made a face he took as not pleasant and hurried away. Pedro thought the child looked very warm in his full body snowsuit and thick gloves, but Pedro didn't think he would have the dexterity to fire a rifle with any accuracy since he couldn't even put his arms down.

"Sorry about that. They have been in and out of here all day. All that snow we got last week, the kids have been playing in the park across the street. I wanted to show you these over here." The clerk took him to a stall. "These are hand warmers. When your hands get cold, you just mash them and then stick them in your pocket and they warm up your hands. I like to also stick them in my boots. They keep your feet nice and warm as well. What kind of boots do you have? If you are going to be out there for very long you should really have bunny boots."

"Bunny boots?"

"They are snow boots, designed so that your feet won't freeze in negative degree weather."

"Do you have them in black?" Pedro left the store. Sure enough there were tons of kids playing in the park across the street. The mother with the child who needed to pee had misread Pedro's face. What she had taken as disdain was actually curiosity. Children amused Pedro. Having never really being a child himself, he found them a constant curiosity. They were like small adults, but none of the concern and weight of life. They did and said the dumbest things and yet parents seemed to go to great lengths to preserve them.

Pedro sat down on a park bench and played one of his favorite games, trying to match the child with the parent. When you are a sniper, you sometimes spend long hours in one location waiting for your target. Small games like this helped pass the time. It was harder with these kids though because they were covered head to toe in clothing. Pedro did not have parents, well parents like these kids did anyway. While they had been genetically altered, an egg and sperm had come together to make them, just in a test tube. There had been much speculation as to where the 'samples' had come from. Unfortunately, Mother had not divulged her source in the records she had left behind. Mother hadn't thought the original source was important, it was what she was going to do with them that mattered. There had been rumors that the eggs at least had been gotten from female prisoners and there was some weight to those rumors. With no records, though, it was impossible to prove. What was clear was that the genetic material had not all been from the same source. The Spartans resembled every creed and color the world had thought to create. Pedro thought there must have been some intended criteria since all of them were tall, thin, and athletic in appearance.

These children looked so open and innocent. When he had worked for the military as a sniper, he had actually been ordered to shoot some children. Some as young as ten. The enemy didn't really care that they were children. They would strap a bomb to anyone. At some point he had befriended a kid in the middle east. Well, as much as a Spartan befriends anyone. The kid had been a street urchin. He hadn't been too bad of a shot actually. One day he had stopped coming around. Pedro hadn't thought of him in ages.

"It's good to get them out isn't it?" A gentleman had

sat down next to Pedro and was attempting small talk. "There will be more than one tired kid on the way home tonight. Which one is yours?"

"None of them." The man made a face.

"So you are just sitting here watching?"

"I was until you got here." Pedro got up and walked off, but he kept watching the kids as he went. One kid took a snowball right to the face and immediately burst into tears. It's mother came to brush the snow off and check for injuries. Pedro couldn't imagine crying over a snowball to the face. He couldn't remember ever crying. But he did wonder about having a mother. From what he knew of genetics, the parts of his DNA that hadn't been messed with by Mother and Father belonged to someone. Out there was a woman who looked like him, who carried the same genetic material he did. His mother. No doubt she would be less than thrilled to find out a Spartan could be traced back to her. That would be if Pedro could somehow trace her.

A snowball landed near Pedro.

"Sorry." The kid yelled. There was no chance of a little Pedro running around out in the world. There had been some talk of allowing Spartans to propagate themselves thereby cutting down on laboratory costs.

What Mother hadn't been able to figure out was how to guarantee the desired genetic material was passed along. Future generations of Spartans may have been able to have children, but Pedro and the rest of his generation were sterile. Pedro picked up a snowball, packed it tight and threw it back. Perfect aim, he hit the kid in the back. His fingers now freezing, he stuck them in his pocket and walked as quickly as he could back to the warmth of his room. A warmth he had no intention of leaving until it was time to leave for the mission.

# 17

Out of caution, Ross calibrated the machine again. More than one scientist's results had been ruined by faulty machinery. She lowered the sample containers to a lower depth, making notations for each new depth, carefully writing down the locations and the current condition of the water. Having taken her samples, she brought the containers back to the surface, one by one, and ran them through the machine. The numbers were even higher.

Either hydrocarbons were coming from the ocean floor, or they were sinking from the surface because they were heavier than water. What was certain was that they didn't free themselves from the earth. Crude oil was definitely in the water column. Either someone was drilling, or a container ship was leaking while transporting it. Ross made sure she was accurate in everything she did. Nils wouldn't be the only person interested in her findings, and she needed to make sure they would hold up against heavy scrutiny. Ross nearly jumped out of her skin when Nils tapped her on the shoulder. She had neither heard nor seen the dingy return to the boat.

"What's the news?" Ross looked behind him, realizing the others had already packed up for the night and headed inside.

"It's good Nilly. Based on our current water depth, I was able to get deeper readings, and they were even higher than I thought they would be. I'll have to look into some things, but off the top of my head, I can't think of any other reason for there to be such high levels of hydrocarbons, nitrogen, and sulfur in the water other than crude oil."

"Keep this somewhat quiet. I don't want news getting out before we officially publish our findings. Let it be a surprise to them."

"The same goes for you Nils. Keep this quiet. I don't want people thinking this is a sure thing, then I find out tomorrow something is wrong with the readings."

"Of course. Ross, thank you, this is fantastic news."

"I told you Nils, if it was here, we would find it."

"The only thing better would be if we could catch them in the act of drilling."

"Well, if this trail keeps getting stronger, we may be able to follow them all the way home. How did your day go? Find anything of interest."

"I didn't find gold, but I found a metal commonly found with gold. I'm going to call my organization tonight and let them know. They can start getting their ducks in a row to get the place protected."

"You are that sure?"

"I will publish my paper just like you will. If the mining companies see that I have found Tourmaline here, they will be all over the place."

"Mining companies read scientific research papers?" Ross asked. Nils shrugged his shoulders.

"Sure, they read scientific papers. They employ hundreds of geologists, biologists, and all sorts of people like us."

Ross didn't feel like being with the others that night, so she grabbed a sandwich and went back to her bunk to review the numbers. She wasn't the only one either. As a result of the productive day, or because of Dr. Lebedev's outburst the night before, everyone seemed to be hiding in their separate corners tonight. Ross was in her bunk lying on the bed looking over the readouts from the day and making notes when her phone rang. She answered without thinking.

"Hello."

"Are you frozen yet?" Sam said on the other end. Ross smiled at the sound of her voice.

"Snug as a bug."

"You were supposed to call me when you got underway, you asshole." Sam said, feigning anger.

"Shit. Sorry Sam." Ross pinched her nose. She had completely forgotten to call.

"Well, obviously you aren't dead, so I'll forgive you. How are things going?"

"Great Sam. Really great. I'm glad I came on this trip. I feel more like my old self than I have in a long time."

"Some people take spa weekends to find themselves. You go on a boat in the arctic north crammed in with half a dozen other people and shared bathrooms. It's definitely not normal, but I'm glad you are having fun."

"I know it sounds strange, but part of what I love is learning new things from my colleagues. Amongst other things, I have found that there are scorpions that live up here, and a microscopic animal called a Moss

Piglet."

"What the fudge are nugget scorpions doing up there?" Sam had been working on correcting her language since becoming a mother. The results were mixed.

"According to the biochemist I'm bunked with, they are as common as house spiders. Not to worry though, the venom on their pincers doesn't have any effect on humans."

"Thank god for that. What the hell are the other things you mentioned...a piglet?"

"Moss Piglet. They are apparently the hardest to kill species on the planet. We sent them into space and they loved it."

"I love our conversations. I always learn something useless." Sam said. "What about your research? Have you found anything there?" Sam had learned over the years what questions to ask when talking about Ross's sciencey stuff. It required no knowledge on her part, but kept the conversation moving.

"Well, Nils has been pushing me to find evidence that someone, namely the Russians, are drilling for oil up here. Practically asked me to make it up if I didn't find any evidence for real. Thankfully, it doesn't look like I will have to put my career on the line."

"You found something?"

"Looks like it. Not enough to prove anything conclusively, but I'll get some more data tomorrow. There are increased amounts of hydrocarbons and sulfur throughout the water column. Something has happened to release it from the ground."

"So ah, how hard did Nils 'press you'?" Sam's voice was naughty.

"Sam! Not that kind of pressing."

"Pitty."

"Good god, Sam. Have you forgotten about Jack?"

"I haven't forgotten Jack. I'm just saying you are on a boat in the middle of nowhere with a hot Nord. It would certainly make the trip more interesting if there was some steamy flirting going on."

"He's cute, I'll give you that, but he thinks he's God's gift to women. I'm not interested."

"I bet that's driving him crazy."

"Odd you should mention that. He said the other night he thought I was mysterious all those years ago when we were on the research trip together."

"Oooohhh."

"I thought he was so busy with all the female

attention he was getting from the other students he didn't even notice me."

"Look at that Ross, breaking hearts and taking names on the seven seas. You're like a sexy, smart pirate. Oh, you should go as that for Halloween!"

"I could. I could dress like a pirate, but instead of a sextant I can carry a microscope."

"That isn't my idea of sexy, but it's close enough. Speaking of sexy, how is Jack?"

"Don't know. I haven't spoken to him."

"Ross."

"Don't give me that, I've texted him repeatedly, and he isn't answering."

"I'll ignore the fact that you've texted your boyfriend repeatedly but forgot to text me..... Do you have any idea why the silent treatment?"

"I think I might actually. After you left the other night, I apparently called him and went into this long ramble about how it wasn't going to work and we might as well admit it now."

"Ross! You were only slightly drunk when I left."

"Sam, I was hammered. The problem is, everything I said was true. I just didn't have the guts to say it sober. If we can't see each other more than twice a year, it's going to be hard to move the relationship forward isn't it? I mean one of us is going to have to make a major change for us to be together, and I'm not sure either one of us is willing to do that. Might as well call it now. What I was hoping was to finish this trip and then go and see him and say all this in person. Not say it in a drunken phone conversation in the wee hours of the morning."

"And you haven't spoken to him since?"

"Nope."

"No offense honey, but that was a dumb thing to do."

"No shit." There was a baby crying in the background. "Is that my baby, what's wrong with her?" Ross said.

"She's tired and cranky. Listen, you want me to call Jack? He might answer if it's me."

"No, don't worry about it. I messed it up, and I'll fix it. Go take care of Ruby."

"Bye." Sam rushed off, the screaming in the background taking on a whole new level. Ross hung up smiling. Talking to Sam always took her out of her serious science self and reminded her that there was a teenager still in her somewhere. Ross looked at her phone. Maybe she should try and call Jack? The truth of the matter was, between Jack,  and Sam's adorably plump baby Ruby, Ross was for the first time in her life thinking of life beyond science.  She was closer to forty than thirty and was an established scientist with several papers to her name and one major scientific discovery. Not to mention she was something of a science hero since she had escaped from the resort last year.  Ross, Sam, Jack and his father Si, held the great distinction of being the only four people in the world to have ever survived an attack by a Spartan.

Ross loved her job, she loved her career, but she also loved the way Jack smelled first thing in the morning. How he created a warm space in the bed, how she felt all tingly inside when he was around.  She missed it more than she really wanted to admit.  Watching Sam transform into a mother had got her thinking about what comes after love and marriage.  It was just her luck that the man who had her thinking and feeling all this lived in Australia and was currently  working on a boat in the middle of the Indian Ocean. *"You know perfectly well it wouldn't be any less complicated if he lived next door."* She thought to herself. *"If only he wasn't so extremely attractive and didn't have an Australian accent. I love the way he calls me 'darling'."*  Ross gathered her shower items.  She needed to go cool down.

# 18

Sam hung up with Ross and put Ruby down for a nap. The conversation with Ross rolling over in her mind the entire time. By the time she was slowly backing out of sleeping Ruby's room, her decision had been made. Ross may get mad at her, but she was hundreds of miles away and couldn't do anything about it. By the time Ross got home, all would be forgiven.

"Sam? Is everything alright?" Jack grumbled. Sam didn't strike him as the type of person who thought much about time zones, but the fact that she was calling in the pre-dawn hours had him a little worried all the same.

"As fine as it can be. What's the matter with you? You sound weird." Sam said.

"You woke me up, Sam, it's three in the morning here."

"Oh shit.  Sorry, I forget you're halfway around the world."

"Well, go on.  You might as well tell me what was so important." Jack said, his eyes still closed.

"I just got off the phone with Ross."

"Yeah, how's she doing?"

"Fine actually, as far as I can tell.  I think the gist of it is that her research is going well."

"Good. Is this why you called me Sam?"  Jack didn't want to hang up on her and go back to sleep until he was sure this was a waste of time.

"You haven't called her Jack."

"I know that Sam."

"I'm calling to see why you haven't called her.  She told me about your phone conversation before she left."

"She did, did she?"

"Ross was drunk, Jack."

"I know that Sam, it was very obvious." Jack leaned his head against the wall.  The coffee maker was all the way out in the kitchen. He didn't want to go that far, but it sounded like this wasn't going to be a quick conversation. Throwing the covers back, he shuffled in that direction.

"You can't take what she said seriously if she was

drunk."

"Sam, this is a conversation I will have with Ross when she is done with her trip."

"I need to explain something though, Jack."

"What?"

"Ross, I need to explain Ross."

"Ross can explain herself, Sam. I don't think we should be having this conversation." If Jack hadn't been half asleep, he would have already hung up on her. But Sam was more awake and quicker than he was at the moment.

"Jack, listen. I am normally perfectly happy to let Ross fuck up her life as she sees fit, but I can't watch this. She cares about you Jack. *Really* cares about you."

"Then she needs to be the one to say something."

"Jack, do you have any idea how much Ross debated coming and seeing you versus going on this research trip? If that isn't proof of how much she cares, I don't know what is."

"But she's there and not here. I lost."

"See, this is what I'm saying. I obviously need to explain Ross to you."

"You're giving me a headache."

"She actually thought long and hard about whether

she should come out and see you or go on this research trip. Now, you think about that. Ross loves nothing more in this world than science, and she actually had to stop and think about where she was going to go. I can tell you from where I sit, it has never been a debate before. It's obvious Jack." Jack's eyes opened and he stood up straight. Sam had a point.

"Jack, Ross is a special person. When they made Ross, they put in a lot of extra brainy bits. She can do things that we can't, she sees the world differently than we do. You can't handle her like you do other women."

"I know that Sam. I know she is one in a million, but none of this changes the problem at hand. We live half a globe away from one another. It doesn't really matter how we feel about each other if we can never manage to see one another." There was silence on the other end of the phone.

"There has to be a way Jack. It can't end this way."

"I don't want it to end either. I've never met anyone like Ross. But right now I can't see a way forward, and drunk or not, neither can Ross. As you have pointed out, she is smarter than most of us."

"This can't be how it ends Jack. Ross has never felt like this about anyone."

"The feeling is mutual Sam, but that's where it stands. I want to talk to her when she gets off this trip. Ross says she's going to come out here once she is done, and I figure that will be that."

"Can't you come out here for a time? Once you've finished with the sharks." Jack closed his eyes and pinched the bridge of his nose.

"I can Sam, but I would only do it for a short amount of time. Si and I are going to get the business up and running once this is over with. Ross could come out here, but she isn't going to give up her career and I wouldn't ask her to. She was right when she said the one who sacrificed would just end up resenting the other. Ross will always be a special person to me, and it's a twisted state of affairs that we can't make it work, but that's life."

Jack hung up with Sam. The smell of coffee filled the kitchen. He thought about going back to bed, but he was awake now with thoughts of Ross rolling around in his head. Taking his cup of coffee, he went out to the deck. The sky black. *'Always darkest before the dawn.'* Jack thought to himself. He closed his eyes and took in the sea air, feeling the salt on his skin. He could no more live in Boston than Ross could live out here. He wanted to see her again though. Feel the weight of her in his arms, watch her snore softly when she slept. Say a proper good-bye.

"What the hell are you doing out here in nothing but your undies?" Si said from the doorway. He was wearing his ever present overalls. Jack was pretty sure he slept in them though he was more than willing to be wrong.

"Thinking. Coffee's ready in the pot." Si ducked back into the kitchen and came out with a cup of coffee and stood next to his son. They watched in silence as the dawn peeked over the horizon. Jack wasn't a fan of early mornings really, but it had its charm.

"Jack."

"Mmm."

"When this is all over with, go to Boston. Stay with Ross for a while, see what happens." Jack didn't look at him.

"What will you do?"

"Don't worry about me, boy. I'll find something to keep me entertained. Ross, she's special, Jack. It'd be a pity not to give it a real chance." Jack wasn't surprised that Si had listened to his conversation with Sam. It would have been hard not to hear it. He was surprised to find his father being so serious now though.

"What am I going to do in Boston, Dad? We were going to start the business back up."

"You could start a business there. It's a different part of the world, son, but there's still water. You could find something. Besides, Boston has one thing going for it this place doesn't."

"Ross?"

"Got it in one."

"What about you?" Si turned and looked Jack square in the eye.

"I've got more days behind me than in front of me, boy. You don't need to be living your life for me. I know you are worried about the distance between you and Ross. No matter what happens, if you are going to stay together, one of you is going to have to make a major change, right?"

"And you think it should be me?"

"I don't care who it is, my boy, though I do think it should be you."

"Can I ask why?"

" Because you're the bloke. Call me an old romantic, but I think it should be the man to make the sacrifices."

"You old softy."

"Ross is a special woman, and they don't come around often. Believe me. When you find one, and you are lucky enough she wants anything to do with you, you hold onto her." Si was looking his son square in the eyes.

"You're being serious aren't you?"

"Deadly."

"But what if….." Si made a pained face, and shooed Jack away with his hand.

"You can 'what if it' til the cows come home. Until you and Ross give it a try, a real try, you aren't going to know for sure. If that means you spending a few months in Boston, then I don't think that's such a huge thing."

"What about the business?"

"It'll wait. You know as well as I do it's going to take some time to get everything together. I can be working on that while you are out there."

"You make it sound so simple Dad."

"Well, it isn't bloody hard boy. What are you afraid of?"

# 19

Ross came back from her extremely long and unsatisfying shower (hoses had better pressure). When she got back to the room, Lillian was in bed and appeared to be asleep. Ross quietly put her stuff away. Settling into bed, she wasn't sleepy. Despite the shower, Ross was still thinking about Jack. If that wasn't enough, they were farther north now and hitting some ice, which made a very worrying sound when you were in the belly of the ship. Ross knew the ship was built for it, but she knew where the nearest lifeboat was all the same. Deciding that the night didn't want her to sleep, Ross pulled her laptop out from under the bed and looked back over the data again. There wasn't anything there she hadn't seen before. Ross thought about starting on the paper and pulled up the screen to start typing.

Fantasies of two hit research papers began to circulate in her mind's eye. Ross's work, as far as she knew, had never been used to spur legislation. She had to admit that she was a little excited to think that the work she was doing here and the scientific paper that would follow, might play a role in protecting the water and ice around them. This could start a whole different career for her. Maybe she would end up like Nils, traveling the world and finding new ways for science to save the planet. Maybe she could find a way of getting paid to go sail the Indian Ocean with Jack. Well, one thing was very clear. She wasn't going to be focusing on anything tonight. Images of Jack kept running through her head. She checked her cell phone to see if he had texted. He hadn't.

Ross got an achy feeling in her heart when she thought about Jack. Maybe she should text him and let him know what she had found? Shuffling through her clothes, she picked up her phone and looked at the time. It was eleven local time, Lord knows what time it was there, probably tomorrow morning. *'He's probably not going to be interested in what you found, much less early in the morning.'* Ross thought to herself. Right at that moment though, she would really love to hear his smooth Ausie voice say.....anything. Just as long as he was talking to her.

Giving up on working and not wanting to stay in the dark room, Ross headed towards the canteen. *'You only had a sandwich for dinner, you deserve ice cream. Today you discovered a possibly significant finding.'* Ross was going to be severely disappointed if no one had thought to bring ice cream, which they very well might have considering how cold it was outside. As she approached the canteen, she heard a noise and froze. Someone else was in the canteen. *'Please don't be Dr. Lebedev.'* She thought to herself. Ross stood in the hallway trying to figure out who it was humming to themselves, and she could hear containers from the fridge opening and closing. Ross wasn't the only one scavenging for food at this hour. Not really in the mood to be sociable, she thought about going back, but she really wanted that ice cream. The person dropped something and released a Nordic expletive. Nils.

"What are you doing up so late?" Nils asked as she came around the corner. He had poked his head from around the fridge and moved over to the counter with some containers.

"Couldn't sleep."

"Come have a celebratory drink with me." He said, shaking the half empty bottle. "It's part of what I confiscated from Dr. Lebedev."

"What are we celebrating?"

"Your discovery, of course."

"Ah Nils. I think it's a bit early for that, don't you?" Ross opened the freezer. Some sadistic person had brought vanilla ice cream. Opening the fridge, she checked to see if they redeemed themselves by bringing chocolate sauce. No luck. *'If the color white had a flavor...'* Ross thought to herself wondering which of her shipmates was the psycho who brought vanilla ice cream without chocolate sauce. She closed the doors in disappointment. Sitting in front of Nils, he slid her a glass.

"Something is there Ross. We may not know what happened, but it is a step in the right direction. At the very least it confirms I was right in asking you to come on this trip." He flashed his charming smile. Nils filled her glass and she drank even though she knew she shouldn't. Ross so far had drunk more on this trip than she had in the year prior. Nils' smile could get her to do things she normally wouldn't. He poured her another vodka, and they toasted before throwing it back. Nils scooted closer to her to fill her glass again. He had his arm over her shoulder. "I am glad you came, Ross. I mean it." His eyes were so damned green and serious. Ross scooted back to put some air between them. "I know it took a lot for you to come on this trip." Nils added. Ross downed her second glass.

"How do you know that?" She challenged.

"I've been following you closely. Not that I had to, it was all over the place when it happened. A bunch of scientists are invited to a resort that gets blown up. The science community weren't the only ones watching. Couldn't believe it when I saw your picture as one of the hostages. You haven't been on a trip since."

"You have been keeping close tabs." Ross was feeling uneasy, but it had more to do with the mention of her being a hostage than the fact that Nils had apparently been stalking her.

"I just want you to know how much I appreciate it. You're a fantastic scientist, Ross. Can I tell you a secret?"

"Sure."

"Back when we were both students, I had such a crush on you."

"On me?" Ross had to laugh. "I'm surprised you

could see me for all the other women throwing themselves at you."

"Maybe that was the attraction. You didn't throw yourself at anyone but mother science. The focus you had, I wanted that so bad. I can't think what I might have accomplished if I had half that focus."

"You haven't done bad for yourself, Nilly. You left a string of broken hearts on that trip, you chair several panels on pollution and other environmental issues, and you have a pretty bitchin man bun going on." Nils threw his head back and laughed.

"It took me two years to grow this man bun. My students seem to like it. They say it makes me more relatable."

"You look like a yoga instructor." Ross smiled. She was attracted to Nils, there was no way around it, but her alarm bells went off whenever she was around him. Who wouldn't be attracted to him? He had a great accent, a jaw bone that looked like it had been chiseled by Michelangilo, and a wicked grin that made you wonder what would happen if you could make yourself just go along for the ride. The grin reminded her of Jack. She should call Jack. What time would it be in Jakarta? Jack always said to call anytime.

"What are you thinking about?" Nils asked. His green eyes searching hers.

"Jack." Ross answered honestly.

"Jack? Who is Jack?" Nils was feeling his vodka. Ross had three shots to his six and that was just while she had been sitting here. He was leaning towards Ross again, but it wasn't in the predatory way he was before so much as it was for support. Ross made a face. What was Jack to her?

"My boyfriend." She answered and a shiver went through her.

Nils squinted his eyes. "You didn't tell me you had a boyfriend."

"Would it have affected my job here?" She was being flirted with and she loved it.

"Maybe." Nils sat up straighter. "Tell me about Jack, is it serious?"

Ross shrugged. "If you watched the coverage of what happened at the resort, you saw him. He was one of the shark wranglers that I was rescued with."

"Please tell me he's the older gentleman and not the rustic good looking one."

"He's not the older one. That's Si, his father."

"You didn't answer if it was serious." The twinkle

was back in his eye.

"It's still going on, which makes it the longest relationship I've ever had."

"But…"

"But when I left the states, we weren't on good terms." Nils leaned in again.

"Oh?"

"He wanted me to come out there to see him. I came here instead."

"Where is he?"

"In the Indian Ocean. They are still looking for the genetically altered sharks that were in the resort. Some of them escaped before it was blown up. He and Si are trying to help track them down. There is a marine biologist in Sydney that is worried about the effects they will have on the natural population."

"Tom Sweed, I know him. Good guy. He's worked with the species before. So why did you come here instead?"

"Well, it wasn't because of you, Nils." Nils grabbed his heart like he'd been stabbed. "I came because you were paying. I told Jack I couldn't afford to fly out there even after he offered to pay half. Truth is, I was afraid to go back. We landed in Jakarta both going and coming. It is where the whole thing started and ended for me. I'm just not sure I'm ready to go there."

"Maybe he can come to you?"

"He did, for Christmas. Met my folks. It's not fair to expect him to come to me again. He has to work as well. I told him before I left that I knew it would never work and this was proof."

"Ouch."

"Yeah. I haven't spoken to him since." Nils sat straight and looked at Ross.

"You want my advice?"

"No."

"Tough shit, you're going to get it anyway." His speech was slurred, but his green eyes were clear. "Call him Ross. I don't know the man, but you don't stick with a girl who lives halfway across the world for this long unless you have some strong feelings for her. Trust me, I've been there. His frustration at your not coming to see him may not have been aimed at you, but more frustration that he couldn't see you period. Trust me, if he was just in it for the sex, he would have been gone a long time ago."

"What was the worst reason you broke up with someone?" Ross asked. What Nils had said hit her in the stomach. He was right, they were both still in it for a reason. She wanted to change the subject and Nils' famously fast paced love life was an easy target. Nils thought about the question for a while.

"I found out her real hair color was brown."

"What?"

"I thought she was a blonde, then I saw her roots. For some reason it seemed like a lie."

"That is a real bullshit reason." His green eyes caught her again.

"Call him Ross, right now."

"I have no idea what time it is in Jakarta or whatever part of the Indian Ocean they are in."

"It doesn't matter where love is concerned, my dear." He took her phone out of her pocket and handed it to her. "Call him." He slid the long way around the bench seat and stood up. He gave her one more grin and a wink, then headed to his bed.

# 20

Ross looked at the time on the screen. With the help of the vodka, she was feeling ready for bed as well, but Nils was right. At that moment she wanted nothing more than to talk to Jack. Even if he sounded as irritated with her as he had the last time they spoke. She pressed the button to call him. It rang several times and then went to voicemail.

"Great," thought Ross, "now I'll be up all night wondering if he's screening his calls or if he just didn't hear it." She rested her head in her hand and was beginning to feel sorry for herself when the phone vibrated on the table. She nearly jumped out of her skin.

"Jack?"

"Ross? What is it, honey?" Ross could hear the wind in the background. He was working on the boat.

He hadn't heard the phone. "Hold on, let me get inside." There was a pause and then the wind in the background was gone. "Everything okay?" Jack asked, sounding slightly concerned.

"I just wanted to talk to you. I'm sorry about how we left things last time."

"It's alright, love. We'll talk when you get out here. How's it going?"

"Well, I will definitely be writing a paper about my findings, and Nils might be able to use my results to get the area protected at least for a little while. That's if the numbers stay where they are."

"I have no idea what you are talking about, but it sounds like things are going well."

"Yeah, they are. How are things there?" Ross could feel herself relaxing the more he talked. Hearing his voice, actually talking to him.

"We haven't found them. Take that as you will." Jack and Si didn't really want to find the boys. Not that there was much chance of finding five specific sharks in the depths of the Indian Ocean. Si had visions of the boys being hacked up by science and he was rather protective of them. He had been assured several times that they simply wanted to tag them so the sharks could continue to be monitored, but Si still wanted to be there to make sure no hacking occurred.

"Nils says he knows the guy you are working for."

"Oh yeah, how's that?"

"Well, Nils works with several organizations all over the world, he said he knows Tom......that's a helicopter." Ross interrupted herself.

"What's it doing there? What time is it there?"

"I don't know. Maybe one of the crew is sick?" With Jack still on the phone, Ross left the canteen and made her way to the stairs that led to the deck where she ran into Nils coming back out of his room. "What's going on?"

"Don't know." Nils said, but the look on his face worried her. They heard three gunshots, and they both froze. Ross had been looking at Nils, recognition and surprise mirrored in both their faces. Ross felt her knees go out from under her. Nils zipped up the coat he had been putting on and ran up the stairs to the deck. Ross watched as his feet disappeared out of sight.

"Ross, what is happening?" Jack said urgently in her ear, but Ross didn't answer. She could hear heavy footsteps running above her. Heading towards the stairs.

"Someone's here Jack. They are on the boat." Ross was frozen to the spot.

"Who Ross...who is on the boat?"

"Pirates, run!" Nils yelled down the stairs.

"Pirates?" Jack yelled into the phone. "Ross, get out of there."

"They have guns, Jack. I heard gunfire." Ross was in a daze, frozen to the spot. How could this be happening? What exactly was happening? She should run, she should do something other than stand there with the phone to her ear asking questions. Hot tears welled up in her eyes. "Ross, can you hear me?" Jack yelled in her ear. "Ross, get out of there honey." She couldn't make herself answer him.

"Ross, run!" Nils had leaned down the stairs to yell at her. There was a gunshot close by, and Nils came back down the stairs on his back, a bullet wound in his chest. His eyes were blank and lifeless. Ross watched in silent horror as a red spot spread from the hole in his chest.

"Ross, honey, what was that?" Jack was screaming in her ear now. Ross couldn't take her eyes off of Nils. There was movement at the top of the stairs. Ross looked and saw black boots at the top of the stairs where Nils had been standing just a moment ago. They were coming. Whoever they were, they were coming downstairs. Ross took a step back and hit the wall behind her. White hot fear ran through her as the black boots on the stairs paused and then took a step down.

Ross was so preoccupied with what was going on in front of her that she didn't see Lillian exit their room and run down the hall towards her. In a blur, Lillian jumped over Nils' body and grabbed Ross's hand, and ran down the opposite side of the hallway taking Ross with her. Ross dropped the phone where Jack was screaming louder and louder. The black boots that came casually down the stairs cut Jack off as they stepped on the phone, crushing it. Pausing for only a moment, the black boots went in the direction Lillian and Ross had gone.

Lillian ran like she knew where she was going. Ross could hear more gunfire behind them, but she didn't dare look. She saw a black form coming down the stairs. He had started in their direction. There was very little chance that they hadn't seen Ross and Lillian take off running. With a start, she remembered Jack on the phone. Where had she dropped the phone? Would Jack be able to call for help? 'No,' Ross answered herself, *'No one knows where the hell you are.'*

"Where are we going?" Ross said, not that it really mattered.

"Shhh. Trust me." Lillian said. They were running through parts of the ship Ross hadn't seen. Every once in a while she could hear  heavy boots fall on the metal floor of the ship behind them.   Lillian seemed to know where she was going, running deeper into the ship. They went through one metal door after another, as Lillian closed the door behind them each time.   They were getting closer to the engine, Ross knew because the noise was deafening.   Going through another doorway, they were in the engine room.   To Ross's surprise, they didn't stop there but went through to another smaller room at the back where they stopped.

"Hide, Ross."

"Hide?"  A new wave of realization ran through her. Ross had been in impossible situations before, but there was absolutely nowhere to run now.  Even if they hid, she doubted very seriously that the person following them wasn't going to search until they found them.

"It's me they want. Now hide."

# 21

Pedro's new boots hit the deck of the ship with a loud thud as he led the team into the wheelhouse. The nighttime captain had radio to his mouth, "Mayday...." Pedro raised his gun and put a bullet between his eyes. The radio fell half a second before the body did. One of the team splintered to the left, following another crew member who had turned and started to run. One shot and the crew member was dispatched with a single bullet to the back of the head. The body fell forward, landing halfway down the stairs. Pedro backed out of the wheelhouse and went down the right side of the ship where there was supposed to be another entrance into the living quarters.

Pedro heard shouting below. The others had heard the gunfire. They would be scurrying like rats now. The third member of their team was taking the same path as Pedro on the other side of the ship. Between the three of them, they would walk the length of the ship, dispatching anyone they came across. A man in a puffer coat popped out of the side entrance, and Pedro got him in the chest with a single shot, not before he yelled something to someone down below. Pedro hesitated for a moment, expecting someone to follow the puffer coat up onto the deck. When no one came, he slowly made his way down in time to see two women run past the stairs and back into the bowels of the ship.

A gun shot was heard to his right as one of his team announced through the headset that they had killed one male still in his bunk. Someone else had got the third crew member coming down the hall. That meant the two women who had run past were the last two targets.

"Going hunting for our last two." He said through the headset.

The others would search the rooms and collect the research equipment. He moved quickly but confidently. They were in no rush. Looking at his watch, they were only six minutes into the mission. A mayday call had gone out, but the ship was so far away from civilization, the response time would be an hour. Probably more. The women were trapped. It didn't matter where they ran, he would find them, and he had plenty of time to look. It was clear they were moving to the back of the boat. It was not a large craft, they were going to run out of places to hide soon, and then he would have them. He could hear through his head set that the others were gathering equipment. Time to hurry up and get this done.

Lillian pointed to a small cabinet at the back of the room. There was no way one of them, much less both of them, was going to fit in there.

"Get up there." Lillian half whispered.

"What?"

"Hide, Ross. Get up there. On top of the duct." Ross looked up and saw the duct work running along the ceiling of the room. Ross hadn't thought to look there, hopefully neither would anyone else. Lillian kept looking behind her while Ross scaled the cabinet as best she could. She was sure at any moment the person following them would burst through the door and shoot her in the back.

Managing to get herself on top of the duct, Ross made

herself as small as she possibly could. Lillian's head appeared next to her. "Stay quiet." Lillian's eyes were sad. "I'm sorry for all of this Ross." Her head disappeared again. Ross listened for signs that Lillian was hiding, but there was nothing.

"Lillian." Ross whispered below. There was no answer. They heard the door of the engine room slam open.

"Stay where you are Ross and don't make a sound." Lillian said with sternness. Ross laid there and listened for the sound of boots on metal. The engine was so loud it was all she could hear. A tear ran down Ross's cheek. There was a sharp intake of air when the door to their hiding spot flung open. Ross opened her eyes and looked in the direction of the door. There was one gunshot and the unmistakable sound of Lilian's body falling to the floor. Ross closed her eyes and tried not to breathe. There was no sound for a while. Ross could hear the person below her pull something metal across the floor. Metal scraping against metal. A head came into view and looked Ross in the eye. The head covered with a black hood, the eyes were the only thing visible. Ross had seen those eyes before. Those emotionless, blank eyes. Ross could not look away.

"Spartan." Ross said. The gun came up in front of her. A flash of light and everything went black.

Those emotionless eyes watched until they were sure she was gone. Watched as the tense form relaxed into nothingness. He had aimed for her head, but she had turned her head at the last moment, and he had hit her neck. It was their training to check for a pulse, but judging by the hole in her and the amount of blood coming from the wound, there was no point. She had said their name right before she died. He had heard it loud and clear. As far as he knew, there were only a handful of survivors that had come across a Spartan. Kneeling down, he felt the pulse of the other one, she was gone. His job done, he went back the way he came, stopping to turn off the engine in the engine room. The boat went silent. The boat, like everything in it, was now dead in the water. "Two females eliminated, heading back up to the deck." He said into his headset now that he could be heard. The others were waiting there with the bags of equipment standing ready. Without a word, he loaded one of the bags onto his back and began to climb the ladder back up to the helicopter. Once in their seats, they signaled to the pilot they were ready. The nose of the helicopter dipped and they were off. Pedro looked at his watch. From start to finish, they had been on the boat twelve minutes and thirty-six seconds.

The three of them were silent for a time, no one congratulated the other on a mission well done. The Spartans didn't do that . There was no wondering about the families the dead had left behind. No concern over who would find them. Someone had wanted these people dead. They had paid the price the Spartans had demanded, and the job had been done. Simple.

They watched as the ship grew smaller and smaller. Pulling the hood off his head, Pedro ran his hand through his hair and said, "I think we have met one of them before." His companion looked at him blankly and shrugged his shoulders.

"What makes you say that?"

"She said, 'Spartan' right before I killed her."

"We don't usually leave survivors."

"I can think of only one situation where there were any." His companion knew what he was talking about. They had all been involved on a mission a little over a year ago to bring down their creator. The mission had been a success, but four survivors had bested one of them and made it back to safety. The Spartans did not take joy in the revenge they had been able to take tonight. The Spartans did not feel bad, mad, or sad about this. They had not felt shocked or surprised. The Spartans felt nothing. To them the fact they had been recognized by one of the apparent survivors was a curious fact. Nothing more.

The helicopter followed the water for a while. Some distance away from 'The Hunter', the pilot gave the word and they pushed the black bags towards the open side doors and pushed them out. The splash of the bags could barely be seen in the night.

"I should let our employer know that we are done." Pedro pulled a cell phone out of his pocket and dialed.

"Yes." Alexi answered.

"It's done. All persons found and eliminated. All equipment destroyed." Was all he said, and then hung up. Pedro then chucked the phone into the water. There was no need for any further communication. Pedro stuck his hands into his pocket where the heat pack he had brought with him returned warmth to his hands almost immediately.

Alexi was in his office looking out over the square. The sun was still rising in the sky, and the office smelled of coffee and cigarettes. His favorite. He was watching as people were flooding into the square on their way to work. It was done. It had been done cleanly and now it was over. Alexi had been playing it over and over in his mind since he had last discussed the plans with the Spartans. There was no way they would be able to trace it back to him or the president. The knot in his stomach finally eased. He smiled to himself that he had managed to take care of this problem and eliminate the Nils Ryeng who had caused him so many headaches over the past few years. There were things to do, but for right now, he would just stand here and smoke his cigarette and enjoy watching the sunrise. A sunrise he could fully enjoy because he knew he would live to see it set.

# 22

Jack stared at his phone in disbelief. He had stopped yelling into it when it went dead. He tried calling back, but it went straight to Ross's voicemail. "Shit." His mind tried to figure out what he had just heard. "Shit. Fuck. Damn." Jack said. Si had left when he saw Jack talking to Ross, he now came running back. He got to the room just in time to see Jack throw his phone down and fumble with the steering wheel of the boat for a second before turning around and seeing Si. Jack had been on boats most of his life. He could parallel park one faster than he could a car, yet he was fumbling. The nerves were vibrating off of him. Something was wrong.

"Get us back to land, Dad. Right now!" Jack's voice was urgent and pleading.

"I'm sorry?" Si moved towards the controls, but he

had no idea what he was supposed to be doing or, more importantly, why?

"Something happened. Take us back to land. To the nearest airport." Jack added hurriedly.

"We're in the middle of the bleedin' ocean, son. We are days away from the closest airport. What's happened?" Jack was bouncing around the cabin like a caged animal. Si turned the boat over and started pulling up the anchor. Jack seemed to calm a bit with some sort of action taking place.

"It's Ross, Dad, something happened to Ross. I've got to get there." Si took his hands off the wheel, pulling up a map, checking the fastest route to Jakarta. "What's happened to Ross?" Si said, typing the data into the computer and setting the course.

"I don't know. She called, we were talking, and then she heard something, and there was a gunshot. Her phone went dead. Someone said "pirates" in the background."

"What the bloody hell do you mean 'pirates'? There is nothing up there. What would pirates be doing with a research boat?"

"There were gunshots and then some yelling. Dad, she was scared. I have to go. I have to go figure out what happened. I think she's in real trouble."

"Are you sure? Couldn't it have been something else?" Si wasn't doubting his son so much as hoping that it was something else. In fact, as Jack explained what had happened, a knot formed in Si's stomach. As impossible as it all seemed, Si's gut knew that every word of it was true.

"You should have heard her. She was afraid. Real fear."

"I'll figure out where the nearest airport is and get us there, but it's going to take a while. In the meantime, you call anyone you can think of and get someone out to that boat."

"Who?"

"If the boat left from a harbor, it had to set a course. Check with the harbor master in that area and tell them what happened. At the very least, they can try and radio the captain and get a status. If the ship can't be reached, call the Coast Guard." Jack went down below where it was quieter and started making calls. He thought about calling Sam, but didn't. He had nothing to tell her, and there was no reason to upset everyone if Ross had just dropped her phone overboard. *What if that's it? Something scared her and she dropped her phone* overboard?" Jack thought to himself. But her voice. That was fear, pure unadulterated fear. His girl was in trouble, and right now it was entirely possible that he was the only person who knew it.

"*How could one woman be that unlucky?*" Si was thinking to himself. He had set a course for Jakarta. Si stuck his head out the cabin door to see where the sun was. They had about four more hours of good daylight. After that he would be completely reliant on the navigation system to keep them on course. It was going to take the rest of the day and all night to get them there. He hoped the engine would hold out because he planned on taking her full steam until he saw the harbor. "*The woman ventures out for the first time in a year and gets herself into another jam.*" Si shook his head. Ross was a smart woman, probably the smartest he had ever known, but damned if he could figure out how she was going to get out of a boat under attack in the arctic waters of the North. Mind you, he hadn't really known how they were going to get out of the last jam either, but here they stood.

"Hold on my girl. We're on our way." Si announced, kicking the engine up as far as she would go.

# 23

The Captain of *'The Hunter'* sent out the mayday at 1:32 am local time. It had been a partial mayday, made all the more urgent because it had been cut short. The operator thought they had heard a gunshot before the line went dead. The rescue boat pulled up alongside *'The Hunter'* cautiously at 2:52am. The boat was dead in the water, no engine noise and no running lights. Despite attempts, no further communication had been made with the ship or its crew. It was unusual for a ship attack to happen in these waters, in fact, no one on the rescue team could remember being called out on one, but then these waters were being traveled more now that the melting ice was widening the lanes.

"Try radioing them again." The sergeant said, not thrilled about climbing onto a dead boat in the middle of the night.

"Nothing, Sir." Radar showed the ship was moving with the current with no one on deck, just a ghost ship.

"Everyone get ready, we don't know what's up there." The smaller craft positioned herself alongside the larger *'Hunter'*, and with coverage, his men began to board.

Climbing aboard, the sergeant scanned the deck with his gun. The only sound he could hear was the water lapping against the boat. "This is the Coast Guard. Come out, hands visible." He shouted. Nothing. The sergeant made his way to the wheelhouse to look for the captain or whoever made the mayday call. Scanning the room with his flashlight, he saw the captain slumped over the controls. He approached and lifted the man's head. Single bullet wound between the eyes.

"Sarg." One of his men alerted him. "There's someone over here." Shot at the top of the stairs, a single bullet wound to the back of his head. Whoever had done this was a good shot and had a steady hand. It wasn't easy to keep his hand from shaking while adrenaline pumped and his fingers stung with the cold.

"There are more down here, Sarg." He heard through

his headset. "No sign of the gunmen." His men having gone the entire length of the ship and finding no gunman, they went about the job of collecting the dead and trying to figure out what had happened here. Leaving one of his men to stay with the dead in the wheelhouse, the sergeant made his way down the stairs meeting another of his men in the hallway below. "Over here, Sir." The man directed him to the single male lying at the bottom of the stairs. Single gunshot to the chest. This was looking very professional. "There is another one in here, sir. This one didn't even make it out of bed." Following the man a short distance down the hallway, he saw an older man lying blank faced and open mouthed in his bed. A single shot to the head. It looked like they had got him before he even had a chance to call out.

"The roster said there was a crew of three and four scientists who chartered the boat. So far we are missing one crew member and the two female scientists. Keep looking."

"One crew member dead in the hallway, Sir." Another of his men reported.

"See if this thing has a data recorder."

"On it Sarg." The man nodded and headed off to the

wheelhouse.

"SIR!! I need some help here." One of the men yelled into the headset.

"Location."

"Past the engine room, Sir. I think she's alive." The sergeant as well as two other men ran down the hallway, past the engine, which the sergeant noted was silent. Past the engine room there was another small room for storage "Down there, sir." One of his men guided him.

"Get a medic down here. Show him where to go." The sergeant said to the private behind him. The man peeled off in the opposite direction to carry out his orders. On the floor was the crumpled form of a woman. "I checked if she had a pulse." His man was applying pressure to the chest wound, his hands and the cloth covered in blood. The sergeant didn't say anything, but he wondered if his man had really found a pulse, or if he had been feeling his own heartbeat. It had happened more than once. You want to find something so badly and your own heart is beating so hard that you mistake it for theirs.

"Move over son, let me take a look." The private re-adjusted himself but was careful to not remove pressure from the woman's chest.

The sergeant leaned down to check for himself, feeling her wrist since that had less blood on it. Nothing. He moved his fingers to her neck and checked again. Wait. He readjusted and felt again. It was there, but it was very weak.

"Get something flat to put her on and get her out of here. Where the hell is that medic?" The sergeant yelled over his shoulder. He patted the young man on the shoulder who had found her. "You stay with her. I don't care what happens, you don't leave her side or remove your hands until the medic tells you too."

"Yes Sir."

The medic ran through the door carrying his bag and quickly assessed the situation. Maintaining constant pressure on her chest, they lowered her from the seated position to the flat back they had brought in. The room was crowded with the three of them and the victim. The sergeant moved out to the engine room and let the medic do what he needed to with the help of his man who had found her and who was still applying pressure. A clean bandage was applied to the wound.

"I need a Medivac to the nearest hospital." The medic yelled over his shoulder.

The sergeant radioed ahead to let them know they had a survivor and would need transport.

"What do you think her chances are?" The sergeant whispered as the men both got out of the way so the victim could be carried out of the room and up to the deck..

"She's lost a ton of blood. Pulse is weak, I'll do what I can to stabilize her until we can get her to a hospital. She'll need a transfusion for sure. Even if she makes it, she's got a long way to go."

"Well, at least she won't die out here in a cold tin can." The sergeant offered. The men out of the room, the sergeant went back into the room to see what clues it might offer. The pool of blood on the floor was hard to ignore. There was so much, it was clotting in areas, and bloody footprints marked the path his men had taken in getting her out.

It was clear she had run in here to hide and been found. The sergeant stood in the storage room looking around and picturing in his mind's eye what had happened here in the very early hours. This was a clean job. The captain was shot while sending out the mayday. *Ping, ping*. Whoever had done this had been quick and efficient. Whichever one of the passengers this woman turned out to be, she had been faster than the others. *Ping, ping.* Judging from the placement of some of the other victims, the attack had been unexpected. They hadn't gotten very far from their beds. *Ping, ping.* What in the world could a research vessel have that someone would want this bad? He would have to find out what they were researching. There was still one body they hadn't found. There was supposed to be another female scientist on board. *Ping, ping.*

"Anyone found another body?" He radioed to his men who were still searching the ship for evidence. They all reported back 'no'.

"Keep an eye out for persons overboard. She may have jumped." If that was the case, it would be a recovery mission, if they ever found her. *Ping. Ping.* The sergeant's thoughts stopped long enough to register the sound of water dripping. Not something you wanted to hear in a boat. Maybe a bullet hole? They may be able to recover the bullet. He walked to the spot where the woman had been found, being careful to not step in her blood. He could see no bullet hole. *Ping, ping.* The sound was farther away. He turned around and saw a metal storage cabinet the same as you would see in many garages. He had been standing in front of it. *Ping, ping.* He opened the door and saw nothing but tools, rags and some cans. *Ping, ping.* The sound was definitely coming from here. Stepping on a bucket, he looked at the top of it where the sound was the loudest and found the source. He watched as bright red blood dripped from the bottom of a metal vent to the top of the cabinet. *Ping....ping.* The blood was slowly coming down the side of the vent, curving under with the shape of the vent and, having reached the center of the vent, dripping on top of the metal cabinet. *Ping....ping.*

"What the hell?" He could see nothing above the vent from where he stood. The bucket was not tall enough, the sergeant looked around. He found a small metal step stool that had been kicked to a corner. Pulling it over, he stepped up, bringing his head above the vent. There was something there, but he couldn't tell what it was. Pulling his flashlight up, he saw Ross's hair first, and then the rest of her. His missing scientist. He reached a hand up and felt for a pulse but couldn't find her wrist or her neck. The angle wasn't great like this.

"Get the medic back down here." He yelled into the

radio. "Hold on honey, we are going to get you." Dead or alive, she was getting out of there.

# 24

Ross was not so easy to get out of the room as Lillian had been. A back board was balanced on the top of the cabinet while one man climbed up the other side of the vent and pushed her onto the board. To keep her level, the men had to carry her out over their heads until they got to a larger area and could readjust her. The sergeant was convinced she was dead, but had informed his men to treat her with as much respect as they could considering the awkward place where she was found. The medic watched and gave instructions from the doorway of the engine room. Putting a thermal blanket over her, they decided to evaluate her fully up on deck. With every passing minute, the sergeant was more sure they were recovering a dead woman. Her form was lifeless, they hadn't been able to feel for a pulse yet, but they were hardly likely to find it with the gunshot wound in her neck.

Having been carried out of the belly of the boat, Ross was laid down on the deck so the medic could look her over.

"Congratulations, Sergeant. You found yourself a live one."

"She's alive!" The sergeant said with no small amount of surprise. The medic handed him a wad of bandaging and held it over Ross's neck.

"Dead women don't bleed. Fresh blood is coming out of the wound. It is much slower than it should be, but her pulse is probably very weak, and she has been lying for hours in a boat that is getting colder by the minute. But, she is mostly dead or slightly alive. Depending on how you want to look at it." The medic smiled at him. While he spoke, his hands were busy fixing a pressure bandage to Ross's neck. "Our woman here was very lucky. A wound like that all the way out here, she should have been dead an hour ago."

"There's no chance she's going to make it, is there?" The sergeant whispered. He didn't want to bring down the mood.

"Probably not, no. But who knows? She's made it this far." The medic turned to his radio.

"Change of plans, I'll be bringing two transports." Chatter came back. "Time to get these ladies on the boat, the helicopter is on its way."

They would come back in the light of day and search the boat for any other clues they could find. For right now, they needed to make sure their survivors were taken care of. With one more look at the dark boat, the sergeant followed his men back onto their craft and sped off towards their cruiser where the helicopter would meet them. It was 3:42 in the morning when Ross and Lillian left 'The Hunter'.

The medic and the sergeant were happy to see that the helicopter was waiting for them when they arrived back at the cruiser. With a sense of urgency, the women were off loaded and transported to the waiting chopper. They would be sent to the nearest hospital in Inuvik Regional Hospital. A remote place that was more used to dealing with chainsaw accidents, but they had seen their fair share of gunshot wounds, and they had a helipad. The medic had called ahead so a trauma team would be waiting for them.

"One chest wound, one neck. Both have a BP around 85/50, heart rate is around 50 bpm. Started

IV's, compression bandages on both. Massive blood loss." The flight medic nodded.

"What the hell happened?" He yelled over the sound of the blades.

"Don't know, but they were the only ones to survive." The flight medic nodded and tapped the pilot on the shoulder. The chopper left the deck of the ship and headed south. The medic stepped back and watched as his patients were flown away. He had somewhat gotten used to this part. Patching them up and sending them on and never knowing in most cases if what he did was enough. It would be a miracle if they made it.

# 25

Having gone home after the morning rush hour to get a shower, hot meal, and a change of clothes, Alexi returned to his office just after lunch time. Feeling refreshed, he was going through his emails when his phone rang.

"Yes."

"Mr. Secretary would like to see you immediately." The woman said matter of factly.

"I'll be right there." Alexi collected his phone and cigarettes from his desk and took off confidently to the security office. He stood tall and walked with purpose down the hallway, confident in a job well done. He nodded to the people he passed, smiled at the ones he knew, and relished in their discomfort at his presence. None of them knew what he had done. If he had done his job right, none of them would ever know that he had orchestrated the well planned attack last night.

"He has asked to see me." Alexi said, approaching the secretary's desk.

"I know." She said smartly. "He isn't here yet, he has asked that you wait out here until he is ready." For the first time, Alexi wondered if he had, in fact, been called down for the congratulations he deserved. Folding himself into one of the chairs, he tapped a cigarette on his knee.

*"Probably already has another issue he wants taken care of."* He thought to himself. Forced to wait fifteen minutes in awkward silence before he was called in, Alexi was ticked off as he entered the office.

"You can go through now."

The Security Chief was standing at his window with a cup of coffee in his hand.

"Any issues with last night?" The Chief asked without turning to look at him. Alexi straightened again.

"No sir. It all went very well. The Spartans called me this morning and said it was all done and taken care of."

"Good, good. And no survivors?"

"No sir, they said everyone was eliminated."

"Even our informant."

"Especially our informant." Alexi said, glad that he could report good news. The Security Chief turned to look at him for the first time, his famous half smile on his face. Alexi's blood turned to ice and his mind swirled. The atmosphere was pleasant, but Alexi had never known that smile to mean anything good.

"It is a great relief to me that it can not be traced back to us. A great relief." Alexi smiled in return. "Especially since seeing the news this morning. Have you seen it?"

"No sir, I was here all night until the Spartans called. I went home for a few hours to freshen up." The chief nodded. He did not seem to disapprove, which was a relief. Placing his cup and saucer on the end of his desk he picked up the remote.

"Then you won't have seen this." Turning on one of the many TV's on the wall that played twenty-four hour news, the video showed aerial footage of 'The Hunter' only illuminated by the light of the helicopter shooting the footage. There were no lights on the boat, Coast Guard boats surrounded it.

"The attack happened in the very early hours of this morning. At this time we have no idea what motivated this attack on a research vessel that had only left harbor a few days ago. What we do know is that out of the three crew and four scientists aboard, there are only two survivors. Both of them are in critical condition and being treated at a nearby hospital. It is not known at this time…." The tv went mute. Alexi went numb. Survivors. Not one, but two. He couldn't bring himself to turn and look at the Security Chief. There was every chance there would be a gun pointed at his head. That was a little messy for the Chief. He would have to be careful where he stepped, as there was a very good chance he was going to accidentally fall out of a high window later on that day. Alexi replayed what the Spartan had said in his head. "He said there were no survivors. He specifically said there were no survivors. I asked." Alexi said, as much for himself as for his boss.

Accepting his fate, he turned around to face it with as much dignity as possible. The half smile was still there, but it had taken on a whole new meaning. "I can see this is a surprise to you." He said calmly. "Sit down." Indicating a chair in front of his desk.

"I will admit, I have wondered about these Spartans since seeing the news. They are supposed to leave no survivors, yet here are two. Don't they check these things?" Alexi was not fooled by the cordial tone. The man was lethal. For all he knew the Chief was stalling until the hit team got there.

"It is in their training to check, Sir. I can't imagine what has happened."

" I have put some feelers out." The Chief leaned back in his chair and sipped his coffee. "It is the worst possible scenario. Our informant is one of the survivors." Alexi silently prayed for a heart attack. That his body would just stop working and he would die. He wiped the sweat away from his forehead.

"I will call the Spartans immediately. This WILL be fixed." He said, having to work very hard to sound indignant instead of terrified. The Security Chief waved his hand to calm him down.

"The Spartans came with a guarantee, you said that before, yes?"

"Yes, and they are going to have to make this right!"

"Right now both survivors are in critical condition. I found out they are both supposed to go into surgery as soon as they are transported to a secure hospital. There is every chance they won't survive the surgery. If this is the case, there is no problem, but I want the Spartans there if they wake up."

"I am so sorry, Sir. I will make sure this is fixed, at no additional cost!"

"Please do. On principle, I think both survivors should be taken care of, but really the only one I care about is our informant. Understood."

"Yes Sir."

"Report to me if there are any other issues." With that, Alexi was waved away and he all but ran from the room. At every moment, he expected someone to approach him and be taken away, but he managed to make it back to his office without incident. There was a freshly made cup of tea on his desk, he looked at it and backed away. It would not be safe to drink it under the circumstances. With shaking hands, Alexi woke up his computer and went to the encrypted email address the Spartans had given him. Alexi was not used to this form of intimidation. When Alexi wanted to get his feelings across, he was used to using fear in his favor. Sending a strongly worded email and then waiting for a reply seemed ridiculous under the circumstances. Waiting for their reply was absolutely infuriating.

"It appears we have a problem." Hesa said, to the other Spartans behind him. "We are actually going to have to honor our guarantee." They were in the middle of packing for the South African trip, set to leave that evening.

"What job?"

"The research vessel. Apparently we left two survivors."

"We don't leave survivors." Dominic added.

"Who survived?" Pedro asked.

"The two female scientists. I'm verifying it now." There was a pause. "They are both in critical condition. One chest wound and one neck, they are going to try and do surgery but because of the nature of the attack, they want to get them to a secure hospital first. I doubt they will survive. It says they were both on the ship an estimated hour and a half before help even arrived. That means it was probably three hours before serious medical intervention was taken."

"Those were my kills." Pedro offered.

"Did you check for a pulse?" Spartans had been trained to always check for a pulse for this very reason. Leaving half dead survivors was so messy. They were known for their clean kills.

"Of course I checked for a pulse. I don't think I did on the neck wound, but I definitely did on the chest wound. There wasn't one."

"Obviously, there was." Dominic offered. "Though I can't imagine either had very strong pulses."

"What do you want me to answer?" Hesa asked.

"We will honor the guarantee, of course." Dominic answered.

"He wants the full might of the Spartans behind this." Hesa said.

"He'll get Pedro. They are already three quarters of the way dead, how many people does he think it's going to take?"

"I'm slated for the South African trip." Pedro responded.

"You'll have to take care of this first." Dominic looked at him. "It was your failure, you fix it." Pedro took his bag back to his room and dug out his only sweater again. It appeared he would be going back to the frozen north.

Alexi received a response from the Spartans in the evening, by which point he had smoked three packs of cigarettes and drunk two bottles of vodka. The day had been spent watching images of 'The Hunter' continue to flash on the screen along with pictures of the scientists and crew members aboard. His failure had been on full display all day. Alexi continued to watch in the constant hope that neither of the survivors had woken up and said anything. Alexi could not remember ever praying for someone to die more vehemently than he was right now.

"One of the survivors was Dr. Ross Halloway, a chemist from Boston. Dr. Halloway is one of the four survivors from the Ikan Hui Resort that was attacked last year by a group of genetically altered soldiers calling themselves Spartans. It is not clear at this time if this was the reason for the attack. Little has been heard from the Spartans since the disaster at Ikan Hui....." the reporter went on. Alexi took some small delight in the luck that a survivor of the Ikan Hui resort was on this doomed voyage. This would leave little doubt as to the motivation for the attack and increase the chances that no one's finger would point at him or mother Russia.

After receiving the email back from the Spartans, Alexi took a deep breath. The Spartans were going to fix the problem. It looked like blame was going to be laid exclusively at their feet. It was time to worry about saving himself. He wasn't sure taking care of the survivors was going to be enough to insure his life, unfortunately. Even if he wasn't eliminated for this, it would only take another small mistake before he found himself stabbed with a syringe on the way to work. Alexi didn't like the idea, but if he was going to do what he planned on doing, he needed to act like it was the furthest thing from his mind. It was now five O'clock. He would leave at six like he normally did. Have his driver stop and get him something to eat on the way home. There was one risk he was going to have to take. He looked up flights from Moscow for the next day. If he was lucky, this time tomorrow, he would be out of Russia. If he wasn't lucky, he would be dead. Either way it would all be over soon.

Being a senior member of staff, Alexi had handlers. Trained men who were there to make sure his loyalty to the party never wavered. And to report him if it did. His driver was not a problem, they had known each other for sometime. The problem was going to be the young man they had recently assigned to watch his house. Eager to prove himself and be of greater service to the party, the youngster took his job incredibly serious.

After cleaning himself up and trying to erase the trauma of the day from his face, Alexi greeted his driver warmly and they made light conversation on the way home. He waved to his other handler already stationed at his house and was greeted with a scowl and a nodd, just like always. So far, so good. Alexi took his dinner in front of the TV like he always did, and then went to bed at the same time he always did. All perfectly normal.

With all being quiet, Alexi peaked out his front window. His driver was asleep in the car. The young man at the back was pacing, no doubt keeping himself alert and awake. Grabbing a screwdriver, Alexi quietly went to his bathroom and made sure to stay out of sight of the window, scraping away the grout that held a certain tile in place. The tile removed, Alexi took from the secret hole the passport and money he would need to make his escape. He looked at the clock on the wall. He was running early. Making his bed, he dressed in the dark, packed a few items in a backpack, and took a deep breath while looking around him. His coffee pot was warm. There was a single dirty coffee cup in the sink. Carefully setting the scene so that when they stormed his house later that day, it would look like he got up and went to work. He even replaced the tile in the bathroom, using toothpaste to act as grout. It would be obvious to anyone who looked, but not as obvious as a gaping whole in his shower.

At four in the morning, Alexi shoved an extra pack of cigarettes in his coat pockets and headed out the door like he was leaving early for work. The young man at the back of the house could not see him, and his driver was still asleep in the car. Getting into the back seat behind the driver, Alexi startled the man awake. Acting quickly, Alexi brought his hands around the front and, using a shoelace, he strangled his driver. It had been some time since he had killed someone with his own hands. He was pleased he hadn't lost his touch. That done, he pushed the man over to the passenger seat and took his place at the wheel. The height difference between the two men was apparent. Alexi contorted himself to where he was the same height as the driver and started the car.

"Where are you going?" The young man came over the radio.

"Bathroom." Alexi answered, doing his best to impersonate the driver's husky voice.

"Ten minutes." It took some restraint to not inform the young man what he could do with his ten minutes. Alexi drove to the airport with a smile on his face. It was five in the morning. The young man would call in when the car wasn't back in twenty minutes or so, but it would not be until seven when it became clear that Alexi himself was not there. Then the real alarm would go up. If he was lucky, it would be another hour before it occurred to them to close the airports. The plane was set to leave at six. He would be landing by eight. Since the name on the passport was not his own, even an alert would not be a problem.

As the plane took off on time, he leaned his head back on the seat and took a deep breath. He had done it. He was free.

# 26

Si was steering the boat. Night had now fallen. Jack was still below deck making calls and Si was dying to know what he had found out. He was also dying for food, but eating seemed stupid at the moment. Finally, Jack's head popped up from below with the look of urgency still on his face.

"What's the word?"

"Not a whole hell of a lot. The Coast Guard wouldn't tell me anything. All they would say was that there had been an incident at sea. Everything I know, I ended up getting off the news." Jack sat down next to him and put his head in his hands. "She's alive, but in critical condition. They are trying to get the two of them to a hospital where they can do surgery. I tried calling Belinda, Ross's mother, but she didn't answer. I have no idea what time it is in Boston." Si didn't say, but his stomach did a flip. He refused to believe this was the end for Ross. There was no denying how serious it was though. He clapped a hand on Jack's shoulder.

"Did they say what her injuries were?" Si asked.

"No. They did say it was a miracle they had survived  as long as they did in a freezing cold ship." Jack was trying very hard not to vomit.   Si looked at his son's tortured face, which suddenly showed all of Jack's forty-one years.

"It'll be alright son.  Ross is a strong woman." Jack's phone rang, and he went back below deck.

"Hello."

"Jack, oh my God! Jack!  It's Ross."  Sam was almost screaming into the phone.

"I know Sam, I know.  I was on the phone with her when it happened.  Do you know how she is, is she alright?"  Jack's heart sank.  Sam sobbed, doing that thing in the back of her throat women do when they are crying so hard they almost throw up.  Jack froze on the phone.  He didn't want her to tell him. He didn't want to hear the words. Si came down the stairs behind him.

"It's Sam....she a...she..."  Jack didn't know what to say.  Si took the phone from his son.

"Sam love, Si here.  Calm down my dear, take a deep

breath. Tell me what happened." Si listened for some time, thumbs looped through his overall strap.

"Where is she now?" Si listened some more. "We are headed to the nearest airport as we speak, but I think it will be a day or more before he actually gets there." More listening. "Don't worry Sam, Jack will take care of it. You stay with Ross's mum and tell her we are thinking of her. We will let you know if we hear anything and the same to you. Okay, okay.....bye." Si hung up. Jack was pacing around the room. Si held up his hands in the international symbol to calm down.

"Well?" Jack said.

"The hospital called Ross's Mum early this morning. She wasn't the one to call you because she had been on the phone ever since talking to the hospital trying to see if she can get out there. They got Ross off the boat and sent her to a regional hospital. The hospital stabilized her but wasn't up for it when it came to her injuries, so they have now sent her to a trauma unit farther south. Sam's in absolute hysterics. They can't tell them what happened because, to be perfectly honest, they don't know what happened."

"Dad....is she alive or not?" Si let out a deep breath and looked his son square in the face.

"She's alive son, but she's considered critical." Jack shivered, his whole body went cold. "Ross was shot in the neck. The boat was in a very remote area. The Coast Guard went out as soon as they got the call but it was still an hour before they got there. By that time, she had lost a lot of blood." Jack set his hands on his hips. Tears formed in his eyes, but they didn't spill over.

"They are transporting her today to the other hospital for surgery to correct some of the damage. There is a chance she won't make it through the surgery, but there isn't another choice." Si continued.

"How much longer until we land?" Jack said, clearly using all his energy to control himself.

Si looked at his watch. "It's nine now. We will go through the night, probably hit the harbor between five and six tomorrow morning as long as the engines don't crap out on us."

"I'm going to make flight arrangements and then pack. I'll take the first shift tonight." Jack went to leave, Si stopped him with an arm around the neck, pulling him in for a hug. Jack let it happen, wrapping his arms around his father's back. Si's voice cracked when he said, "It's going to be okay, my boy. She's going to be okay." They both knew Si had no way of knowing that, but Jack did feel better hearing the determination in the old man's voice.

The engines held, and despite their agreement, they would take turns steering the boat. They were both on deck when the city lights of Jakarta appeared on the early morning horizon. Jack stood next to Si, tucking in his starched white dress shirt. Si noticed without comment it was the same shirt Ross had spilled shrimp down when they had first met. With that and a clean pair of jeans, a freshly shaved face and combed hair, Jack was looking smart. Much better than the scraggy pirate he had looked the day before.

"Almost there son. What time is your flight?"

"Eight."

"You'll have plenty of time. Are you sure you don't want me to come with you?" Si asked. He hadn't said anything, but he had packed a bag when Jack wasn't looking and had his passport in his back pocket. He was only a little offended that Jack hadn't noticed that he, too, was wearing his best shirt and had also shaved away his pirate beard.

"No, it's alright Dad. I may not be coming straight back and there is no reason for both of us to miss out on work." The man's face said it all. He thought he was going to collect her body. They pulled up along the harbor, and before Si had closed the space between them and the dock, Jack had jumped off, duffle bag in hand. Before Jack could take another step, his phone rang. It was Ross's mother.

"Belinda?"

"Oh Jack." The woman was crying, and it broke his heart. Jack was terrified she had called to tell him it was all over. "Sam said she called you."

"She did. I'm actually on my way to the airport now."

"I told her not to ask you to go. I didn't want to bother you."

"It's no trouble Belinda, she didn't ask me, I was going to go regardless."

"Thank you, Jack. I can't thank you enough. I can't go. Jimmy is still recovering. I have been on the phone since I found out yesterday trying to figure out how I can get out there. Sam offered to stay with him, but she has the baby."

"It's not a problem, Belinda. I'll bring her back to you....no matter what happens." Jack was controlling himself, but it was taking a lot of effort. Belinda wasn't bothering to control herself.

"They shot her in the neck, Jack. In the neck. How is she going to survive that?"

"She's a strong woman, Belinda. The strongest I've ever known. If anyone can do it, it's Ross."

"She's a scientist. I don't pretend to understand what she was researching, but why would anyone want to shoot a bunch of scientists? I just keep thinking how scared she must have been, Jack." Jack thought of the last image he had of Ross. The fear in her voice. He knew exactly how scared she had been. A tear spilled over and dripped down his face. Seeing this, Si jumped off the boat and stood next to him, his face covered in angst.

"She was hiding." Belinda continued. "She had hidden herself so well the Coast Guard almost didn't find her. You always want to be there when your children need you. It doesn't matter how old they are, or how stubborn. I wish I had been there, Jack. I can't tell you how much it means to me you are able to do this. I've spoken to the authorities this morning. They have her on a secure ward at the University of Alberta Hospital. Authorized people only. I called and told them you were coming. I know I was assuming a lot, but you seemed the next logical choice."

"Not a problem."

"Thank you, Jack. Ross thinks a lot of you, I'm glad you are going to be there with her."

"I'll call you as soon as I know something, alright love?" Jack hung up and wiped more tears away from his face.

"What's happened son?" Si asked softly.

"Her mother is a lovely woman. The best kind of woman and right now she is sitting there wondering if her daughter is going to be alive in the next minute and there isn't anything she can do about it. Ross's dad is poorly, he can't fly and Belinda can't leave him. Jimmy can't do for himself right now. She was calling to see if I would go up there and keep an eye on Ross."

"Did you tell her you were already on your way?"

"Yeah. Listen Dad, they are going to have her on a secure ward. I don't know how often I will be able to reach out. If um….if she doesn't…..I'll take her home to her folks." Jack bit his lip. Si grabbed his son by both shoulders.

"No matter what happens, if you need me, you call. I'll be there in two shakes of a lamb's tail. Give her a hug from me." Si slapped his son on the back, and Jack ran down the dock to a taxi.

"You betcha she's still alive. God willing she stays that way." Si said to Jack's back. His gut told him Ross was still in trouble. He hoped like hell Jack got there before anything else happened, but it would be a long journey. Plenty of time for more shit to hit the fan.

# 27

The last thing Ross could remember was the blast of the gun that was pointed at her. She was incredibly confused as to why she was standing in her lab back in Boston. At least she thought it was her lab. Her lab had never been this clean and void of people before. Even the trash cans were empty. There was a clear liquid bubbling away over a bunsen burner. *'You should never leave something unattended on the burner.'* Ross thought to herself.

She liked it, having the whole place to herself, but she still couldn't work out how she had gotten here.

"Oh shit, I'm dead." Ross thought to herself. She looked herself over as if to find what she had died of. "I was shot. The bastard shot me." Ross looked around her. This couldn't be it. Where was everyone else? She wasn't going to have to spend the rest of eternity here was she? It would be her luck she would make some ground breaking discovery that would cure cancer or something and she would be dead when she did it.

"Hey ya Ross." Ross turned around to see Nils, complete with man bun, sitting on a stool at the other end of the lab. Ross's eyes went to where the red stain had appeared when he fell down the stairs on the boat. It wasn't there, which was a relief.

"Nils." Ross said with surprise. He had never been to her lab before, he hadn't even been to Boston that she was aware of.

"Hey, Ross."

"You're dead. Aren't you?" Ross remembered him lying at her feet. A bullet whole in his chest.

"Yeah. I'm dead."

"So I'm really dead? I was kind of hoping this was one of those out-of-body experiences. I guess it's for real. I should have known my heaven was a chem lab. Or is this Hell? Have I been cursed to an eternity of searching for scientific proof and never finding any? I guess it's not as bad as constant grant writing. "

"Ross...shut up." Nils said. Apparently, she could still ramble when she was dead. Ross found that a little disappointing. To be honest, she found being dead a little disappointing. There wasn't anything specifically she had wanted to still do in life, but it was disappointing all the same that she would no longer have the opportunity.

"You aren't dead. Yet." Nils informed her with those bright green eyes shining.

"So what is this?"

"I don't know what it is called, but we are somewhere between being alive and being dead."

"Do I get to choose what happens?"

"Ross, you seem to be under the assumption I am some sort of guide, and I'm not. I've been dead only a little longer than you have been 'mostly' dead."

"Is there someone who can help me? I mean I have questions. It seems unreasonable to just put me here and give me no instructions." Nils just smiled.

"Ross, I came here to tell you something."

"Other than I am stuck someplace between living and dying with no idea how to get me out? That seems like more than enough."

"I need you to understand something about the attack."

"Lillian knew about it, didn't she?" Ross wasn't sure how she knew this. But she knew it.

"Yeah. So did I." Ross thought she should be mad. She thought she should be absolutely raging, but she wasn't. "We knew it was going to happen, Ross. I'm sorry. We knew the ship was going to be attacked. We didn't know how bad. I wouldn't have chosen to be shot in the chest."

"Yeah, I saw you leaving this world a slightly different way."

"Heart attack with a French model?" Nils said smiling.

"Or falling off a mountain because you were flirting and not paying attention." Ross answered. Nils shrugged. "You knew something was going to happen? Why didn't you warn us?"

"We thought they were just going to scare us and take the research. I wouldn't have asked you to come if I had known it would end so badly." Pictures were flashing in Ross's mind. Nils on the floor, Lillian and her running. Suddenly, Lillian's being quick enough and having the presence of mind to run away made sense. She had the benefit of knowing what was happening. Ross was remembering not only the blast, but the cold eyes before the blast.

"Spartans." She said out loud.

"Spartans?" Nils asked.

"Spartans attacked the ship. Why would Spartans care what we were researching?"

"Who the hell are Spartans? The Russians attacked the ship."

"Trust me, they were Spartans."

"The only people who would have cared what we were doing were the Russians. They are the ones that approached Lillian before the trip. Threatened her." Nils stated.

"I have to go back, Nils. I have to tell them it was Spartans."

"Lillian has a copy of the research, Ross. She has it all on a zip drive. You have to get it from her and publish it." Ross heard what Nils said, but all she could think about was making sure they knew it was Spartans.

"Ross, promise me."

"I will, Nils. What happened to her? She was with me. We ran down the hallway together, but I can't remember what happened to her." Ross was looking around the room to see if Lillian was trapped between living and dead as well.

"She's closer to death than you are. I'm going to go see her next and apologize to her."

"She hid me, Nils. She hid me and then waited for the gunman." Nils was fading away, like the white light in the room was absorbing him.

"Tell them Ross. Go back and tell them everything."

"How do I get back, Nils?" Ross was more than willing to live and spread the word about what had happened, but how the hell was she supposed to get back. *'I mean they could leave instructions, a map, something telling you where to go. To continue living, go out the door and take a left. If you would like to continue to the afterlife, take a right. How hard is that?* Ross said to herself.

"Ross." It was Jack's voice, but she couldn't figure out where it was coming from. She searched the room waiting for him to appear like Nils had.

"Jack? What are you doing here?" For a horrifying moment, Ross thought something had happened to Jack out at sea and now he was dead. What a choice that would be, going back to tell everyone who attacked the ship or staying in a pristine lab with Jack. *"That would be my luck, the only place we can manage to be in the same place at the same time is the afterlife."* Ross thought to herself.

"Ross, honey, wake up." It sounded like he was

coming over a speaker.

"Jack, where are you? It was the Spartans." Ross started walking towards Jack's voice. The room kept going and then it was black. Ross tried to open her eyes and couldn't. Jack was still talking to her and all she wanted to do was answer him, but she couldn't make her eyes open or her mouth move. It was incredibly frustrating.

# 28

It had taken almost a day and a half of travel to get to Ross's bedside where he was currently pleading with her to wake up. He hadn't showered, he could smell himself, and he was so tired he was starting to feel sick. As it turned out, getting to the hospital had only been half the battle. Belinda hadn't been joking when she said Ross was on a secure floor. All he had wanted to do when he got there was see Ross, but he had to get through security first. When he had told reception who he was there to see, he had been greeted by three armed police who had then taken him to a room in the basement where he had to convince an Inspector Dufort from Interpol that he was who he said he was. Jack would have been impressed if he hadn't been so annoyed. They took his picture and fingerprints, after which a stern looking nurse informed him that once he was on the secure ward, he would not be allowed to leave. He was then escorted by an armed guard to the elevator and Ross's floor.

Leaving the elevator, the guard took him to the nurse's station. "I'm looking for Dr. Ross Halloway please." At this point, Jack was nervous. He was expecting someone at every turn to tell him he was too late, that she had died. When the nurse pointed him to a room behind him and said, "Second room on your left." Jack then worried what he was going to see. Hospitals weren't his favorite places to begin with, but he really wasn't sure how Ross was going to look and what his response was going to be.

His heart beat faster. All he knew was what Belinda had told him. There was a window to her room, but the curtains were closed and he couldn't see anything. With a deep breath, he put a smile on his face and opened the door.

The sight of her broke his heart. The smile dropped from his face and his hand covered his mouth. She didn't even look like Ross, she was too still, too pale. Jack had seen Ross sleep, and even in her sleep, she was more alive than this. Her head was turned towards him so as to accommodate the bandage covering her left shoulder and neck. The lips that had been so red the last time he saw them were pale and chapped, blending in with the pale face. There didn't look to be any life in her at all. If the EKG machine behind her hadn't been showing a steady heart rhythm, he would have thought her dead.

Jack had thought he would run to her when he saw her. On the long flights from Jakarta to Canada and then up to Alberta, Jack had plenty of time to visualize the moment when he would finally see her, and it wasn't anything like this. He stood frozen in the doorway, taking in the room and getting used to Ross as she was now. Jack sat down gently in the plastic chair provided for the guest and reached for her hand. The warmth of it reassured him that she was still there.

"I'm here, my girl." His voice was forced. He didn't want her to hear the fear in him. He kissed her hand. "Oh Ross. What kind of trouble have you gotten yourself into this time? You sleep for now. I'll be here when you wake up." Jack took her hand and rubbed it against his cheek which was covered in bristly hair after thirty-two hours in transit. He watched her face for any sign that she knew he was there. She gave him nothing. *'I'll be here when you wake up my love. Whenever that is.'*

Leaning his head against the bed, closing his eyes.

Footsteps woke him, and he nearly jumped to find a woman standing next to him.

"Morning." The woman said, smiling. She moved to the other side of the bed and listened to Ross's chest and checked her bandage.

"Are you the doctor?" Jack asked in a hoarse voice.

"I am, you are?"

"Jack. Her boyfriend. Can you tell me how she's doing?" The doctor looked down at Ross's chart, no doubt making sure he was supposed to be there.

"She was very lucky, really. The investigators think she must have been shot at point blank range given where she was found. The only thing we can think is that she instinctively turned her head when the gun was fired, and instead of hitting her in the head, it hit her in the neck. Somehow, it missed her carotid artery which would definitely have killed her in a matter of minutes. It did hit several smaller arteries and vessels that all come together in that area, which explains all the blood loss. For whatever reason, whoever attacked the ship shut down the engines and power to the boat. When the Coast Guard arrived, the ship was almost as cold inside as the air outside. Lower body temperature slowed the blood loss in both patients and may have saved their lives. They were able to stop the bleeding at Inuvik Regional, which was the nearest hospital to where she was found. Reconstruction of the vessels was done here. Dr. Halloway will recover to a normal life though she may have some weakness on that side. We won't know more until she wakes up."

"When do you think that will be?" The doctor shrugged her shoulders.

"Whenever she is ready. Her body went through a lot. She has lost a lot of blood, which was traumatizing, and now her body is having to adjust to the blood we have introduced. She does have a healthy amount of pain medication on board which will obviously have a sedative effect, but really, her body is taking this time to heal itself. It may look like she's just lying there, but her body is hard at work doing what it needs to make itself whole again. We will just have to be patient." Jack nodded his head.

"Is she out of the woods? Is there any chance she could...pass?"

"We are cautiously optimistic. She was in surgery yesterday for twelve hours. She did well with anesthesia, and has done well since. I wish I could give you more, but really we are just going to have to wait and see how she does."

"Thank you." She gave him a squeeze of the shoulder as she passed.

"Page the nurse if there is any change." The doctor said and left the room.

Jack squeezed Ross's hand. What the hell had happened on that ship? They had come close to dying when they were attacked at the resort, but to be shot at point blank range...she must have been so scared.

"I'm still here, love. You take your time." Jack sat back in the chair and tried to make himself comfortable. He had managed a nap and splashed some water on his face. He ventured out of the room and got a cup of coffee and a Snickers out of the vending machine. After speaking with the doctor, Jack had called Belinda. The thought had crossed his mind to call Sam, but to be honest, he wanted to close his eyes for a moment and then he would call Sam. He had shot off a text to Si and let him know he was there and that he would call him later.

Leaning back, Jack rested his feet on the hospital bed and closed his eyes. His phone vibrated in his back pocket, the ringtone telling him it was a FaceTime call.

He pressed the button and Sam's face (extremely close up) came into view. "Hey Sam." Jack sat up, his voice was husky.

"Jesus Jack, what happened to you?" Genuine concern on her face.

"The last time I slept was three days ago Sam. It was also the last time I showered."

"Sorry." She hesitated for a moment. "How is she? Have you seen her?"

"I'm here with her now. I should warn you Sam, she doesn't look great. The doctor said she's doing well, but she isn't quite out of the woods yet." Sam played with the necklace around her neck in a way that reminded him of Ross's hair twirling when she was nervous.

"I spoke with Belinda already." Sam said. "Let me see her, Jack."

"Someone to see you, Ross." Jack said, turning the phone so that Sam could see Ross. Jack heard Sam's intake of breath at the shock.

"Ross, it's Sam here, Honey. Are you listening to me? You need to wake up and get back here. Do you understand me? This wasn't the plan, Ross. We are supposed to go together after having outlived our husbands. Remember? We are supposed to get kicked out of the nursing home together. Ross honey, I need you to wake up. I need you to help me raise Ruby because, to be perfectly honest, I think she is going to be one hell of a teenager, and I'm just not sure I can handle it. I need you. Ruby needs you. Jack needs you. You have a lot of people here Ross who need you to wake up." Sam's voice was breaking. Jack flipped the phone back around. Sam was fanning the tears. "Jack, she looks…."

"I know." Jack said.

"I want to smack her, but I don't think they'd let you stay if you did that." Sam sniffed. "Jack, I can't do this. I need her. I can't do life without Ross."

"You aren't going to have to. She is tough, and what she lacks in toughness, she makes up for in stubbornness." Sam half sobbed and half laughed.

"Keep repeating blatantly wrong scientific facts to her. Tell her Darwin was a hack and that the planet is flat. Ehhh, tell her Madam Curie was lucky. That she wouldn't have been anything if it weren't for her husband. That should get her up. She nearly punched a guy in college over that one." Ross had never been able to leave an incorrect fact lay. Resulting in many awkward social interactions. Sam's lip began to quiver again. "Also tell her every hour that I love her, and I can't live without her."

"I will, Hon." Jack couldn't handle much more of the women crying. If Sam didn't cheer up soon, he was going to break down and join her.

"You okay, Jack? You look like hell." Jack asked himself the same question. He felt like only one thought had occupied his mind since Ross had dropped that call, and now that he was here, all he wanted was for her eyes to open.

"I was going to call it off, Sam. She'd been trying to get me and I had ignored her because I didn't want to do it while she was on the trip. But I was going to tell her it was over. I don't even know why I called her back that day." Jack buried his head in his hand. "What if I hadn't? When would we have found out what had happened?" The sick feeling returned to Jack's stomach like it did every time he thought about that night. Would it have been Sam or Belinda that called to tell him? What would he have done then?

"Thankfully, we don't have to worry about that. Si said you were already back to land when Belinda called you. I can't tell you how much it means to us that you are there. That someone she knows and loves is going to be the first thing she sees when she wakes up."

"I will be here. I promised her."

"I know you will, Jack. Keep talking to her. I'm serious about the bad science facts, it absolutely drives her nuts. If anything will get her back from where she is, it will be that."

"It won't be hard. I don't think I know a lot of accurate science facts."

"Take care of yourself, Jack. Let me know the instant there is a change, I don't care what time it is. You hear me?" Sam pointed her finger at the screen and gave her best 'Mom' face.

"Yes, ma'am."

Sam blew him a kiss and signed off. Jack checked for signs that Ross had heard any of what Sam had said. Taking her hand again he said, "What do you know about global warming? I personally think it's all made up. I mean the planet has always had spells of hot and cold weather. What makes right now any different?" Still nothing. Jack spent the rest of the day looking up scientific falsehoods in search of the one that would annoy Ross so much it would bring her back to him.

# 29

Pedro was fully aware that being sent back to clean up his mess was a punishment. Not that he had any hard feelings about it. He had no feelings at all other than feeling cold. They had received word that against all odds, the two survivors had actually survived their surgeries. The plan for Pedro to kill them (again) was now in place. It would be both simple and more complicated. They were on a secure ward. Nothing as bold as a helicopter and a gun could be used for this mission. Pedro was slightly more confident this time because he hadn't killed this up close and personal since he was just out of training. Now that he was a little more experienced, finishing the job should be easy. He pulled his bag out of the car and headed towards the small plane sitting on the runway. He only needed a small bag because he didn't intend to stay for long. In fact, his travel time would take much longer than the mission itself. He had gotten himself to Paris. A private plane was waiting to take him the rest of the way.

"I'm ready to go whenever the pilot is ready." Pedro said. His foot was on the first step when he heard the man say, "We aren't going to wait for the others?" Pedro turned around slowly.

"Others?" The man was going to bruise himself if he wrung his hands any harder.

"There were five of you for the original mission. It was assumed that the same would be coming on this mission." The man was trying not to appear frightened and failing in every way. The Spartans did not feel fear, but it didn't mean they didn't recognize it in others. It was actually a very useful tool when you knew how to use it. The Spartan stood too close to the chubby little man and said, "When I was in the military, I once killed five people in a well defended compound in the middle of the desert and was back at camp for breakfast. I think I can handle two severely injured women in the hospital with a handful of armed guards by myself." The chubby man's eyes grew large. "Do we have a problem?"

"No, no problem."

"Then let the pilot know I'm ready." Pedro turned back towards the plane and hopped up the stairs. Tossing his bag in one chair, he sat in another. The engines of the planes revved up. He hadn't lied about his ability to kill. Didn't need to. To say he wasn't concerned about this mission was an understatement. He had barely given it a thought.

The chubby little man approached the cabin of the plane and gave the thumbs up to the pilot. Backing away, he bent down to make sure that the device was where he was told it would be. Under the belly of the plane there was a small box with a little red light letting him know it was active. He watched the plane taxi out to the runway and then hustled back to his car where he quickly called his boss.

"Are they off?" The familiar voice asked.

"He is off. There was only one."

"What do you mean there was only one?"

"Only one Spartan arrived for the flight. He said he was all that was needed for a mission like this." The line went dead. Not for the first time, the chubby man was grateful he was insignificant. His one job here had been to meet the Spartans and call when the plane was away. They didn't even know his name and so he was fairly confident there would be no repercussions for delivering bad news.

The Chief of Security slammed down the phone. He did not deal with disappointment well and the fact that only one Spartan had shown up for the mission was aggravating. He would add that to the list of things he would yell at Alexi about when this was all done. Not letting himself get distracted, the chief picked up the phone again and gave the order to continue as planned. He then turned his chair to look out the window. He would wait here until he had heard that his orders had been obeyed. Taking a deep breath, it felt good to be in charge again. The down side of his position was that he had to delegate. He relished the good old days when he could complete the mission to perfection without having to rely on anyone else.

Five hours into the flight, the plane was over the Atlantic in the dark of night. Pedro rested his eyes since there was little time to get any sleep once they landed. On the belly of the plane the little box's light went from red to green. Immediately following, there was a blast of fiery light in the quiet night sky. Those parts of the plane, not instantly consumed by fire, fell silently into the ocean below.

The chief's phone rang and he answered without a word, and a smile curled his lips. Still with no word spoken, the chief hung the phone up again. No one crossed him, not even a Spartan. Pressing the button on his desk phone, he said, "Get me Alexi." There was a long pause before his secretary came back and said, "Alxi Stanovich was reported as missing by one of his handlers fifteen minutes ago. They just called to say they found his driver strangled to death in a car at the airport."

"Why is this the first I'm hearing about it?"

"It was going to be part of your security meeting this morning. They are still trying to figure out what has happened." The secretary answered, not responding to his angry tone. The chief cut off the conversation. Nothing made him more angry than desertion. How dare Alexi run away! There was no point in closing the ports and stations, which is no doubt what his security meeting would suggest. The man was already out of the country. It didn't matter though, he would be found and he would pay for turning his back on his country.

At the very moment the plane was exploding over the

Atlantic ocean, Jack was making another plea for Ross to wake up. Something she desperately wanted to do. She could hear Jack, she could even feel him holding her hand against his scruffy face, but she couldn't make herself open her eyes.

"Do you think the earth could be flat? I mean, how do we really know what shape the planet is? I watched some of those videos online, and I have to say, they make a good argument." Ross's eyes flew open and stared blankly. She looked around, and finding Jack, grabbed his shirt with her good arm and pulled him in close.

"SPARTANS." She said it loudly and slowly so he would be sure to understand. Jack did understand. Ross had finally made her way through the darkness and got her eyes and mouth to do what she wanted them to.

"Spartans?" Jack questioned, searching her face for any sign that she hadn't meant to say what she did. Ross was serious.

"Spartans." Ross said again, calmly this time. Jack smashed the button for the nurse and squeezed her hand. The blackness was gone, the relaxed feeling she had when she was in the lab, was gone. The pain was very present. The sudden movement caused a red hot pain up her neck and down her back and left arm. Jack watched as her face went from animated to white as a sheet again. Surprise filled her eyes as the pain took over.

"Ross, honey. Lay back. You are okay, you hear me? You are in a hospital, you are safe." The pain did not fade. His touch convinced her he was really there, and she teared up.

"Jack! Oh Jack." Ross clung to him. "I saw his eyes. I saw his eyes." She tried to explain. Jack believed her, she could tell, but he was trying to calm her down, which she didn't understand because if there was a time to panic it was now!!

"Relax, honey." He leaned into her, being careful not to touch her for fear of hurting her. He stroked her cheek and kept eye contact with her. "You're safe, we'll tell them. Okay, we are going to tell them." Ross nodded her head.

"It was the Spartans, Jack. It was the Spartans. I saw them." Ross wanted to tell him everything, everything that had happened, but the nurses and doctor came into the room and took over. Ross was laid back on the bed, and they started asking her a series of questions and inspecting the bandage on her neck. Her morphine was dialed up to help with the pain.

"What happened?" The doctor asked. Jack was frozen to the spot, standing near the door so that he was in Ross's line of sight but out of the way.

"I told her the earth was flat. She just sat up and started yelling." He almost whispered it. The doctor gave him a look. "She hates it when you get scientific facts wrong." Jack explained. The doctor nodded.

What had she been thinking about to bring her out like that? It was clearly important to her that they knew it was the Spartans who had attacked the ship.

"She knows who did it. I need to speak to that inspector fella." Jack said, finding some of his voice. Ross was watching from the bed, she nodded her head in agreement. The adamant eyes that were locked with his were now growing foggy.

"She's on a lot of pain medications, we will let her rest and then see what she has to say." Jack's back got straighter.

"I need that investigator now. If she's right, then she, the other survivor, and everyone in this hospital is in danger. These people don't leave survivors, and if they know she's alive, they are probably a little pissed about it." The doctor rolled her eyes.

"Who are these people who are after her?" The doctor asked. Ross seemed more relaxed, and the doctor seemed content with her bandages, so she turned her attention to Jack. How was he going to describe a Spartan without it sounding crazy?

"Remember a while ago, it was all over the news, a resort full of scientists was attacked?" The doctor leaned back on her heels and crossed her arms over herself.

"Yeah, by some people calling themselves Spartans. The military had designed them for war."

"Do you remember there were four survivors?"

"Yeah."

"You're looking at two of them. We, along with two others, are the only four people to ever survive an encounter with a Spartan. We barely got away last time. Now, she said she knows who it was and that it was a Spartan. If that is the case, they will kill whoever they have to to get what they want, and if that means killing everyone from the front door to here, that's what they will do. I need the investigator now, please!" The doctor looked like she was debating whether or not to believe him, but the fact of the matter was these two victims had been placed on a secure ward for a reason.

"I'll call the investigator, but I'm going to have to dial back her morphine to make it to where she can even understand what they are asking her."

"As long as you crank it up as soon as they are done." The doctor adjusted and then left. Jack looked around him, with a new awareness. Ross was asleep again in the bed, but she looked more like herself. The color was back in her cheeks. He had seen the fire in her eyes when she looked at him. She was injured, but she was there. He could deal with the wound on her neck. As long as she was the same Ross, he could deal with that and worse. Ross had only been awake for a few minutes and most of that panicked, but it was Ross. He ran his hand through his hair and took a deep breath.

"It had to be fucking Spartans." He whispered to himself.

# 30

Inspector Louis Dufort had arrived in Canada twelve hours after the attack on 'The Hunter'. He had been trying to track down where the Spartans were when he got the call. His first task was to secure a floor of the hospital to insure the safety of the survivors as it was hoped they would be able to shed valuable light on what happened. Dufort exited the elevator on the secure floor in a foul mood. He had just returned to his room and gotten into bed after viewing the crime scene on the 'Hunter' which was now moored in harbor. It had all the hallmarks of a Spartan attack, but did absolutely nothing to shed light on why it had happened. A wasted trip that had taken hours on a plane where he had not been able to smoke or sleep (thanks to the turbulence) and now he had been called away again.

With a grumble, he stomped off the elevator. "What is it?" He asked the nurse sharply.

"She's awake, and talking." The nurse answered, giving him a steady glare that seemed to be a unique talent of her profession.

"Which one?" Dufort's mood had instantly brightened.

"Dr. Halloway." While Dufort wanted to know what both of his survivors could remember of the night, Dr. Halloway was the one he had eagerly been waiting on. It was a well known fact in his department that Dr. Halloway was one of only four people who had ever survived a Spartan attack, so if Spartans did this, she would know. Dufort ran a hand through his hair to tame it and made some effort to straighten his tie. He wished he had shaved but there wasn't time.

"When did she wake?"

"We called you immediately. Her boyfriend is with her and insisted on it."

Dufort had forgotten about Jack. He entered the room quietly. Jack was leaning over Ross stroking her hair and saying something to her. When Dufort entered the room, Jack turned to him. The man looked like hell. Bags under his eyes from lack of sleep and a ten o'clock shadow.

"Good evening. I understand Dr. Halloway is back with us." Dufort tried to look as pleasant as he could. He found his 'normal' face tended to scare people. Dr. Halloway, through some struggle, sat herself up a little, and looking at him squarely, said, "It was Spartans." Before she leaned back into her bed.

Dufort tried to not let the excitement show.

"You are sure about that?" He asked.

"I saw his eyes." Dr. Halloway said. Dufort almost jumped with joy. As you can imagine, it can be hard to identify a genetically altered killer that looks in every way like a normal human. Law agencies had been trained to identify them by the one distinguishing characteristic they had. Emotionless, dead eyes.

"Did he say anything to you?"

"No." Dufort could see this conversation was costing her, so he would try to get out what information he needed quickly.

"Any idea why they would attack your research ship?"

"We were there to prove crude oil drilling was taking place. Nils was convinced it was the Russians."

"Did you find proof of such a thing?"

"Yes."

"Thank you very much, Dr. Halloway. I will be in touch with you more tomorrow, for right now I will let you rest." Dufort folded up his notebook and walked out the door.

"She knows what she's talking about." Jack said, following him.

"Oh yes?"

"She's seen them before. Spartans. She was at...."

"Ikan Hui resort last year. Both you and her along with her best friend Samantha and your father were held hostage for the better part of eight hours before you made your escape. Making you the only four people to survive a Spartan attack." Dufort knew his brief. Jack stepped back.

"Yeah."

"I have been investigating the Spartans since their existence became known. I was put on the case because the attack on 'The Hunter' had all the hallmarks of a Spartan attack. Thanks to Dr. Halloway, now we can confirm it."

"What are you going to do about it?"

"Dr. Halloway and the other survivor are on a secure ward. The Spartans haven't done much to come after you since last year, we don't think the attack on the ship was motivated by revenge. More likely, if there is a repeat attack, it will be instigated by whoever hired the Spartans to begin with. If the Russians are behind it, we will have to be on our toes. They don't like to fail." Dufort didn't say he suspected they would not be coming for Dr. Halloway, but the other survivor. "Tell me Jack, do you know what they were studying out there?"

"Just what she told you. She mentioned something about hydrocarbons I think, but to be honest, I don't understand a lot of what Ross tells me when it comes to her work."

"Did she know they were chasing the Russians before she went on the trip?"

"Not that she mentioned."

"Has anyone reached out to you or Dr. Halloway before the trip in regards to what Dr. Halloway was studying?" Jack was beginning to catch on to what the inspector was leading to.

"No. I didn't even know who else was on the trip."

"It is strange, don't you think? A research ship being attacked in such a violent way? I am with you, I don't really understand what they were studying or how it would be applied, but it was upsetting someone, no? Thank you for coming and getting me as soon as she woke up. If she thinks of anything else, please let me know. I have to go bring my team up to speed."

"So we just sit here?" Jack was not good at waiting. Dufort patted him on the shoulder.

"Hopefully, by the time the doctors are ready to discharge her, we will have the people responsible in custody."

"And if you haven't caught them by then?"

"We will go to plan B."

Dufort really did need to reach out to his team and let them know there was little doubt they were now looking at another Spartan attack. Before he did though, he wanted to see Dr. Petrov one more time. He had reached out to her like he had Dr. Halloway when she had first come round, but she had not been able to remember the attack. He might as well try again while he was here. Knocking gently on her door, he entered without waiting for a reply. Dr. Petrov was a small woman, but her eyes let him know she was not to be underestimated. Her body may be weak at the moment, but it was clear she was still a woman to take seriously. She looked away from the TV to watch him enter the room. Lillian was watching the news again, in constant worry that they would find out she had known all along what was going to happen.

"I wouldn't watch too much of that if I were you." Dufort said, trying to be jovial.

"I keep expecting to hear that I died on the ship."

"How are you feeling?" Dufort asked, taking a seat next to her. The nurses said she was refusing the full amount of pain meds. To Dufort that meant one of two things. Guilt or fear. He thought there was very little chance she was going to come right out and tell him anything, but after being an inspector for so long, he was good at at least figuring out if there was something there to tell.

"I don't like the way the pain meds make me feel, but they insist on giving me something." The bandage over her chest was massive, giving Dufort some idea of the wound underneath. He would have taken as many pain meds as they would give him.

"I just came from next door. I thought you would like to know that Dr. Halloway is awake. She has been able to provide us with who attacked the ship." Lillian's blood ran cold for a moment.

"Who was it?"

"Do you know what a Spartan is?"

"Sounds familiar. Are they the ones who attacked the ship?"

"It seems like it. Dr. Halloway, in the brief glance she got of them, knew exactly who they were because she had seen them before."

"The attack at the resort?" Lillian said.

"The same. Do you remember anything about the person who shot you?" Lillian could remember just about every aspect of that evening. From when she heard the helicopter overhead. The realization that it was happening. Seeing Ross standing in the hallway and then running. She remembered the running more than anything, but she didn't want to tell the inspector. Not while she had pain meds on board. Getting out of this without any blame was more than she deserved, but she couldn't help taking measures to try and hide her involvement in the attack. Lillian didn't trust herself to not say something revealing while she was on pain medications.

"He was wearing black."

"He?"

"I assume. He seemed male. He walked in and shot me." That had really been it. She barely had time to realize what was happening. They both watched the news for a moment. The footage taken the morning after the attack of the ship floating dead in the water. They hadn't even removed the bodies yet. As she watched it, Lillian thought about Nils lying at the bottom of the stairs. The surprised look on his face. He had really expected them to be able to beat this. Idiot.

"Where were you when the attack happened?" Louis had already asked her this question, but he had already gotten more out of her this interview than the last. Might as well try for more.

"In my room."

"What made you leave your room?"

"Noise. I don't remember what." She knew, saying it was the helicopter would cause more questions. "I got up to see what the noise was."

"Why did you run to the engine room?" This one was a question he had asked before and one she had given a lot of thought to answering. The truth was she had been looking for a hiding place and thought the engine room was a good one. The small room behind it, she had hoped, would go unnoticed.

"I just ran." Was the simple answer she had come up with.

"Why not go upstairs?" Dufort thought he was doing a rather good job of making this feel more like a conversation than the interview it was.

"There was someone on the stairs." To be fair, this was an honest answer. Lillian was very aware of the black figure on the stairs as she ran past it. At the time she had expected to be shot at as she passed.

"Who was at the top of the stairs, do you know?"

"A black figure." She was starting to tire.

"Dr. Petrov, I've been trying to figure out why the ship was attacked. I can't think of why someone would want to attack this particular ship and kill scientists. What were you studying?" Lillian's head was resting more on the pillow.

"We were trying to prove that oil drilling was happening by showing the effects of oil in the environment. I was trying to prove that insects had been exposed to oil in the environment."

"Why would someone want to kill for that?"

"No one is supposed to be drilling there, inspector. The ice is melting, where our ship was found would have been solid ice all year round a few years ago. Because the ice is melting, new shipping lanes are opening up, and new resources are being made available. As is usually the case, government agencies have not gotten ahead of the problem and the place is unregulated."

"So whoever is drilling out there is making pure profit off of what they are able to drill." Lillian nodded in answer. "But Nils knew someone was out there? How?"

"Something about drilling sounds being picked up on radio."

"Did he know who it was?"

"He said it was Russians."

"How would he know that?" Dufort asked. Lillian managed a smile.

"I'm not sure he did know for sure. They were the logical choice. They are close to the area, they have made it known they are interested in the resources that might be in the area. Nils thought the fact that it was being stolen was evidence enough. He didn't think very much of the Russian's idea of playing fair." Lillian made all the signs she was growing tired. In her previous interviews with Louis, he had been sympathetic to the fact she was recovering. She was not above using this to her advantage.

"I'll leave you alone, Dr. Petrov. I'm serious about the news though. Don't watch too much."

# 31

Dufort left Dr. Petrov's room and nodded to the nurses as he passed, then made his way to his office. His lack of sleep forgotten for the moment, he walked quickly and with purpose, making notes in his ever present notebook. It was not a long trip from the ninth floor to his basement office, but he did not want to forget a single thing, and so made note of it while he walked. Getting to his office, he quickly tucked a piece of nicotine gum in his mouth. He felt a bit calmer and picked up the phone to update his supervisor. While he waited for her to answer, he put Dr. Lillian Petrov through the system. Something he had already done, but this time he was looking for something specific.

"What do you have for me?" There was no chit chat, which Dufort appreciated. Who had time for it?

"Dr. Halloway is awake and was very eager to tell me

who shot her."

"Who?"

"A Spartan."

"Is she sure?" The eagerness was clear in her voice.

"As you know, she has seen a Spartan before. She said their faces were covered but she was able to see their dead, cold eyes perfectly before they shot her."

"We've been getting murmurs that they were active again. Any idea who hired them?"

"Russia has been brought up more than once."

"Why would Russia care about a bunch of scientists?"

"They were there to prove someone was drilling for oil up there. Dr. Ryeng had apparently heard that there were sounds of drilling, but no one could figure out who was doing it. The team was up there to prove there was oil drilling happening and get the place protected."

"So we know why? We suspect who? Now we just need to know how."

"I was hoping you could help me with that. I hate to stereotype, but Dr. Petrov is Russian born, and from what I can gather, she left Russia under tense circumstances. I'm trying to figure out if she has had any contact with someone in the Russian government or what hold they would have over her." Dufort said.

"You think she may have had something to do with it?"

"The Spartans don't do anything without planning it out. They would have needed someone on the boat to give them information. Aside from that, I can tell she isn't telling me everything."

"She's just woken up from a complex surgery to fix a gaping chest wound. How can you tell she's withholding information?" Dufort's boss pointed out.

"It's a feeling. She's playing me, and she's doing a good job of it despite the pain meds. It has me wondering where she learned such skills."

"She's lived in England for the better part of a decade now. What makes you think she would work for Russia now?"

"A genius like Dr. Petrov would have been of great interest to the Russian government. The fact that she left under tense circumstances makes me think she wasn't willing to play their games. I'm wondering if they caught up to her."

" You don't think she would have assisted willingly?"

"I don't. Everything I have been able to find out about her is that she left Russia suddenly and has never looked back. Why would she go to such lengths to show her loyalty now?"

"What about your other survivor? Could she have had anything to do with it?"

"I don't think so. I can't say for sure, but I think she was in the wrong place at the wrong time. I can't find any reason for her to have sympathy with the Russians."

"I'll see what I can find out for you. I can't say finding out that the Spartans were responsible brings the investigation forward much. They leave very little evidence behind." Dufort chose not to focus on the lack of Spartan evidence right now. He would continue to assume Spartans were involved.

"Speaking of evidence, have we found the equipment yet?" He offered.

"Nothing yet. I think they dumped it in the ocean. Lord knows where it is now."

"Dr. Petrov is still claiming she can't remember anything though she remembered more today than the last time I spoke with her. I'll see if I can't find out from Dr. Halloway what equipment there was. It might help to at least know what we are looking for."

"Good work, Dufort. Let me know if you learn

anything else."

"I am a little concerned about security. If this is the Russian's, I think the chances of a repeat attack increases."

"Agreed. Do what you need to. I want to get the Spartans and whoever hired them, which means we need those witnesses."

The doctors and the inspector having left, Jack went back to Ross. He had not been able to help himself. Being careful of her bandages, he had pulled her close to him and kissed her. It was clear the pain meds were taking their effect. Not wanting to let her go, Ross leaned heavily on Jack's chest, resting her head on in the space under his chin. Jack thought he should move. Let her lay more comfortably, but selfishly, he stayed. He absorbed the weight and warmth of her. They had just finished FaceTime with Ross's parents. They had discussed Facetiming Sam, but after speaking with the inspector and her parents, she was exhausted and asked to take a break. No doubt Belinda was informing Sam of the news.

"I'll let you lie down and get some sleep." Jack went to move, but she grabbed at his shirt with her good arm.

"Stay." She said, softly.

"Sure."

"I feel better with you here." Ross clung to him in a way she had never done before. Like she was afraid he would disappear. Jack wanted to hold her tight, but he didn't know where to touch her so that it wouldn't hurt her. He laid down and let Ross position herself.

"Maybe I should get on that side, and then you can lean this way." Jack got up and went around the bed to get on the other side. After some finagling, they managed to get comfortable. Ross leaned against him and nestled in. She let out a deep breath and Jack felt her relax against him. He thought she had gone to sleep when she said, "I'm glad you came, Jack."

"Of course I came. I didn't know what had happened to you. I wasn't willing to wait and find out."

"We didn't leave things on the greatest of terms." Jack rested his lips on the top of her head.

"Ross, I don't even know what the right word is for what I felt when I heard those gunshots on the other end of the phone. Then you disappeared and the line went dead. I could have swum here at that point. There would've been no stopping me until I saw you."

"I feel better with you here. I'm sorry I scared you."

"Yeah, please stop doing that. I speak for your mother and Sam as well." Ross tried to laugh, but the movement hurt.

"Ross, can you remember what happened that night?" Jack's voice was quiet and calm. She didn't answer him right away. The scenes of that night flashed in her memory, but she didn't want to remember them. Ross closed her eyes to try and make them go away, but the memory only got stronger.

"I couldn't sleep that night, so I went to the canteen. Nils was already there. He wanted to toast the findings of the day. My findings. I had found proof. There was crude oil drilling occurring, no doubt about it. I was going to write a great paper about it when I got back, and it was going to help protect the area." The morphine was taking hold. Jack could feel her relaxing more into him. "I told Nilly about us. He was hitting on me. I'm pretty sure he was hitting on me. I'll have to ask Sam to be sure. I told him about us to make him stop. Told him we had a fight. That I wasn't sure where we stood. He told me to call you. I was surprised, I thought he was going to make a move, but what he said made sense. After he left, I called you. You didn't answer right away." Ross paused. The pause continued. Jack had thought she had fallen asleep and then he felt her shake with tears.

"He ran up on deck. We heard the guns, and he ran up on deck. They shot him in the chest. He looked so surprised when he landed on the ground. You were yelling in my ear. I could see them coming down the stairs, Jack. Big black boots. I didn't move. I couldn't move."

"You did move, my love. That isn't where you were found."

"Lillian, Dr. Petrov, rushed past me and grabbed my hand." Ross had just remembered that part. Lillian jumping over Nils and grabbing her hand. "We ran down the hallway. I dropped the phone when she grabbed me. We ran the entire length of the ship, past the engine room to this little storage area. She told me to hide and I did. Up on top of something. I can't remember what it was." Jack was hoping she didn't remember too much of what had happened next. No one needed to remember being shot. "She didn't hide. Lillian just stood there and waited for them. We could hear his boots on the metal floor getting closer. I didn't like her to begin with, but she was all right." It dawned on Jack she didn't know.

"Ross, Lillian survived the attack." Ross tried to push herself up so she could look at him. Jack had to help her. "She did? But they shot her."

"In the chest. They found her on the floor beneath where they found you. She is in the room next door."

"Lillian's here? I'll have to go see her." Ross's eyes were growing very heavy.

"You need rest, love." He eased her back down and she found her spot again on his chest. She was quiet for a moment and then said, "I don't remember being scared, Jack. I know I was, I must have been. I just remember those eyes. They were the same as Sarah's. Blank. Nothing behind them at all. They are going to come back for me, aren't they Jack?"

"No."

"Yes they are. Spartans don't leave survivors. I've survived twice now. That has to be pissing them off a little."

"It would if they got pissed, but thankfully Spartans don't get angry."

"Oh yeah." Ross could feel the exhaustion pulling her under. She wanted to tell Jack everything. Wanted to apologize to him for not coming to see him, for thinking it was over between them, but she just didn't have the strength anymore. She leaned her head back against Jack's chest and closed her eyes.

"You take a nap. We'll have plenty of time to talk when you get up." Jack whispered over her.

# 32

Ross slept for a few hours. To his surprise, laying in a bed for the first time in days, with Ross tucked up next to him, Jack got the best few hours of sleep he could remember. It was Ross moving that woke him up some hours later.

"Jack?"

"Yeah?" He was blurry from sleep and had to force himself awake.

"I'm absolutely starving." Ross said. Jack rolled over and hit the button for the nurse.

"Madam is hungry." He informed the voice that answered over the speaker.

"I also have to pee." Ross added, somewhat shyly. Jack thought he could help her with that one on his own, and after some shuffling, Ross managed to get herself into the bathroom and back out again. To his surprise, this minimal amount of effort drained her face of all color. Jack supported her back to her bed and helped get her comfortable. By the time they were done with all that, Ross's cheeseburger and fries had arrived. Some color returned to her face as she dug in. It wasn't until that moment Jack realized how hungry he was. "I don't suppose…" Jack turned around to ask if they could order him the same just as the nurse was producing a tray for him.

"Oh, thank you. You're a cracker." Jack said, with much gratitude. Ross watched with sharp eyes as the nurse smiled at him and continued to look at him as she walked out of the room. Jack didn't see it. He only had eyes for his food.

"She fancies you." Ross announced.

"Don't be silly." Jack answered around his food. Ross still couldn't figure out if he was full of shit or if he really had no idea the effect he had on women. "Don't tell me you're jealous? The poor woman took pity on me. I can't leave the floor Ross. Not even for food. If it weren't for handouts, I'd have eaten nothing the vending machine didn't provide."

"Of course I'm not jealous. Look at me. What does she have that I don't have? Accept clean hair. Clothes.

Teeth that have been brushed this week. How could I possibly be worried about her being more attractive than I am?" A smile covered Jack's face. It was rare to get a full smile that lifted both sides of his face. Usually all you got was a sideways grin. "What?" Ross said.

"Glad to see you still have your sense of humor is all." They were quiet for a while, concentrating on eating. "This is what we ate after Ihan Hui, you remember?" Jack said after a while. Ross nodded her head.

"I also remember we found a fun way to burn off the calories afterwards." Jack added. Ross dared a glance in his direction. His sly grin was in place.

"Not much chance of that happening this time, I'm afraid." Ross said, indicating her arm and bandaged neck.

"That's alright. I grill a mean burger myself. Plenty of time for burgers when you are feeling better."

"After I eat, do you think I can go see Lillian?" Ross said, changing the subject.

"Not sure that's a good idea."

"Why not? You said she was right next door."

"Ross, the color drained from your face after you went to the bathroom. I'm not sure you should be moving around a lot."

"You could help me."

"I'm not sure I want to. I don't want you hurting yourself."

"I can't just lay here Jack, I need to see her. Could she come here?"

"I doubt it, she is recovering from a chest wound. I got the general impression from the nurses that they were slightly more surprised she survived her surgery than they were you."

"Jack, she hid me. She could have climbed up there herself and left me down on the floor, but she didn't." Jack shoved some fries in his mouth and said, "Hang on." Jack got up and went out to the nurse's station. When he came back, he had a wheelchair. Ross had already pushed her tray away and was doing her best to swing her feet off the bed when the inspector appeared behind Jack.

"Going for a trip?"

"Ross wants to visit Lillian." Jack informed him. Dufort pursed his lips.

"I am not sure I can allow this. Dr. Petrov cannot remember what happened that night. I cannot have the only two witnesses talking to one another. Dr.

Halloway, you are more than welcome to cruise around the floor if you feel up to it, get a change of scenery. I cannot, however, have you talking to Dr. Petrov. I hope you understand." Ross had one leg swung over the side. Her forehead was sweaty from the effort it had taken to get that far, and she wasn't looking pleased that Inspector Dufort was telling her it was all for nothing.

"What if I promise not to talk about that night?"

"I don't think..."

"I just want to see how she is. You can come too if you want." Dufort looked at Jack who simply smiled and shrugged his shoulders. While he still wasn't thrilled about them seeing each other, he couldn't think of a good reason to stop them if he was there to make sure nothing important was said, or if it was, he was there to hear it. With a returned shrug of his shoulders, he went to the bed with Jack and helped get Ross into the wheelchair.

"I was hoping we would be together a little longer before you saw me like this." Ross said in Jack's ear as he lifted her out of the bed and lowered into the wheelchair.

"Oh yeah, at what point in our relationship were you

planning on getting yourself shot in the neck?"

"You know what I mean." Talking helped her take her mind off the fact that her neck and shoulder were screaming at her. Ross didn't know why she needed to see Lillian so urgently. At this point, she wasn't sure it was worth the pain, but having gotten so far, she wasn't going to turn back.

Jack lowered her down and let her settle herself and allow a little color to come back to her face.

"Ready?"

"Ready." Jack flipped the brakes on the wheelchair, and the three of them went the short distance down the hallway. Inspector Dufort knocked on the door and poked his head in. Lillian looked startled.

"Visitor for you." Dufort noted that the startled look did not go away at the mention of this. Dufort realized he wasn't the only one who expected a second attack on the survivors. "Are you up for seeing Dr. Halloway?" Lillian nodded. He opened the door and stepped back while Ross was wheeled in. Lillian's face said it all Ross thought. It went from surprise to horror.

'How bad do I look?' Ross thought to herself.

"Ross!"

"Hey, Lillian. How are you?" Ross painted a smile

on her face, but it didn't last. She could see the tears welling up in Lillian's eyes, and they began to well up in Ross's as well. Lillian's injuries didn't look all that bad from here, but she was obviously in pain and moving just the little bit that she did hurt her.

"Oh god, Ross, look at you."

"I was lucky. They think I turned my head when I saw the gun. Otherwise, he would have gotten me in the head. What about you?"

"It should have killed me. One shot to the chest, barely missed my heart." They stared at each other for a while. There wasn't anything else they could say. They had survived. For whatever reason, they had survived despite the skill of the shooter. Despite being in a remote location, despite having been out there for so long without help.

"For whatever reason, the attackers shut down the ship before they left. Most likely because it would send the ship adrift. We think it may have saved you though. At the time the Coast Guard found you, the temperature on the ship was enough to slow your blood flow, but not enough to kill you. Another half an hour or so, and the temperature would have gone down to the point where it would have been too late."

Dufort offered. "On the flight to the hospital, it was noticed that your wounds were bleeding more than when they loaded you. Thankfully, the medical staff was present and able to staunch the bleeding at that point." The two women sat there in silence while he spoke. Half an hour from death. Ross remembered she had been that close to death once before.

"Thank you, Lillian." It was like being shot in the chest again for Lillian.

"For what?" Ross looked at Dufort.

"I can't really say right now. But thank you for what you did. You saved my life." Lillian stared blankly at her, a tear escaping her. Ross was not looking at her when she said this, but the inspector was. Lillian's mouth was open like she was about to say something else, but didn't.

"I'll let you get some rest." Ross said. "Come down and see me if you feel up to it." They nodded at one another and Jack turned Ross around to leave the room.

"Ross, thank you for coming and seeing me. I'm so sorry this happened." Ross nodded again and Jack rolled her out of the room. He looked at the clock as they passed the nurse's station. They had only been in there three minutes, Ross looked exhausted.

"You think that will do you for a bit?" Jack asked.

"I just needed to see her. Jack, how bad do I look?"

"Why do you ask?"

"Everyone who sees me seems shocked and horrified."

"Well, not to put too fine a point on it, darlin, but you've looked better. You have a rather large bloody bandage on your neck, and you go from a pasty gray color to a washed out pink color." Jack lifted her back into bed, and for the first time she noticed the needle mark in the bend of his elbow. He got her back on the bed and helped her get her legs back under the covers and got her comfortable with her pillows.

"Jack?"

"Hmmm."

"I needed blood didn't I?" He looked at her with sad eyes. "I'm getting the impression it's a bit of a surprise that I made it."

"No love, we aren't going to talk about that."

"How much did you give?" Not for the first time, Jack wished she wasn't quite so smart. With a sigh of resignation, he said, "Two pints. They wouldn't let me give more." He wouldn't look at her, instead doing a thorough job of tucking her blankets around her legs.

"Jack? Do we have the same blood type?" His face had gone dark and he wouldn't look at her.

"I'm type O. I think both you and Lillian got some."

"How long have you been here Jack?"

"This is my fourth day."

"You sat here for two days watching me sleep?" Like a slap in the face, it hit her how fast he must have moved to have gotten here as quick as he did. Ross didn't know where exactly he had been in the Indian Ocean when she had called him, but he was not near land. Jack and Si would have had to make for the nearest city with an airport. Ross roughly worked out how long a flight from Jakarta to where she was in Canada would take. He had not left her side. Part of that was because he couldn't, but he hardly ever left the room.

"Come here." Her voice was soft, and he turned, she was holding out her hand to him. "Come here Jack." He leaned over her. Ross stroked the stubbles that now covered his face. Pulling him forward, she kissed him. Jack leaned his head against hers.

"I'm not sure how I feel about your blood running

through my veins." Ross said.

"Beggars can't be choosers." She laughed and immediately regretted it. Jack could tell how much pain she was in because when it was really bad, Ross almost crawled in on herself. He leaned back up and punched the button for the nurse.

" Are you needing more meds?" The nurse asked as she came in.

"It's been a big day, I went next door." Ross answered.

"I know. It's news all over the floor." The nurse nodded and amped up her drip a little. Ross held onto Jack's hand, and as soon as the nurse was gone, he kissed her on the head and said. "You rest up now my brave girl."

"Stay with me Jack?"

"You know it." She had meant forever. They had been about to part ways permanently, and now that he was here in front of her, she didn't want to let him go again. As of yet, she still hadn't figured out how they were going to make it work geographically speaking. With the amount of morphine rolling through her, the chances of her coming up with something was slight. He would be here when she woke up though. They could figure the rest out later.

Inspector Dufort stayed behind after Ross and Jack had left Lillian's room. The brief visit seemed to exhaust Dr. Petrov, but her mind was still sharp. It did not escape her notice the inspector had stayed behind. "Is there something I can help you with, inspector?"

"I was wondering if seeing Dr. Halloway brought back any memories of that night?"

"No."

"What did she mean when she said you saved her life?" The inspector asked. Lillian closed her eyes as if the words themselves pained her.

"When I came out of my room, she was standing at the bottom of the stairs. Whoever they were, they were coming down the stairs right in front of her. When I ran past, I grabbed her hand and she followed me. That is all." Dufort accepted this. He didn't think it was all of the story, but he accepted it.

"I've been doing some digging on you Dr. Petrov. Can you tell me why you left Russia?" Lillian looked almost bored with the question.

"As I am sure you are aware, people with certain aptitudes are often recruited by the government. I didn't want to work for the government. They didn't like being told no. It was made very clear that they would make it hard for me to stay if I didn't help them. All I wanted to do was science. I went where I could do that. Thankfully, Cambridge accepted me."

"You, of course, knew what happened to people who told the government no. Just a few months before you left for London, your brother was found dead of mysterious circumstances." This got a flash of surprise and anger from Lillian.

"He was poisoned."

"Apparently, large amounts of heroin were found in his system. His death was ruled an accidental overdose."

"My brother had never used drugs in his life. As I'm sure you know, he was part of a resistance group that opposed several policies of the President. He had been arrested at several protests. He was beaten severely after one of them. Demetri didn't overdose, he was killed." It was the most animated he had seen Lillian.

"Your parents lost both their children only months apart. First Demetri, and then you a few months later. From what I understand, you haven't seen them since you left." Sadness filled Lillian's eyes at the mention of her parents.

"Because of the circumstances under which I left, I can't return."

"So if someone from the Russian government approached you and asked for your help, you wouldn't accept?" Lillian did not respond to this immediately.

"Thankfully, I have never had to make that decision."

"I don't want to add to your worries, Dr. Petrov, but I did want to let you know that in carrying out my inquiries, I have been unable to locate your parents. We have not been able to ask a lot of questions, but my colleague spoke with their neighbors, and your parents haven't been seen for a few days. Do you know if they were taking any holidays?" Lillian felt frozen to the spot. She herself had not heard anything in regards to the plan she had put in motion before she left, but she had not thought anything of it since there was virtually no way to reach her. For the briefest of moments, she thought about asking the inspector for help.

"They didn't mention anything, but they may have gone to visit my aunt. My mother says she hasn't been in the best of health." Lillian made up on the spot. The inspector seemed to accept this and left her on her own. Lillian closed her eyes and let a tear escape. If only the bullet had found its mark and saved her all this pain.

# 33

On the way back to his office, Dufort's phone began to ring. The caller ID said it was his supervisor.

"What do you have?"

"A high ranking member of the Russian government has just handed himself over to authorities in Helsinki." Dufort walked faster to his office for privacy.

"How high ranking?"

"Secretary of the Security Council. He is telling authorities there that he knows what happened on 'The Hunter'."

"And does he?"

"The local authorities are still making sure he is who he says he is, but my intelligence is telling me that a member of the President's cabinet has, in fact, gone missing within the last few days. She didn't know who exactly, but apparently, the President is in an extraordinarily bad mood."

"I'll be on the next flight to Helsinki." Dufort said, already starting to gather the items off his desk.

"Don't. I have already sent another agent out to interview him." His supervisor seemingly had no idea the effect this would have on Dufort. His temper rising, Dufort threw the items back down onto the desk with such force that his cigarettes flew out of the packet.

"This is my case." He managed to say with a little calmness.

"You are needed where you are, Inspector. As we have discussed before, there is a very good chance a second attempt will be made on the survivors. I need you where you are. Obviously, you will be kept up to date on any developments." Duforts' anger went up a notch, mostly because his supervisor spoke the truth. His survivors were still very much at risk, especially since the press seemed to have taken on the story. There was hardly an aspect of that night or his survivors that had not been revealed to the world. They were making much of the fact that Dr. Halloway had been attacked by Spartans before. It really didn't make much sense to pull him away now and replace him with someone new. Taking a deep breath, Inspector Dufort said, "Can I send the investigator some questions I would like answers to?"

"I'm sure that would be alright. We are sending Inspector Maes, I believe you have worked with her before?" Dufort calmed down a little. Inspector Maes was one of the best inspectors he had ever seen. A tiny little thing you underestimated at your own risk. She had twice as much patience as he did (which wasn't saying much, but did come in handy) and managed to get information out of her suspects when no one else had been able. Inspector Maes claimed there was no great secret to this, but Dufort suspected that, like so many other people, they thought because she was small and cute that she would not throw the full force of the law at them. Something Dufort had never seen her fail to do. If he wasn't going to question this defector, at least it was Maes going in his place.

"I have her contact information, I will send her a list."

"You have a few hours. Last I heard she was still enroute." Dufort hung up and bent down to pick up a cigarette that had fallen on the ground, then outside for a much needed smoke.

"I am beginning to feel a little bit like a celebrity."

Ross said, sitting up in her bed and finishing her pudding.

"People waiting on you all the time?" Jack answered.

"There is that, but every time I travel now, it makes the news." They were watching the national news, getting updates on how the investigation into the attack was going. "Strange to be the person they are talking about again." They were trying to link the attack on 'The Hunter' to Ikan Hui based completely on the fact that Ross had been at both locations. "What do you think the chances are they are right?" Ross asked.

"Slim to none." Jack replied. "Spartans have had a full year to kill you and they haven't."

"We ruined their 'no survivor streak'." Ross pointed out.

"Spartans don't feel emotion. Besides, why would they just go after you? Four of us survived."

"I just don't know how our research would cause anyone to kill us."

"There's a lot of money in oil. People have killed for less."

"There was no way we were going to figure out who they were. I joked with Nils I could follow their trail all the way home, but not really. All we were going to do was prove someone was drilling so we could get protection for the area. There is a chance they would have been able to drill without detection for some time."

"You said you have proof there was drilling going on though, right?"

"Yeah."

"Which means you found proof that there was crude oil. If word got out there was crude oil, there were going to be a lot more people wanting a piece of it....."

"Would you kill people for that?" Ross asked. "Or would you be glad you got free oil for so long and go away so that no one ever found out who you were?"

" Dad had a fishing buddy back when we were kids. Always came back with huge fish. I mean Dad would do the typical thing of making the fish bigger for the story. Steve could prove it, he had what looked like sea monsters stuffed and mounted on his walls. Dad used to always ask him where he found such large fish, but Steve would never tell him. Told Dad if he shared it, then everyone would have large fish on their walls and there would be nothing left for him." Ross sat back and listened. Si had a penchant for telling stories. Ross could just imagine him sitting in a bar, drink in hand, telling fish stories. Jack seemed to be following in his footsteps. "One day Dad was bringing his boat in, and there were police cars all over the dock. He pulls up just in time to see them putting Steve in the back of the car with his hands behind his back. Never knowing Steve to break the law in his life, Dad ran up to him and asked him what was going on." Jack paused.

"Well? What had he done?"

"Steve had been in the bar the night before, bragging about his latest catch. Some guy called him out and told him he was full of shit. Accused him of lying, and that was the reason Steve never told anyone where the fishing spot was, because there was no fishing spot. Steve brushed it off, but the next morning when he went fishing, the guy from the bar followed him. Steve beat his skull in with a shovel."

"Jesus."

"He then put the body in the boat and took it around to the main dock where he called the rozzers and confessed on the spot. Told my Dad he was truly sorry for what he had done. He hadn't meant to kill the man, just keep him from knowing where his fishing spot was."

"So your point is, people will kill to protect what they have."

"Exactly."

"That would explain why they destroyed the data. So all proof of the findings would disappear as well. Jack, whoever did this then, whoever hired the Spartans, can't be too happy there are survivors." Ross and Jack made eye contact.

"That's why you're on a secure ward, love. That's why Interpol sent the inspector."

"That's all well and good, but what happens when Lillian and I are healed, what will they do with us then?"

"I don't know love, but you are going to be okay. I'll make sure of it." Jack said, taking her hand in both of his. In all truth, he had been giving this eventuality some thought. He had a plan he was forming, but he didn't want to mention it to Ross just yet. They fell quiet just as the report said, "A private plane flying over the Atlantic exploded mid-flight today. The plane left France this morning carrying one passenger and a crew of three. It is not known at this time what happened. There was no distress call made from the cockpit. The plane was heading for Alberta with a layover in Greenland." And then the reporter went on to the next story. Jack had stopped eating his Jello. To quote his father, something didn't feel right in his belly about that story.

"Did they say the plane was heading for Alberta?" Ross asked. Jack nodded his head. His mind was spinning, and he didn't dare look at Ross for fear that she would see it. Sarah had done a lot of work in France as a hired hit man. To be honest, he didn't know where the Spartans went when they weren't trying to kill Ross, but France seemed as good a place as any. "Jack, do you think they could have been...?"

He did. Jack was absolutely certain that whoever was on that plan was heading for this hospital and Ross.

Several thousands of miles away, Alexi was watching the same coverage from his room in Helsinki. His hands shook as he brought the cigarette to his mouth. He had almost waited too long to get out of the country. He wasn't sure why that Spartan had been eliminated, or the meaning behind it. Alexi had no doubt that the chief of security was behind it. The fact that his arrangements with the Spartans had been scrapped, and no doubt another plan put in place, would have been directed right at him. It was clear that though Alexi had made everything right, he had made an unforgivable mistake and would have been eliminated.

Picking up the phone in his room, he called the number on the business card he had been given. "Yes, inspector. I just thought of a few more details I thought you might find interesting." Alexi put the phone down. So far, he had only given enough detail and answered enough questions to convince Interpol he was legitimate. Now he wanted the chief to pay. Alexi wanted to make the chief so mad, his fat little face turned purple and burst. He would tell Interpol everything he knew. Which was considerable. Alexi gave no more thought to the two women lying in hospital beds in Alberta even though he knew that someone would be sent to kill them. Even if it wasn't a Spartan.

# 34

Lillian was watching the news as well and coming to much the same conclusion Ross was in the other room. It was the third time the story had cycled through, and they had not mentioned who was on the plane, but Lillian couldn't help but think whoever was on it was heading for them. She paid little attention to the nurse when she walked in to check that the IV was still flowing. If Lillian had looked properly at her, she would have noticed that the nurse was not one of her regulars. As it happened, Lillian didn't look at her until, out of her peripheral vision she saw a syringe.

"No pain meds. Thank you." Lillian said. Still watching the news. The nurse paid no attention. "I said no pain meds." The nurse continued as if she hadn't heard. It was then that Lillian noticed she had not seen this nurse before. The nurse placed the needle in the IV port.

"No pain meds." Lillian said in Russian. The woman looked up. Lillian grabbed her hand, which the woman shook off.

"The President sends his regards." She answered in Russian, pushing the plunger into the IV port. Without thinking, Lillian ripped her IV out of her arm and reached for the nurse's button. The nurse threw herself onto Lillian, aiming the syringe like a knife at Lillian's neck. If the needle landed right, there was enough poison left to kill her. "Traitor!" the nurse yelled in Lillian's face. She was holding the nurse off with all of her strength. Lillian looked the woman in the eye, seeing the woman's hatred and determination. With a great deal of pain and guilt, Lillian thought, *'Let her. What does it matter?'* Lillian dropped her arm, resignation in her eyes. The nurse raised up with a smile on her face.

Things happened quickly after that. A real nurse entered the room to see why Lillian's heart rate had shot up. She hit a red button next to the door, which immediately alerted everyone that there was a situation in Lillian's room. The nurse then put the fake nurse in a headlock and dragged her off of Lillian. At that point, more people entered the room. Lillian had surrendered, she had closed her eyes to accept her fate. When she looked again, there was no one there.

Lillian was surprised to find she wasn't dead. She knew she wasn't dead because she was in a hell of a lot of pain. She was bleeding from where she had ripped out her IV, blood covering her arm, her hospital gown, and the bed linen. Her chest wound was on fire, and Lillian was a little more horrified to see that a fresh red stain was spreading over what had been a clean white bandage. The pain started at the front of her chest and went all the way to her shoulder blade. So sharp it took her breath away, Lillian laid back and tried to catch her breath.

More people entered the room. Lillian looked over to see the Inspector run in. When Lillian managed to sit up, she saw armed guards. Her attacker was on the floor. She was vaguely aware of the medical team standing just outside the door. "Get her out of here." Dufort yelled. The medical team could not come in until they had secured the attacker. "Clear the room." The fake nurse was carried out by the security team. They had no sooner cleared the door than Lillian was rushed by the medical staff who instantly got her positioned on the bed. Lillian saw lights passing overhead. They were taking her somewhere. Where were they taking her?

"Wait!" Lillian yelled. "Inspector!"

Dufort appeared next to her. Taking her hand. "I remember now."

"We have to stop the bleeding." The doctor said.

"I will be here when you get back."

"The nurse. She's Russian." Lillian said, then they wheeled her away. Dufort stayed where he was as Lillian was wheeled quickly down the hallway. There was more Lillian needed to tell him, but she had given him enough to work on until she was able to tell him more. Pulling his phone out of his pocket, he phoned his super. It went to voicemail. "I have confirmation the attack originated with the Russians. I'll have more for you later." He then called Inspector Maes. There were a few more questions he had for this so-called informant.

Jack and Ross knew something was going on. They heard voices next door and then an alarm. Jack went to go see what was happening, and he was pushed back into the room by an armed guard who then closed their door and stood in front of Ross's room. "What's happening?" Jack yelled through the door, but he got no response. He turned to Ross. "Come on." He pulled back her covers and picked her up.

"Where the hell are you taking me?" Ross asked.

"To the bathroom. Hide in there until I figure out what the hell is going on." Ross let him pick her up, grabbing her IV pole as a way of helping.

"What good is that going to do?"

"I don't know, but at least they won't be able to see you, and they'll have one more barrier between them and you." Jack looked the same as he had that day at the resort. Not being in much of a position to argue, and being a little more afraid than she was letting on, Ross let herself be hidden in the bathroom. In the shower stall, to be exact. Jack even closed the shower curtain. Feeling extremely vulnerable, standing there in a hospital gown and little else, Ross looked around for anything she could use to help herself. Grabbing the small bottles of shampoo, she read the back quickly. 'It'll burn the bastard's eyeballs for a while.' She said to herself. She popped the cap and stood at the ready. It was bugging the crap out of her not knowing what was going on.

Ross jumped out of her skin when Jack knocked on

the door. "Ross honey? I'm coming in."

"As long as you are alone." Ross said. Jack came in slowly, Ross was still poised with the shampoo bottle just in case there was someone with him.

"You okay?" Jack asked before coming any closer. He didn't want to say anything, but she looked a bit mad.

"What the hell happened?" Ross was not okay. She was getting rather tired of fearing for her life.

"A fake nurse attacked Lillian. They just hauled her out kicking and screaming." Ross couldn't help it. A relieved tear escaped.

"Did she do it, did she kill her?"

"No. No, they got to her in time, but they had to take Lillian into surgery. Her chest wound started bleeding." He came up to Ross and wrapped an arm around her. She was still holding the shampoo bottle at the ready.

"Jesus Christ, Jack!" Ross finally let the shampoo bottle go and melted into Jack's arms. "I am so tired of being scared." Jack led her back to the room and her bed. The guards were still standing in front of Ross's door, which was fine by him. They had no idea if Lillian was the target or if Ross was also threatened.

Jack was humming. He got Ross back into bed, but he couldn't sit still. He paced like a caged lion.

"Jack. I have to get out of here." Ross said, saying the same thing he was thinking.

"Where do you want to go?"

"Anywhere. I'm a sitting duck here." She was trying not to cry, but the pain meds had been making her more emotional. Without hesitating, Jack opened the door and demanded to speak with the inspector.

"He's questioning the suspect, " was all they would tell him. Jack went back and sat with Ross and texted Si. He had a plan, but he wanted to run it by Si before he said anything to Ross.

Dufort left the makeshift interview room. With a nod, the local authorities entered the room and took the fake nurse into custody. Checking his phone, he had a text message from the nurse's station letting him know that Dr. Petrov was coming out of surgery and had asked to speak with him. He was desperate for a cigarette, but things were finally starting to move on this investigation. Popping a piece of nicotine gum in his mouth, Dufort made sure his notepad had enough space and then he headed up to the ninth floor again.

"Dr. Halloway would also like a word with you."

The nurse said, when he appeared out of the elevator. *'I bet she does.'* Dufort thought to himself.

"Has Dr. Petrov asked for me?"

"They said she came out of anesthesia asking for you."

"How groggy is she?"

"Surprisingly awake." Dufort thanked her and made his way to Dr. Petrov's room. Lillian was sitting like a stone in her bed. A fresh bandage covered her chest. Dufort was relieved to see that the blood that had been dripping down her arm was cleaned up.

"How are you feeling?" Lillian looked away from him and it was then that he noticed she was crying. "Dr. Petrov?"

"I lied, Inspector. Someone did reach out to me. I knew the attack on *'The Hunter'* was going to happen." Dufort slowly took out his notepad and sat down. Keeping his voice calm and even, he said, " Do you know who this person was?"

"Yes. I had been approached by him before when I was a student in Russia. Alexi Stanovich. He is the Secretary Of the Security Council. You don't turn him down and live for very long. He killed my brother."

"Did you help him willingly?" Lillian shook her

head.

"No. Of course not."

"What did he offer you?"

"He didn't offer me anything. It was what he was going to do if I didn't. I thought if I didn't help him, he would kill me. I was okay with that. He must have known that would be my answer. He said he already had people at my parents' house and if I didn't agree to help, they would be dead. That I could not do."

"What information did he want?"

"Nothing too serious. How many people were going to be on the boat, what kind of boat, where we were going, what kind of equipment we were going to be using. That sort of thing. I almost convinced myself it wouldn't be so bad, but I knew as well as you do that whatever they were going to do with the information wasn't going to be good."

"Did you know they were going to attack the ship?"

"Yes. They were only supposed to steal the equipment. They said they just wanted to scare people away from the area."

"Did you know they had hired the Spartans?"

"No."

"Why didn't you tell anyone?"

"He said if I told the authorities, he would kill my parents. I thought about doing it anyway. I really did. I told Nils Ryeng about it."

"Why him?"

"He called me the same night I was asked to help. I was in a weakened state and he could see it."

"You dated him for a while, no?"

"A little over a year."

"He didn't want to cancel the trip?"

"No, of course not. To Nils the end always justified the means. He thought he could outsmart them, bless him." Lillian was sinking more and more into her pillows. She was no longer wound tighter than a drum. Dufort had seen it before. It had nothing to do with her pain meds. She was off loading the burden that had been weighing her down. A guilty conscience was being released.

"Out smart them how?"

"We figured out they wanted the research. It was clear that they did not want our information released to the outside world. Nils had me download all my research and Dr. Halloway's every night on a thumb drive that never left me. He did the same with his research and Dr. Lebedev's research. The idea was that we would let them attack the ship, destroy the equipment and laptops, think they had won, and then publish our papers anyway. Nils was even going to make a show of trying to stop them, really sell it."

"Wouldn't they kill your parents once you had published?"

"I put into motion a plan to get my parents out of Russia. I did it before I left, using what friends and contacts I have left. I haven't yet heard if they were successful. I realized while on the ship that the science we were doing, the place we were working to protect from greed, was worth more than the lives of two old Russians. I love my parents. Don't get me wrong. But there are things under that ice mankind has never seen, frozen in the ice since before man started walking upright. There are discoveries there that may very well change how we look at the world, and they will strip it clean of all its natural resources before anyone has a chance to protect it . How does that compare to the lives of my parents?"

"Letting them kill your parents would only delay them. They would still find a way to get their hands on what they want."

"But I wouldn't have blood on my hands. The day

before the attack, I told Nils I wanted to tell the others what was going to happen. Then at least they would know and maybe we could fight back. Obviously, we didn't know exactly what was going to happen."

"That's why you were out of your room and running down the hall before anyone else knew what was going on." Lillian nodded.

"I had found the utility room when I was exploring the ship. I selfishly thought that I might be able to find a hiding spot. When I saw Ross standing in the hallway, I couldn't leave her there. They were coming down the stairs, she was standing there in shock. Nils at her feet."

"You gave her your hiding spot." Lillian turned her head slowly and looked Dufort in the eye.

"They were just supposed to attack us. Scare us. It became obvious that they were there to kill us. I couldn't just leave Ross there. It was all my fault."

"Have you heard from anyone from the Russian government since the attack?"

"Not until today. I got the general impression that they aren't happy I'm alive."

"Is there anything else you would like to tell me?"

"I lied to you before. I could remember what

happened. Every moment of it. I didn't tell you because I didn't want to be blamed. I worked very hard to build my body of research. I would like to think that I am respected amongst my peers. All of that will change once they realize what I have done. They will hate me."

"And now?" Dufort asked. Lillian did as close to a shrug as she could manage.

"It doesn't matter. What does it matter when compared to the lives of the people lost?" Dufort closed his notepad.

"I think you will find people more forgiving than you think." Lillian scoffed. "Your peers, they are English?" Dufort asked.

"Mostly."

"They have never lived in a country which asked them to do such things in the name of patriotism. If they had been given the same choice, what would they have done?" Lillian squinted at him.

"You do not blame me?"

"I think you should have reached out to the proper authority. I also understand that your experience with government would not garner trust. Whether what you did was criminal, probably. I will see what I can do."

"You are going to help me?"

"As far as I can. You have suffered for your decision." He indicated her wounds. "I think if you continue to help us in our investigation, an arrangement could be made."

"I will help in any way I can." Dufort nodded.

"If you think of anything else, let me know. For now, I will let you rest. You've had an eventful day."

"Was she going to kill Ross as well?" Lillian asked, Duforts' back.

"She isn't saying much, but from what I can gather, you were the only target. You know too much."

"That is why I decided to tell you. They can kill me now and it won't matter. You will know everything I know." For the first time, Dr. Petrov gave a little smile.

"Rest well." Dufort said, and he left her room. Before taking another step, he made a reminder for himself to check in on Lillian's parents.

# 35

Dufort left Dr. Petrov's room and paused, rubbing his hands over his face. He had seen numerous Dr. Petrov's in his time. She had made it. She had a career that by all accounts was well respected. It had been ten years since she had been in Russia and had seemed to have gone out of her way to assimilate into her new English life. They had still gotten to her and made her into someone she could not look at in the mirror. Forced to make an impossible choice. He had meant what he said, he would do all he could, but there was only so much he could do. With a deep breath, he turned left and headed for Dr. Halloway's room. He knocked before entering and found her sitting up in bed with a pained look on her face and a sympathetic looking young man manipulating her arm.

"You are looking quite well, Dr. Halloway." Dufort

lied. Jack sat nervously, both knees bouncing and looking like he would pounce on the physical therapist who was hovering over Ross.

"I'm not completely convinced they got all the bullet out." Ross said through gritted teeth. Dufort moved around the bed. The therapist had taken the bandage off so he could be sure to not cause more harm than good. He was not a medical man, but he had seen a few gunshot wounds, and Ross had been extremely lucky. The bullet seemed to have gone out of it's way to not hit anything. The therapist caught him looking.

"The bullet passed through the trapezius muscle. It entered here,' he gently placed his finger where Ross's neck met her shoulders, 'traveled two inches before it exited here, shredding everything in its path." There was a slightly larger wound at the back of Ross's shoulder. "Your trapezius muscle controls the tilt of our head and the control of your shoulder. All those little movements you did before without thinking are going to hurt for a bit. If you keep doing your exercises, it won't hurt forever." The therapist said this last part to Ross who was looking like the pain was getting the better of her. Bringing her arm back to its original position, the therapist then helped her lean back in the bed. The stitches in her neck prevented them from getting too crazy with the physical therapy, and it hurt like hell while they were doing it, but even Ross could tell the improvement. Her arm was able to go in wider circles than it had been three days ago.

"I'll see you tomorrow, dear. You did good work today." He placed an ice pack underneath her shoulder and left, giving a nod to Jack.

"I know he is trying to stay positive, but I sit here while he lifts and rotates my arm. He's doing all the work." Ross said.

"You aren't complaining about it either." Jack added.

"How is Lillian?" Ross asked Dufort.

"She is going to be fine. I believe there was some damage done to the healing of her wound in the scuffle, but nothing too bad all things considered."

"How did the bloody woman get up here? This is supposed to be a secure ward." Jack said, rather tartly.

"Yes, I have had a word with the head nurse. No one was supposed to be put on this floor unless they had a work history here with the hospital. Considering the mystery surrounding your case though, there have not been many volunteers. So when a well-credentialed nurse with experience in trauma and a clean background check volunteered, they took her."

"Was she a Spartan?" Ross asked.

"No, she's a Russian national. Though her paperwork had her as American and, to be honest, she does speak rather good English with an almost flawless accent." Dufort knew because the woman had called him a bastard in four different languages, including English, and with flawless accents each time.

Ross found herself pausing before asking her next question, thankfully Dufort saved her the trouble.

"It looks like Dr. Petrov was the only target." Dufort helped himself to a seat. "We have been looking at the crew, and even your fellow researchers, for an informant. The attack was carried out in such a way that we think the attackers must have had a certain amount of information beforehand."

"You think there was someone on the ship who was giving them information?" Jack offered. Dufort nodded.

"It had to be one of the crew." Ross said, not able to think why any of the scientists would offer information that would harm anyone.

"We know who the informant was, and it was not a member of the crew." Dufort left it there and watched as reality dawned on them.

"Lillian?  But why?"  Ross said, with sadness.

"It was not by choice.  You will have noticed that Dr. Petrov is Russian?"

"Yes, but she left years ago, she told me she couldn't stand the place."

"This is true, but unfortunately for Dr. Petrov, her parents did not leave with her.  The Russian government was planning on attacking your ship, they had a beef with Dr. Nils Ryeng, and they didn't want him finding out what they were doing.  They used Dr. Petrov for some basic information they could pass along to the Spartans.  Lay out of the ship, equipment that was being used, how many researchers and crew were on board.  Dr. Petrov knew there was going to be an attack, she knew they would destroy the research. She did not know they intended to kill everyone on board."  Tears were running down Ross's face.

"Why didn't she tell us?  Nils would have called off the trip if he had known."  Dufort shook his head.

"According to Dr. Petrov, Dr. Ryeng knew.  He knew what position they had put her in and thought he had found a way to fix it to where the Russians would be happy and not kill Dr. Petrov's family, and protect the research so it would still be published."

"He was wrong." Ross said, starting to get a little pissed, but something niggled at the back of her mind.

"So what happens now?" Jack asked.

"Well, we have an informant who might be able to point us to the individual in Russia who is responsible. We are pursuing that line of inquiry."

"What happens to Ross? They are talking of discharging her."

"You will go back to Boston where I have arranged for twenty-four hour security until the matter is settled." Ross and Jack looked at one another. Dufort was somewhat surprised to find they were not more relieved than they were.

Dufort left them because Dr. Halloway looked like she could use a moment to herself. Jack surprised him by following him out to the hallway.

"Was there something else?" Dufort asked.

"I was wondering if another option might be possible for Ross. Security wise. After she leaves here?"

"What have you in mind?"

"My boat. It's in the middle of the bloody ocean." Dufort smirked.

"I'm not sure I could get an agent to agree to guard

Dr. Halloway on a boat in the middle of the Indian Ocean."

"No offense mate, but I wasn't thinking of inviting one." Jack explained what he had in mind.

"It is not procedure, but I can't argue with your logic. That being said, I would need Dr. Halloway to sign off on it before I could allow it."

"Understood." Jack turned back, going into Ross's room where she was sitting smiling, holding Jack's phone up in front of her.

"Jesus Christ, Ross. They said she tried to stab that woman with a syringe." Sam's voice screeched.

"Sam's been watching the news again." Ross explained to Jack as he came back in.

"Only after she failed to get the poison to her through the IV." Ross matched her hysteria with calmness. Like it was everyday that people around her were almost killed.

"I thought that was supposed to be a secure damn floor you are on?"

"It is a secure floor. I can't say much about it, Sam. They are thinking of discharging me in a few days." Ross tried to change the subject. Unfortunately, this had the opposite effect.

"What the hell are they thinking? You were shot in the neck, lunatic nurses are trying to kill people, and they are just going to send you home?"

"What are they supposed to do with me?"

"I don't know. But sending you out into the world injured to fend for yourself doesn't seem like a good idea." Sam said rather emphatically. "Don't they have a secure bunker or somewhere they can put you?"

"Sam!"

"I'm sorry, honey. I want to see you so bad it hurts, but I mean, look at those stitches. Someone really tried to kill you."

"Now I have a good excuse for not wearing those off the shoulder tops you are always trying to get me into."

"No, but you are going to rock the one shoulder look."

"Sam...seriously."

"Ross, you have one good looking shoulder left. I think you should make the most of it."

"I just realized I have nothing to wear home." Ross looked at Jack with amazement that neither one of them had thought about it.

"What about your luggage?"

"Evidence." Ross replied. "They haven't returned it

to me. Lord knows where it is."

"You want me to send you something?"

"Could you?"

"Absolutely. I'm sitting here wanting to be useful. Give me a list." Sam propped up her phone and got paper and pen.

"I need everything. I haven't got a stitch."

"No undies?" Sam said, winking. "How many times have you given Jack a thrill going to the bathroom?"

"Only Ross could make a hospital gown look sexy." Jack said, from his perch.

"I'll go to your apartment later today, get everything, and have it overnighted. Hopefully, it gets to you in time."

"How's Carbon?" Ross felt bad she hadn't thought of poor Carbon before now.

"Your neighbor is still taking care of him."

"When you go to my place, give him a kiss on his nose and tell him I love him."

"I will absolutely not do that. Jack, you need anything?"

"I'm fine, thank you though."

"Sam. I've been through enough. Please don't send me anything 'bold'."

"I make no promises. Okay. Keep me posted. I love you honey."

"Give Ruby kisses for me." Sam signed off and Ross felt exhausted. It had been a busy day.

"Have you really been sneaking a peek at my butt?" Ross asked Jack.

"I wouldn't say I've been sneaking. It's been fairly out there for me to see."

"Jack."

"Hmmm."

"Come home with me?" Jack looked at her blankly. "I'm sure the security the inspector has arranged is fine, but I would feel safer with you there. Plus.....I don't want you to leave." There, she said it. Jack looked at her and how tired she was. Now wasn't the time to bring up his plan, plus he hadn't heard back from Si.

"I'll do whatever makes you feel safe." He said. Ross nodded her head and closed her eyes.

# 36

Alexi sat nervously tapping his lighter on the table having just finished telling the inspector everything he knew and handing over what evidence he could to back it up. She was not saying anything though. He had expected something, especially from a woman. A smile. Some sign of gratitude, something. But she was just looking over a file and occasionally making notes. He was waiting for the right moment to ask for a favor.

"I was wondering if there was something you could do for me?" Alexi asked as meekly as he could manage.

"And what would that be?" Inspector Maes asked without looking up from her file. Alexi was having a very hard time having little to no power here. When he spoke, he was used to people looking at him. Usually, with fear. The fact that he no longer commanded enough respect for this female inspector to even look at him when he spoke was testing him.

"I was wondering if my location could be moved soon? I fear my government might have found out where I am and that my life might be in danger." This time she at least looked up at him.

"You already have an assumed name. We are housing you in the embassy, which is extremely secure. You are safer there than if we were to send you somewhere else." Alexi tried to paste a charming smile on his face.

"You are probably right. It's just this plane exploding and the attack on Dr. Petrov makes me a little nervous." Alexi had heard about the attack on Dr. Petrov while he was being interviewed. He was slightly surprised to find he was glad Dr. Petrov had once again escaped.

"We haven't been able to link that back to the Russian government yet." The inspector said.

"Oh, it was them. I had arranged for the Spartans to correct their mistake in letting the two women live. They were to board a flight in Paris and fly to Alberta. With that event and the attack on Dr. Petrov happening so close together, I can find no other explanation."

Alexi said, not for the first time.

"Then why was there only one passenger on the plane?" Maes responded.

"Obviously, a last minute change in plans."

"You are thinking they got rid of the Spartans. Highly trained killers, known for their accuracy, and then sent in one of their own people?" When she said it like that it sounded ridiculous. Well, it was ridiculous. It was a decision not made out of logic but revenge.

"The Chief of Security has a very short temper, and he was extremely upset about two survivors. I'm sure that changing the plans I had made in such a dramatic fashion was in part meant to be a message for me. He believes in using Russian power for Russia."

"Then why hire the Spartans in the first place?"

"The President had been asking for them since he learned of their existence. It was well known that anyone who was able to get him in contact with the Spartans would be in great favor. The Chief would not dare come between the President and that."

"Are there any other missions the President was planning on using the Spartans for?"

"Not that I am aware of." Alexi answered. "I really do feel like I am a sitting target at the embassy. It is probably the first place they will look for me." Alexi knew it would be the first place he would look.

"Are you aware of any spies in our embassy?" The woman asked cooly.

"No."

"Neither are we. While we verify everything you have told us, we will keep you close at hand. In the meantime, arrangements are being made for a more permanent situation for you. You understand, though, that you arrived rather unexpectedly. It might take a few weeks." Alexi understood perfectly what she was saying. He calmly thumbed his fingers on the table until they took him back to his room. He would have to be very careful. Alexi's reputation had gotten him far in Russia, but apparently it was going to keep him in place here. A high ranking Russian official didn't leave the country often. They were going to make sure they got every drop of information out of him before they set him free. And then who would want him? No one. It would be the same as inviting a serial killer to live next door. Sure, he said he would never kill again, but who would trust him? Alexi kicked himself for not thinking that far ahead before he left. Maybe it would have been easier to shoot himself.

With Ross sleeping comfortably, Jack went out to the hallway to call Si and run his plan past him before he brought it to Ross.

"What do you want from me, boy? Sounds like you have thought of everything." Si said. Jack could hear the wind blowing in the background.

"Tell me if you think it really is possible."

"Of course it's possible. As long as Ross goes along with it."

"Am I being selfish? I've wanted to get her out on the boat for ages now."

"Listen son, she goes back to Boston, she will have strangers taking care of her. At least out here she will have two guys who know her and would never let anything happen to her. Besides, we will see anyone coming from miles away."

"I haven't said anything to her yet."

"Don't push her son. If she would feel safer back home, you go with her. I'll be alright here." It made Jack nervous being away from the boat for so long. Jack had so much time at sea, he didn't really feel comfortable surrounded by people on land anymore.

"How are things on the boat?"

"Had a small shower the other night, got a little

bumpy, but I had a few drinks and got bumpy with it. Glad to report it's all okay today." Jack ran his hand through his hair.

"Please don't drink while I'm gone, Dad. If something happens out there, you have to be able to think straight."

"Relax boy. I'm still tied up in the harbor."

"Why?"

"I didn't want to be out to sea if you called me and said something else had happened, so I stayed here." Si hadn't wanted to get too far because if Jack called him and told him Ross had died, he was going to be on the next flight to Canada.

"She's out of the woods now, Dad."

"I know. I thought about going back out, but then I saw on the news that crazy nurse attacked the other woman, so I thought it would be best to not get too far away."

"I need to get her out of here. I've never felt so helpless in my life. Ross was hiding in the shower with nothing but a bottle of shampoo to protect her."

"Get her back here, Jack. No one is going to be able to protect her better than we can. I wonder if they are still selling illegal firearms in the market here? All we have is a flare gun. I'll ask around." Jack pinched the bridge of his nose.

"Don't do anything just yet, Dad. I'll let you know what she says."

"While you're at it, ask her if she wants me to get her a gun. She seemed pretty handy with one at the resort, and you know what Americans are like. She might feel safer with one on board." Jack hung up with Si and got his thoughts straight in his mind. That was all he needed, Si getting picked up for trying to buy a grenade launcher from the market. How was he going to get it back to the boat? Hide it in his overalls? When he walked back into the room, Ross was waking up.

"Did you have a nice nap?"

"I did. Jack, I want to go see Lillian again." Ross was already getting herself out of bed. Jack noticed she wasn't having as much trouble as she did before and wasn't waiting for him to get her a wheelchair.

"Are you going to walk it?"

"I'm going to try. I want out of here, and I would like to walk out of here." Ross said, making sure to pull her gown tight behind her. "I would also like to wear underwear again soon." Ross added.

"Let's not rush things. I've rather enjoyed being

surprised by your bare bum staring back at me." To Ross's surprise, she found walking relatively easy. Also to her surprise, she was rather winded by the time she got to Lillian's room.

"Lillian?" Ross said. Lillian slowly turned her head from the window to the gentle voice that had said her name. Ross didn't know what she expected. Lillian had been attacked and repaired since the last time she had seen her. So, she was a little surprised when Lillian turned and smiled at her.

"Ross, what are you doing here?" Likewise, Lillian thought Ross looked almost normal. Ross had color in her cheeks and a twinkle in her eye. To Lillian, Ross looked lovely.

"I wanted to see you. How are you doing after the attack? That must have been a hell of a surprise."

"Not as much of a surprise as you would think. Hello, my name is Lillian." Lillian addressed Jack.

"Jack." He answered. "Ross's boyfriend." It felt strange to Ross's ears to hear the words 'boyfriend'. Thanks to her and Jack's distance from one another, she had not had to introduce him to anyone or worry about each other's titles.

"She's lucky to have someone like you around."

Lillian held out her hand and Jack shook it. Lillian had thought she could change the subject, but Ross didn't want to.

"What do you mean it wasn't a surprise?" Ross asked.

"It was clear after the attack that I was supposed to die on that boat. Well, we all were, but especially me." It was hard now that she was looking at Lillian to see her in any way cooperating with the Russians. She had seemed to want nothing to do with them when they had talked on the boat, which seemed like a year ago.

"Why did you do it?" Ross asked before she could sensor herself. Lillian just smiled. It was almost impossible for people to understand unless they had lived in similar environments.

"He was in my house when I got home from work. Alexi Stanovich. He is known in my country as "the reaper." He doesn't actually kill anyone, but a visit from him brings death. I thought he was there to kill me. When I fled Russia, it was because they wanted me to work for the government. That year though, they had killed my brother for resisting the government. They made it look like a drug overdose. They thought his death would pressure me into agreeing, but I got out instead. I was fine with him killing me. Really, I think I had been expecting it since I got to England."

"He didn't threaten to kill you, though, did he?" Jack asked.

"No, he wanted information about the trip, and if I didn't agree, he would kill my parents. The information he wanted didn't seem dangerous in any way, and with my parents at stake, I convinced myself it would all be fine in the end." Ross was starting to get angry. She felt bad for the situation Lillian had found herself in, but the fact remained, she could have warned those on board.

"You still could have told someone." Lillian looked Ross in the eye, prepared to take the judgment that was coming to her. She knew this would be the first wave of recrimination from those who would judge her for the decision she had made.

"I wanted to. I really did. It didn't take long for me to regret my decision. I wanted to call the trip off completely, but Nils said no."

"Nils knew." Ross said it as a statement, not a question. Somewhere, she seemed to remember Nils apologizing. Flashes of Nils in a white room came back while Lillian continued to talk.

"Nils was in London. He called not an hour after Alexi Stanovich left. He could tell I was in a bad way, and after a few glasses of wine, I told Nails what had happened. You knew Nils. You knew how he was. He was convinced we could have it both ways. If we called the trip off, they might kill my parents. So he said to do the trip like normal. We knew it was the research they wanted. Nils came up with a plan so that they would think their mission was accomplished and then months later, when my parents were safely out of the country and the rest of you were all back home, we would hand you back your research and you could write your papers. If they came after anyone, it would be Nils and myself for getting past them, and we could live with that."

"My laptop. You were stealing my research." Ross said.

Lillian nodded. "Nils was stealing Dr. Lebedev's, and I was stealing yours. Your research, along with my research, was updated on a thumb drive that stayed on me at all times. Nils thought he could have it both ways, Ross." Ross had to admit, it sounded like something Nils would do. "He had come up against people like this before and come out on top. He thought for sure he could do it again."

"Arrogant shit." Ross said, Lillian smiled.

"Yes, he was. Unfortunately, being an arrogant shit had served him well in the past. I wanted to tell you, Ross. I should have told you. Nils had an extraordinary way of making you feel safe, though. Like it was all going to turn out okay. It's what I found so wonderful in him. Even if it wasn't true."

There was silence before Lillian felt a sudden rush of guilt. Why hadn't she just told Ross, nevermind what Nils thought? Why had she let him decide what happened in the first place? Would any of it have been different if she hadn't said anything to him to begin with? Probably not.

"Can you ever forgive me?" Lillian said, before she knew what she was doing. Ross was the first of her colleagues to know that she had played a role in the attack, and right now, it was very important that Ross forgive her. Ross didn't answer for a moment, which surprised no one as much as Ross. Lillian was sad. She was recovering from two attempts on her life, she had to flee her home and her family to live a life of freedom, and having accomplished all of that, she had landed herself here. That being said, Ross couldn't help feeling betrayed that Lillian had said nothing.

"It's okay, Ross. It's more than I deserve, I know."

"I forgive you." Jack said. The two women turned and looked at him in surprise, having completely forgotten that he was there.

"You do?" Lillian asked.

"You hid her. It's obvious now that you had scouted that location for yourself. When it all started to happen, though, you grabbed Ross and did everything you could to make sure she survived, and for that, I will always be grateful." Jack held out his hand to Lillian, which Lillian took, still surprised. Jack kissed it.

Ross could still not place the conversation, but images of Nils in a white room kept appearing in her mind. *"I'm sorry Ross."* He was saying. Not completely understanding why the image was important, Ross knew one thing for sure. Lillian was telling the truth.

"I forgive you too." Ross was remembering those few minutes before the Spartan caught up with them. Lillian hadn't tried to hide herself. She had stood there with more bravery than Ross could imagine, and waited for her fate. "Next time, tell me we are going to be attacked, though. I might be able to find an even better hiding spot." A tear escaped Lillian's eyes.

"Thank you, both of you. It's more than I deserve. Ross, if you will open that drawer, I think there is something there that will interest you." Ross did as she was told. There was nothing in the drawer. "At the very back, there should be a pack of gum." Ross saw the pack of bright green wrapping. She held it up in confusion.

"In there you will find a thumb drive with your research on it. It was current. Your most recent discoveries are there. Go write your paper, Dr. Halloway." If Ross hadn't forgiven Lillian before, she would have now.

"What about the others? What about your research?"

"Mine is on there as well, but after all of this... once it comes out that I played a role in it, I doubt anyone would publish it. Unfortunately, Nils had the other thumbdrive with his and Dr. Lebedev's research. I don't know where that is, but Nils told his organization about your research, and it may be all they need to gain protection for the area."

"Thank you, Lillian." Ross had honestly not thought about her research since the attack, but holding it in her hand now, it seemed so precious. Like the whole trip hadn't been a complete disaster.

# 37

Ross was so thrilled with having her research back that she didn't notice she walked back to her room like normal. Her shoulder throbbed, but she was not showing the signs of fatigue she had been before.

"Ross." Jack said.

"Hmmm." Ross was trying to find a suitable place to hide it. She looked around the room, but she was afraid that if she hid it as well as Lillian had, she would forget it.

"Are you looking forward to going home?" Ross turned and looked at him.

"Of course I'm looking forward to going home. Are you saying you've had a good time? I'm sure the nurses will miss you." Jack had looked into the eyes of sharks on a regular and frequent basis. Large sharks that would kill him with one bite, and still he was not as scared then as he was right now. Ross wasn't what you would call a girly girl. She was not going to respond the same way women in romantic comedies do when the boyfriend suggests they move in together. There was, in fact, every chance that Ross was going to run for the elevators. Especially since Jack's home was a boat on the ocean.....six thousand miles away from Ross's apartment in Boston.

"It's just....I've been thinking."

"Jack, what is it?"

"I've been thinking about when we leave here. If you want to go home to Boston, if that is what will make you feel safe, then that is what we will do."

"But?"

"But I think I could take better care of you on the boat. Si and I could protect you better that is. We would be in the middle of nowhere. No one could come within miles of the place and us not know about it ahead of time." Ross said nothing, which left Jack not knowing what to do.

"You asked Si about this?"

"Of course. He was all for it. Said he knew we could do a better job since we cared so much about you. Care more than a bunch of people who didn't know you."

Ross looked at the pack of chewing gum still resting in her hand that contained all her data. Then she thought about her apartment and all the familiar things there. Her cat Carbon, her bed. Oh God, her bed. Sam. Her mother was absolutely losing her mind. Then she looked into those green eyes of Jack's. Those pleading eyes. Eyes that were somehow showing love and fear at the same time.

Ross had seen Jack and Si in action, and if she were honest, there were no two men in the world she would trust more than them.

"I'm not sure I can ask you two to do that Jack." She finally said. Her pulse was running fast. The stream of words running through her head were fast and contradictory, making it very hard for her to form a coherent sentence. Jack already had a gnarly looking scar on his thigh from what they jokingly called their first date. Ross still felt guilty about it. If she had gotten on the ferry with the others, Jack probably wouldn't have been shot. Jack always pointed out that he most likely would have been blown to bits, but Ross didn't think so. Asking him and Si to rescue her again seemed a bit much to ask.

"You aren't asking me. I'm offering." Jack said.

"I know, but I'm not sure it's fair all the same."

"Ross, if you don't want to go...." Ross held up her hand.

"It's not that. It's not. I got you two in trouble last time Jack. I don't want to do that again."

"Do you still want me to come to Boston with you then?"

"I do. I'll also understand if you need to go back. Obviously, I can't expect you to put everything on hold just because I went out and got myself shot."

"Which wouldn't have happened if you had come to see me." Jack was a little disappointed that Ross seemed to once again be avoiding him and the boat.

"I know Jack. You were right, but up until the ship was attacked, it felt so good out there. I was so worried about getting there, but once I was on the boat and doing my research, I was me again. I wasn't a survivor, I wasn't afraid. I was just Ross, kickass scientist, making discoveries and taking names, and I was really excited that my work was going to play a role in getting that place protected. Now I'm a survivor again." Jack still didn't know how to respond. "I think that is a long way of saying, I need to think about it." Jack walked up to her and cupped her face in his hands.

"I won't lie and say my offer is completely selfless. When you dropped that phone, I feared the worst Ross. I thought you were gone, and I don't ever want to feel that way again." Jack didn't cry. But his jaw was clenched so tight with emotion Ross feared his teeth would shatter.

"You being with me may not change anything. I don't think knowing the Sparartans or the Russians are coming would change the outcome." Ross pointed out.

"I know. But we'll go down fighting, and I want that opportunity. I've spent more time on water than land, Ross, and if there is anywhere I know I can make a stand, it's out there."

"I don't want to be the one to get you shot again. You still have a scar from the last time I got us in trouble. I still feel guilty about that. I can't bring this to your doorstep."

"And I can't handle another call like the one I got. Think about it Ross. The sea is a great place to clear your mind and heal."

"I'll think about it. I'll let you know dinner time, all right?"

"Okay. I'm going to go for a walk okay?" He kissed Ross. Like a man kisses a woman. Jack hadn't kissed her like that since she woke up. If he wanted to make her lean towards going with him, it was the right move. Who wouldn't want more of those kisses?

"That's cheating." She said, he flashed her a sly grin and a cocked eyebrow in response. Jack had no sooner closed the door before Ross dove for the phone and called Sam.

"You okay? What happened?" Sam said in a worried voice.

"I'm fine. Sort of. Just found out that one of my fellow scientists helped with the attack."

"What!"

"That's not why I'm calling. Jack wants me to go to the boat with him instead of coming home." There was a long pause.

"You just found out that the attack on your research trip that resulted in you almost dying was an inside job, and you are freaking out because your boyfriend wants you to move in with him for a while?"

"Lillian had a lot going on, okay. Tell me what to do about Jack."

"What do you want to do?"

"I haven't got a clue. I want the comfort of home so bad. But I also want the comfort of Jack. He makes me feel safe. I kind of hate that he makes me feel safe. I should be able to make myself feel safe. I'm a grown ass woman with a Ph.D. and a handgun. On the other hand, being out on a boat far away from the rest of the world is appealing."

"Forgetting for a moment that seeing your best friend was not listed in the reasons you want to come home, go where you feel safe, Ross, and stop questioning what you SHOULD be feeling. Honey, you gave us all the scare of a lifetime. You have been in a life and death situation for the second time in as many years. This time you were shot in the neck and minutes away from death. Physically you are not one hundred percent and whoever is going to be protecting you has never seen a Spartan. Jack and Si have."

"So you are saying what?"

"I'm saying that as much as I want you back here, I want you safe. I want you to feel safe. If it were me, I would be going with the devil I know and not the devil I don't. Spartans can hide in clear sight Ross. Jack and Si know what they are looking for." Ross took a deep breath.

"I'm moving in with a boy, Sam."

"A really cute boy who would die before he let

anything happen to you. You've done worse." Ross laughed.

"That's part of what I'm afraid of. That I'm bringing trouble to them."

"They are big boys, Ross. They play with sharks for fun. They can handle trouble. I think Si kind of likes it."

"What am I going to tell my mother?"

"She's going to be disappointed, but since there is a chance you are going to come off that boat pregnant, I think she'll forgive you."

"Sam!"

"Seriously, Hon. We all just want you safe."

"She saved my research."

"Who?"

"The one who helped the attackers. She and Nils knew it was going to happen. They knew they wanted the research. So, she copied my research every night onto a thumb drive. He did the same with his bunk mate. Lillian just gave it back to me. I'm going to be able to publish a paper after all."

"Oh honey, that's really good. It wasn't all for nothing then, was it?"

"No. And it means the bastards don't win."

"Ross. Do you have to publish it?" Sam asked.

"Why?"

"Honey, the people who hired the Spartans wanted that research. They know if you publish, that it will prove what they were doing and prove that the land needs protecting right?"

"Right."

"What's to stop them from coming after you if they know you have the research?" Ross looked at the pack of gum in her hand. How was something so small so dangerous? Ross had never dealt with dangerous information before. "Just hold on to it for a bit, Ross. Don't tell anyone you have it and hold onto it. You can always publish later if they manage to catch the people responsible."

"Yeah."

"You okay?"

"I don't know. I really don't know. How did life get so complicated?"

"It has a way of doing that. Go with Jack, honey. Recover from your injuries. Enjoy being away from the madness of civilization and being harder to find. Heal. Then get back here as soon as you can." Ross sat there for a moment examining her feelings. She tucked the pack of gum into her robe pocket. It wasn't a great hiding spot, but it would do for now.

To her surprise, she missed Jack. He had only been out of the room for ten minutes, but she wanted him back. *Go with him.* Ross told herself. *He's been after you for months to come see his world. It's not too much to ask, all things considered. But what if I hate it?* She asked herself. *How can you hate being on the ocean with Jack?* Ross couldn't think of anything.

Ross picked up the hair brush and ran it through her hair. She wanted to look as good as she could when she told Jack. Putting one foot in front of the other, Ross walked down the hallway where she knew Jack would be. He had rolled her there in the wheelchair several times. It was the only place on the floor where there were windows overlooking the outside world. Ross's window overlooked the hospital's air conditioning unit. He was standing there, arms braced on the window ledge looking fixedly out the window. He turned when he saw Ross, and he rushed over to grab her arm.

"I'm fine."

"You look pale, you feel okay?" Jack said.

"Yeah. A little winded. I'm fine. I called Sam."

"She wants you to come home I guess." Ross leaned against the wall. It had been a week since she had been outside, she realized.

"Actually, she thinks I'd be safer with you. She said you and Si know what you're doing when it comes to Spartans. The people that would be protecting me in Boston don't know what a Spartan looks like."

"What do you think?"

"I think she's right. I really do struggle with bringing all of this to your door, Jack. I also struggle with needing someone else to make me feel safe. The fact of the matter is, you do make me feel safe. As Sam pointed out, I'm wounded, and no matter which way you slice it, I am going to be relying on someone else for my safety. I would rather it be you and Si than some strangers."

"So you are going to come to the boat?"

"Looks like it." Ross smiled. "I am rather looking forward to getting away from civilization for a while. Breathing fresh air. Feeling sun on my face."

"You're gonna love it, you'll see." Jack cupped her face again and kissed her. "I love you, honey." Jack froze. He hadn't meant to say that out loud, even if it was what he felt. Jack studied Ross's face for her reaction. Ross's eyes grew large, her face went pale, and she started to sink to the floor.

"Ross?" Jack supported her as she fell. Her eyes rolled back in her head and she passed out. "Ross?" Jack tapped her face, nothing. Looking around in a panic, he found the emergency call button. Letting Ross go for a moment, he pressed it and went back to her. It was a small floor, there were only two patients. It didn't take long before people showed up and pushed him out of the way to get to Ross. Jack was left as a spectator while they checked Ross over and carried her away.

# 38

"So, what did our parakeet have to say?" Dufort asked, as a way of a greeting.

"He's a slick bastard who had obviously thought about what he was going to say. I strongly suspect he was more hands- on than he implied. You are going to love this, he got us the phone number used to contact the Spartans. "

"Please tell me you tried it." Dufort said.

"I did. Of course, I did." Maes answered.

"And?"

"Well, it doesn't go to their secret lair, unfortunately. It sends you to a person who can get in touch with them. A sort of secretary, if you will, who asks what you are calling for, takes your info, and then says someone will call you back." The hairs on Dufort's neck were standing on end. This was closer than they had ever gotten to the Spartans before. "I am waiting for a call back. They weren't able to tell me how long it would take before I could expect to hear from someone.

"I'll keep you posted. One interesting thing that came up in conversation was that the attack wasn't supposed to be lethal in the original plan. The Russians thought it would be better to make it look like a pirate hit. Scare everyone, make other scientists think twice before coming to the area. Dr. Nils Ryeng kicked it up a notch. He had apparently upset the president on another matter, so when he found out he was heading this trip, the president decided to terminate them."

"So this was about revenge?" Dufort said.

"Sounds like it, just not in the way we thought. Alexi left because there were survivors. With the president having a personal stake in it, he knew there was no room for error. As for why he handed himself over....I think he wanted to stick it to the Russian Security Chief. I get the general impression he almost hated the man. He obviously thinks he's past it. At the same time, he knows the President is going to put a price on his head. While he's worried, Mr. Reaper also thinks he can outsmart them." She said.

"Any idea why the Russian government is looking for all this extra cash? I mean, selling whales, stealing oil. Are they trying to fund something?"

"It's not the country that is looking for the money, but the President. You have to pay a lot of money to the oligarchs if you want to be president. They are starting to call in their debts. With interest."

"Good Lord, what a mess." Dufort didn't need to point out.

"I'm just hoping that if we catch a Spartan, being the logical creatures they are supposed to be, they will give us the lead back to who hired them, and we can at least get who is responsible for this attack."

"No offense, but I hope that doesn't happen until I get there." Dufort told her.

"Well, go get your patients home." Dufort hung up with a smile on his face. While he would have loved to interview Alexi himself, he knew his colleague had done a good job and the investigation was moving forward. They now knew who was responsible, they just had to prove it.

With a slap on his desk, Dufort got up and went to go find the doctor in charge of his patients. He had done all he could on his end to make sure they had security when they went home. Local agencies in both London and Boston were just waiting for Lillian and Ross to return home. Dufort got in the elevator and went to find out when they could both be discharged so he could move onto more interesting things.

Dufort got off the elevator on the ninth floor to find Jack pacing the hallways looking worried. There was a tangible sense in the air that something had happened.

"What happened?" He turned and asked Jack. The man looked like he was about to explode.

"She walked down the hallway to talk to me. We were just standing there talking and she turned white. Her legs went out from under her and she passed out."

"What do they think happened?"

"I don't know. They came running and took her away. I haven't heard anything since. I don't even know where they took her." Dufort's eyes widened at this. He didn't know where she was either. Why hadn't they called him?

Jack picked up on this, and a whole new level of panic took over. The two men rushed to the nurse's desk. Jack let Dufort take the lead.

"Where in the name of Satan and all his demons is Dr. Halloway? More importantly, why was she taken from the floor without my knowing?" Demanded Dufort, almost coming over the counter at the nurse who was looking less than impressed with him.

"She's right here." Ross said from behind them. Jack was relieved to see that normal color had returned to her face. He let out a big sigh and kissed her forehead. "Are you trying to kill me, woman?"

"Not on purpose." Ross answered.

"What happened?" Jack asked, the doctor standing behind Ross.

"We put Dr. Halloway on blood pressure meds to lower her blood pressure and allow the veins and vessels we fixed to heal."

"Basically, I moved around too much." Ross said.

"And for that she had to leave the floor?" Dufort piped up. His face almost purple.

"There was obviously a concern that the ligatures we used had slipped and that she was bleeding from somewhere. We needed imaging to confirm this. We can't bring the machines up here, so Dr. Halloway had to be taken to the machines." The doctor explained as patiently as she could manage.

"I should have been informed." Dufort's voice was rising. Jack took the wheelchair and let the doctor defend herself against the inspector while he got Ross back to her room.

"It was an emergency. Surely, some allowance can be made for that." The doctor said, sounding calm if not a little irritated.

Jack closed the door to the room. They could still hear them going at it, but it was muffled.

"I'm sorry, Jack. I thought I felt funny because I hadn't walked that far since the injury."

"The important thing is you are all right now." Jack said, holding up the covers for her.

"I didn't mean to scare you again."

"Well, you don't get all the credit. I was worried enough and then the inspector came up and he clearly didn't know where you were, which he seemed concerned about. For a split second there, I think we both thought you had been kidnapped."

"Jack, what we were talking about before I fell..." Jack held up his hand.

"I'll go wherever you want me to Ross. If that's back to Boston, I'll go to Boston. You need to heal and that will happen faster if you are comfortable with where you are. What I don't think I can do is not come with you wherever you go. I know you like your privacy, but I'm not sure I'm capable of depending on complete strangers to keep you safe." A smile came over Ross's face.

"I never thought of myself as a damsel in distress."

"Ross, you aren't..."

"Mostly because there has never been a knight in shining armor around when I got in trouble. Unless you count Sam. But you're here now, and as much as I hate to admit it, I feel a lot better knowing you are going to be standing guard."

"You want me to get you something to eat?" Ross grabbed his hand and brought it to her face.

"Get me out of here, Jack. Take me to your boat. We'll hide out there until all this blows over."

"You still want to go?"

"Now more than ever."

Jack went out to the nurse's desk to interrupt the doctor and the inspector. The man was practically leaning into the doctor. Not that she seemed to notice.

"Excuse me. Dr. Halloway would like to know when the earliest she can leave would be." Dufort stopped talking and turned slowly to Jack.

"She wants to leave?"

"No offense mate, but she can't get out of here fast

enough."

"Well…..?" Dufort turned to the doctor.

# 39

Sam's clothing package arrived the evening before Ross left. 'Oh goody!' Ross had said, when the nurse brought the package in.

"It looks like they searched it." Jack said.

"Yeah, they didn't seem very worried about hiding the fact either." Ross added. The paper around the package had barely been re-wrapped. Ross lifted the lid of the box, which no longer fit on top because the contents of the box would not allow it. "By a man who had never folded laundry before apparently. There was no way Sam would have sent a parcel arranged in such a haphazard way." Ross pulled out one item after another and was shocked to discover how much she had missed having clothes. Fashion was definitely more of Sam's thing. Ross always thought that wearing clothes was about not distracting others or embarrassing herself. Now, she thought they were beautiful. Not able to wait until the next day, Ross took the underwear out and immediately put them on.

Jack watched with hidden amusement as Ross shimmied her way into a pair of underwear and then threw her head back and said, "Oh yeah, baby. That feels good." Jack let out a chuckle. "What are you laughing at?"

"A man usually likes to hear that when a woman takes her undies off, not when she puts them back on."

"I've been mooning the floor for too long. It's nice to feel covered." That being said, Ross left the bra where it was until the next morning. She didn't feel like being *that* normal yet.

With a pang of gratitude, Ross smiled at the flannel shirt Sam had sent along with other button up shirts. It was a pink and lime green plaid shirt, which is more color than Ross normally liked in her flannel, but she couldn't bring herself to be annoyed. The clothes had been chosen carefully and with love. Nothing that had to go over her head. Not even her bra. Sam had managed to find one that snapped in the front, which must have taken some effort.

"Sam thought of everything, didn't she?" Jack said,

looking at the clothing on the bed.

"She's good like that."

"I'm kind of disappointed though. I would have thought Sam would take advantage of the opportunity to get you into girly underwear. These are rather granny-like. I'm not sure I know how to operate a bra that opens in the front." Jack said, holding them up. Ross snatched them back.

"Much the same as the others, just a different location." Jack gave the half grin she had come to love.

"Hopefully, I'll get some time to practice with it." Ross had a hard time sleeping that night. She was tempted to wake Jack and leave early, but their flight was set and they had to wait for their guard. It was strange not being in control of your own movements, and Ross would be glad when all this was over and she could go where she wanted when she wanted.

"You awake?" Jack asked.

"Yeah, can't sleep."

"You nervous?" Since Ross had agreed to go with him to the boat, he had spent most of the waking hours assuring her that he and Si would be able to protect her. Going so far as to repeat Si's offer to buy a gun on the black market.

"I know it sounds strange, but I honestly just want to get out of this hospital. I think I will feel better once we are on the boat." Jack smiled, and reached out for her hand, which she took.

"You'll love it. I know you will." He wouldn't be able to stand it if she didn't. He loved Ross and he loved the ocean. It seemed impossible that they wouldn't love each other.

"Why do you love it so much?" Ross had never asked him this before, which seemed strange when she thought about it, but also made complete sense. In her mind, he loved the sea like she loved science. She didn't want to stop talking though, and she didn't want to talk about Spartans or her injuries, or anything remotely related to what the next twenty-four to forty-eight hours might include.

"We just understand each other, really." Jack said, in his soothing Aussie accent. "I can tell what the next day is going to be like by how she acted the day before. How far away a storm or high winds are by how tall the waves are. I seem to lack those goal posts on land. Things seem to constantly surprise me. It's hard for most people to understand."

"No, I get it. Chemistry is like that for me. It's this

thing most people don't understand or are almost completely unaware of, and I just get it. It's the rest of the world that baffles me."

"You sure you're okay with this? Going out to the boat? You can change your mind Ross, I'll understand. Si will cry, but…."

"No, I'm still okay with it. I keep thinking about my apartment and a Spartan knocking at the door. I wouldn't know until I opened the door and saw those dead eyes." A shiver ran down her back. "I'm not sure I could handle that."

"You wouldn't have to, love."

"I know, you would be there."

"That, and you would be dead. I mean a Spartan isn't going to miss you twice at point blank range, is he?" For some reason, Ross found this hysterically funny instead of horrific.

"You're an asshole." She said, between laughs. They continued to talk until the sun slowly illuminated the sky.

Sam had packed flip flops for the boat and a low heel boot for the flight. Having gotten herself dressed, Ross looked at herself in the mirror and gasped. She looked like herself. Herself when she let Sam dress her, which was more than she cared to admit. Ross pulled her hair over her good shoulder and put it in a low ponytail. She looked cute, which was more than she thought she would look.

"Hello darlin." Jack said, as she came out of the bathroom.

"I know, I look like a normal person." Jack smiled.

"You look fantastic." Jack meant it. She had color in her cheeks, and she no longer looked like a patient in a hospital. Any doubts Jack had about taking her to the boat vanished. Ross would be fine. The salt air would do her good, and as she had said, they could hide out until all this blew over.

Dufort stopped by shortly after breakfast to give her passport back to her. He had retrieved it from her belongings that had been taken into evidence. Quite nicely, he had offered to grab her anything else she might want from her belongings, but Ross wasn't sure she wanted to see any of them again.

"You will have an armed escort until you board the boat in Jakarta. After that, you will be on your own." Dufort said. He was not entirely sure he should be allowing this. But he also shared their worry that the police in Boston would not know a Spartan until it was too late. The three of them had managed to survive the Spartans before, there was no reason to think they wouldn't be able to do it again.

"Thank you for everything, inspector. What will you do with us out of your hair?" To Ross's surprise, a genuine smile crossed the man's face.

"Hopefully, I'll catch a Spartan."

"You know where they are?" Ross said with surprise.

"I can't speak of an ongoing investigation." But the smile on his face said it all.

"Does that mean Lillian is going to be going home soon as well?" Jack said.

"It does. She is recovering nicely. Unlike yourself, she has agreed to our protection. Hopefully, she will only be a day or two behind you." That was good news. Ross went down to Lillian's room on her way out to say goodbye.

"Oh my God, Ross. You look normal. It gives me hope." Lillian didn't look so bad herself. She was smiling, and her complexion was pink and healthy.

"The inspector said you are going home in a few days as well." Lillian's smile grew deeper.

"Did he also tell you I have a homecoming present

waiting for me when I get home?"

"No."

"My parents. My parents are going to be there waiting for me. They may actually be there now."

"Lillian! That's fantastic. How?"

"I still have a few contacts in Russia. Before I left for the trip, I asked them to get my parents out. Provide the documents they would need to get out of the country under the radar. Obviously, I couldn't keep in contact with them. I wasn't sure what was happening, if Stanovich had already killed them or not. I mentioned it to Dufort, and he said he would look into it. He came in this morning and told me they were on English soil. "

"Lillian, that is just fantastic. I'm so glad they are okay. Listen, I would love to stay in touch and maybe even collaborate on this paper. Here's my email address. Let me know how everything turns out okay?" They gave each other a hug. Ross hugged all her nurses and doctors and stepped onto the elevator. She was finally leaving the ninth floor.

*We take the outdoors for granted.* Ross realized this when she stepped outside for the first time in a week. Fresh air hit her face, and the warmth of the sun. She stopped walking and turned her face up, letting the sunlight soak in. Jack gave her hand a gentle tug, and she reluctantly got into the car. Thankfully, where she was going, there would be no shortage of sun. Her armed guard had joined them in the elevator while they were still in the hospital. His name was Gunner, and he looked the part. Ross would have been disappointed if he had been a small string bean. Gunner worked out and probably consumed protein powder on a regular and frequent basis. She wasn't sure he knew what kind of opponent a Spartan would be, but Ross was confident that if they saw a Spartan, she and Jack could easily hide behind Gunner's left bicep.

Ross wasn't sure what the protocol was for interacting with your armed guard, so she shook his hand and said, "Thanks for coming with us," which sounded awkward. Jack seemed to nail it with a firm handshake and a manly nod. Gunner didn't strike her as a talker, so she might be spared any further awkward conversation.

Jack and Gunner went into protective mode as soon as the elevator doors opened. Ross had been so happy to leave the hospital, she had forgotten this didn't mean it was over. They tucked her into a sedan and went to the airport. Ross thought she would be nervous about flying. Usually, she's nervous before trips and plane rides, but maybe because of all that had transpired, Ross had no fear. *'Your neurons that perceive fear are fried.'* Ross thought to herself. It was the only logical explanation. I mean, you couldn't take a chemist who had spent most of her life in a lab and put her in these situations and expect there to be no permanent damage.

Ross watched as the earth grew small below her window and disappeared into the clouds. For a brief moment, she had worried that the flight crew could be Spartans. Gunner assured her they had already thought about that, and he was confident they were not Spartans. So Ross put her headphones on and watched a movie. By the time they landed in Jakarta, Ross thought she would go insane if she had to spend another minute on a plane. Because of security, the three of them held back and let the rest of the plane get off. Gunner went first, then Ross, then Jack. Ross wondered if Beyonce got the same treatment. She fished around in her bag that Sam had sent and found a pair of sunglasses and put them on. Sticking her nose in the air, she left the plane with her inner Beyonce shining.

"Really." She heard Jack say behind her.

"I just want to look the part."

With nothing but two tote bags as luggage, they moved through customs rather quickly. Ross noticed with a smug grin that being back in the Jakarta airport was bringing back memories of when she had walked down the same hallways with Sam a year ago. How they had piled into the hot bus when they made it through customs. The drive from the airport to their hotel, which had taken them through crowded streets. They stepped outside and the hot air hit them. Ross turned to Gunner like she was going to say good-bye.

"I'll see you to the boat and make sure you get away okay." They got into another sedan that had been arranged. The crowded streets were even more claustrophobic in a sedan. More than once, Ross grabbed Jack's hand because it looked like the car next to them was going to collide with them. When they got to the dock, it was identical to the one where she and Sam had gotten on the cruise ship that had taken her to the resort. Also where she had said good-bye to Jack and Si. Memories were washing over her, and she was glad that Gunner and Jack were there because she was extremely distracted. Someone was waving to her, and for a moment she panicked, until she noticed the person waving was wearing blue jean overalls.

"Si!" No one was more surprised when Ross started running towards Si. She had not even been sure she was capable of such a thing. Gunner started running after her, yelling at her to stop. Ross paid no attention. For reasons she wasn't able to process at the moment, she was extremely happy to see Si. Jack was running as well, trying to explain to Gunner (who was reaching for his gun) that Si was friendly. Si had made it down the dock and was standing next to the road when Ross caught him in a hug. She hadn't seen him since the last time they both stood on this dock, and he hadn't changed one iota. He had a short white beard, but other than that, he was the same.

"How are ya, darlin'?" The salty sea dog's voice cracked.

"Oh, Si. I'm so glad to see you." Ross was a little out of breath.

"You're glad to see me? I'm glad to see you. I thought you were a goner, girl."

"I almost was." There were tears running down her face. By this point, Gunner and Jack had caught up.

Gunner didn't look pleased, but he didn't say anything.

"Sorry." Ross said, Gunner just rolled his eyes and tried to catch his breath. Big guys don't run so well. Jack, on the other hand, was smiling. Out of breath, but smiling.

"Si." Si said, taking Gunner's hand almost by force. "Jack's father."

"I know." Gunner said. Si had been included in the security brief. "I will see you all off." Gunner seemed to be ready to be rid of them. No doubt he wanted to sleep. He herded them all back down the dock where Jack and Si's boat was waiting. Ross had been looking for a small little thing. This was a decent sized boat. Jack, eager to get out on the open water, untied the boat while Si kicked the engines up. Ross thanked Gunner for helping her, then she gave him a hug, which he tolerated well. Ross no longer cared that it was awkward, she was grateful to him, and hugging him was the only way she knew to show that.

Gunner stayed on the dock until he was nothing but a small dot on the horizon. Ross let the wind whip around her and soaked up the sun on her face. She looked around, Si was driving/ steering (what was it when you were on a boat?) them further out to sea.

Jack had taken his dress shirt off and was sorting out some ropes in his undershirt.  This had been the right decision.  Ross felt safe. Safer than she had at the hospital, safer than she had since she left her apartment eight days ago.  It had only been eight days, and so much had changed.  Ross chose not to think about what else might happen in the next eight days.  She liked how she felt right now, so she was going to hold onto it for as long as possible.

# 40

At the same moment Ross and Jack were reuniting with Si on the docks of Jakarta, Alexi was stepping out of the consulate in Helsinki for a much needed smoke while housekeeping cleaned his room. He was still wearing the same suit he had been wearing when he arrived. They had offered him clothes, but to be honest, they were of such low quality, he could not bear to be seen in them. The questioning had slowed to a near stop, so for the most part, his days were his own. Something he was getting used to. That and the boredom.

The sun was out today. Alexi took a long drag and leaned his head against the stone wall letting the sun hit his face. He had been told that he could leave the consulate, but only between certain hours. This was as far as Alexi felt safe going. He knew his government would be looking for ways to get rid of him. He knew too much. At this point, they might even know he could prove some of it. Within the walls of the consulate, there was some protection. Some security. Though he longed to go for a walk, get a drink, see the sites, he dare not go too far. It wasn't all bad, he had struck up friendly conversations with most of the staff. The daytime receptionist was particularly nice. Nice to look at as well. Beautiful red hair.

Alexi took another drag on his cigarette and let his mind wander. He was fifty-two years old and starting over from scratch. They hadn't asked him where he wanted to live, and it had been made clear that it would most likely be anywhere they could find to put him, but that hadn't kept him from dreaming.

Alexi had always lived in busy, dirty cities. He could just see the water from his room here at the consulate, and it had him thinking. Thinking about his childhood for the first time in a long time. His father took them fishing in the summertime. Summer vacations spent in a shack in the middle of the woods. He hadn't thought of those summers in ages, now he wanted nothing more than to be in that cabin in the woods with the early morning mist still hanging low over the water. Evenings spent next to the fire.

Everything seemed to make sense there. He hadn't cast a line in several years, but Alexi could see himself fishing on the river on a nice day like today. If he got a big enough place, he might build himself a sauna.

This was Alexi's favorite thing to do these days. He didn't understand enough of the language to watch TV. For the most part, he was left to daydream about what his new life was going to be like. He had lived a life ruled by death and corruption for so long, he wondered if he could live without it. So far, he missed the fear people felt when they saw him, but nothing else about his former life. Whatever happened, he was at last his own man. His every move would not be watched for signs of flagging support for the party. He would not have to fear insulting the wrong person. *I am free.* He said to himself. Taking the last drag, which brought the cigarette to the nub, he flicked it into the street and let the smoke out of his lungs slowly.

While Alexi was finishing his cigarette and daydreaming about the next chapter in his life, the recently hired maid finished vacuuming his room. That done, she gathered her items and headed back out the door. With gloved hands, she locked the door and sprayed the handle, being careful to not inhale until she was a few steps away. She then threw the spray bottle and the gloves in the trash and moved to the elevator.

Alexi looked around one more time at the busy people moving along the street. For the most part they looked happy. Alexi smiled to himself. He had done it. Most people didn't retire from his job. He had known that when he took it, but he had managed it. Correctly reading the situation, Alexi had managed to get himself out of the way just at the right moment to avoid being forced into retirement. He had known what information to safely keep for future use. The right information that would be of interest to Russia's enemies. Information that would make them forget who he had been and what he had done. He had managed it all brilliantly, and now he would be able to enjoy the rest of his life in peace. A light rain had started to fall, so Alexi moved back into the consulate.

Walking through reception, he nodded to the security guard there and stepped onto the elevator. Alexi took a key out of his pocket and turned the handle to let himself into his tidy one bedroom apartment with high ceilings and tall windows that thankfully opened. There was a small bedroom and a kitchenette so he could make himself coffee in the morning. Alexi went over to the window. The rain had picked up in the short time it took him to get back into the building, and the people below were running for cover. The one thing Alexi loved about the consulate was their library. He found their selection of spy novels to be fantastic. Most of them were in English, which was fine. Alexi sat where he could hear the sound of the rain and the noise on the street and picked up the book. Licking his fingers, he turned to the page he had left off that morning and sat back for an afternoon of reading.

He had read no more than a chapter when he felt dizzy. He took a sip of coffee, but the room danced in front of him. He stood up and almost fell back down to the couch again. Worried, Alexi stumbled towards the bathroom to splash water on his face. It felt like the room moved under him, and he went down on his knees. He was now convinced he had been poisoned and he tried to get up, get himself to the phone or the door, but his legs would no longer answer him. Alexi tried to crawl, knowing his life depended on his getting help, but they too were slow and sluggish. "Help." He called out, but the word didn't come out right. Someone would hear him yelling though, so he kept yelling until that was no longer possible. Sticking his finger down his throat, he tried to make himself vomit, knowing perfectly well that if he was already showing signs, it was too late. Dark spots appeared in his vision. He could no longer take a deep breath.

Alexi knew he was dying, and had the thought not been so terrifying, he would have probably been able to tell you the name of the poison and which lab it had come from. Lying down on the floor, he was no longer able to move his arms, every breath a struggle. Alexi knew that a neurotoxin had been used on him. It had attacked his musculoskeletal system, making it impossible for him to move. The fact that it was taking so much effort to breathe meant it had hit his respiratory system, and if that didn't kill him, it was only a matter of time before it hit his cardiovascular system. When his heart stopped, it would be over. Now lying face down on the floor, Alexi tried to concentrate on breathing, hoping that someone would find him before the lights went out. He could see the dust underneath the chair.

The curtain descended quickly after that. The light went out of his eyes. No one had heard his calls. Even if they had, they probably wouldn't have answered. Alexi Stanovich was not discovered until the next morning when the kitchen became concerned after his dinner and breakfast were retrieved untouched.

At the same moment Alexi was calculating how long he had to live based on his symptoms, Lillian was getting out of a black sedan in front of her house. Like Ross, she had an armed escort. Unlike Ross, her armed escort was going to stay with her until she was declared safe. Lillian got out of the car wearing clothes that were not hers. Not having a close friend like Sam, Lillian had to rely on Inspector Dufort, who had kindly offered to find some suitable clothes for her to wear home. She had told him her sizes, but the clothes hung on her loosely because she'd lost weight while she was in hospital. Despite that, the clothes were lovely. Lillian had been surprised that a man like the inspector had been able to find clothes in her style.

"Thank you so much inspector. These are lovely." She had said, giving him a kiss on the cheek. He stood there grinning at her. Right before the moment turned awkward, the phone had rung in her room. Dufort had practically jumped over her to answer it. Speaking briefly with the person on the line, he had then turned to her, his grin broader now. "It's for you."

"Who is it?" Who in the world would be calling her

here?

"Just...go on." Dufort had pressed the receiver into her hand. Lillian was a little fearful when she said, "Hello."

"My little Kot! Is it you?" Her mother said on the other end of the line. "Where are you? When will you be home? I'll make a stew." Her mother asked. At the sound of her mother's voice, Lillian began to shake with emotion.

"Mama, where are you? Are you okay?" She managed to say without her emotion coming through.

"We are at your house Kot, but you are not here."

"And Papa?"

"He is here too. Where else would he be? When are you coming home?" Lillian could not keep control any longer. Her legs went out from under her and she fell to the floor. Dufort caught her and eased her down. The only thing that got to him more than a woman crying was a strong woman crying. Lillian shook with heaping sobs. He took the phone from Lillian and did his best to explain the situation.

"Where is the supermarket?" Lillian's mother asked. Dufort got off the phone with them and sat down on the floor across from Lillian who was managing to regain control of herself.

"How?" She asked.

"You did most of it yourself before you left. I tried to track them down. They had gotten out of Russia but couldn't get into England without the right visas. I got them the right visas and arranged for transport to England and then your house. They are under a twenty-four hour watch and will remain so as long as this goes on." Lillian grabbed his hand and crushed it with what strength she had.

"Thank you. A thousand times thank you." She had then lost control again, and despite his normal attention to protocol, Inspector Dufort provided his shoulder for her to cry on.

"I wish you would allow me to move all of you to a safer location. You will have twenty-four hour security, but you know better than most that may not be enough." Dufort was leaning his head against hers. Lillian had managed to stop trembling, soothed by the thought that she would be there in less than twenty-four hours. She leaned up to look at him with tear filled eyes.

"And you know, inspector, that it does not matter where I go. I have spent a decade hiding from them, just to find out they knew where I was all the time. No, I will not spend anymore of my life hiding. When I get home, I will see my parents for the first time in a long time." A smile crossed her face. "I will eat my mother's food  for the first time in a long time, and listen while my father grumbles at the TV. For the first time in a long time. I will show them the life I have created for myself. No inspector. It's time for me to go home." Dufort nodded his understanding.

# 41

It had not taken them long to get the boat out of the harbor and into open water. Looking all around, Ross saw nothing but ocean. It was both frightening and liberating all at the same time. She had gone to bed early in her own cabin. Jack promised her privacy and he had delivered. The problem was she didn't like it. If she hadn't been so damned tired, she would have gotten out of bed and crawled into Jack's. He had been next to her every moment of everyday for so long, she felt lonely without him around. Ross's arm was stiff from all the movement the day before, and the stitches were starting to itch.

"Don't scratch it." Jack said from behind her. He came up behind her and kissed her stitched neck. It was successful in taking her mind off the itch. " One more week and I will take those out and lovingly kiss where each was placed." A shiver ran down Ross's back in the best possible way. "How did you sleep?" He whispered in her ear.

"I can't remember the last time I slept that well."

"It's the rocking of the boat, just rocks you to sleep. You want coffee?"

"No thanks." Ross left Jack at the coffee maker and went to the front of the boat and saw Si at the wheel.

"Permission to come aboard, Captain." Si broke into a wide smile.

"Of course. How are you feeling?"

"Good actually." Ross caught him looking at her stitches. "Looks better now than it did."

"I know. Jack showed me when he FaceTimed me. You hadn't woken up yet. You nearly had it there, girl." The smile all but disappeared from his face.

"He was aiming for my head. I turned at the last minute. So they tell me."

"Wasn't your time then, was it? You know as well as me that if a Spartan wants you dead, you usually die. I would have missed you, you are one of a kind. I don't know what I would have done with Jack if you hadn't come back. When you dropped that call, I had to keep him from running across the water." Ross was uncomfortable with this. She wasn't sure she would have acted the same if Jack had been in her spot. Maybe she would have. She certainly would have wanted to be next to him when he woke up. Jack appeared in the doorway carrying two cups of coffee. He handed one to Si.

"I let you two sleep in since you traveled yesterday, but we need to get some work done." Si said.

"Anything I can do to help?" Ross asked. Jack turned and smiled at her.

"Come on out, I'll show you what we've been doing." Jack showed her the grid pattern they were using to make sure they had covered the area they wanted to. Si steered the boat, while Jack monitored the system that was lowered into the water. "This basically reads the chips we placed in the boys. It has a thousand meter range in all directions. If we find one, it will ping the number back up to us, and we will know exactly which shark we found."

"Have you had any hits?"

"Not one." Jack said, not sounding disappointed.

"You've been doing this for a year and you haven't found anything? I'm surprised they have kept you out here." Research funding was very much based on results. Ross was curious as to how they were getting funding if they hadn't found anything.

"I wouldn't say we haven't found anything. After a few weeks of searching in vain, we were asked if we would send a camera down with the system. See what we could see. We have compiled a rather interesting list of fish species, some of them not previously known to inhabit these waters." Jack said, rather smugly.

"Seriously?" Ross's ears picked up. Though she was on a much needed leave of absence from work, Ross wasn't entirely comfortable with no work to do. There was the paper to write, maybe. The idea of making new fishy discoveries had her attention.

"We lower the equipment in the morning and then I go to the galley to monitor the camera. When a fish swims past, the camera automatically takes a still picture which is sent to our database. The lab back in Sydney has been rather pleased with the results."

"What kind of fish?" Jack took her down in the galley and showed her the chart he had made, complete with pictures of each species. There were simple tally marks next to each picture.

"This is impressive, Jack. A lot of work has gone into this." She knew the chart was for himself. The lab back in Sydney would want to make their own chart and it would probably be something more technical than tally marks.

"This is what has kept us entertained for all these months. No one has searched this ocean like this. We are literally scanning the entire ocean here. It's very labor intensive, but we are finding all kinds of stuff." Just then a grainy picture came up on the computer screen. It took Ross's eyes a minute to make sense of what she was seeing. It was a large eyeball. There was no color to the picture on the screen. "Is it that one?" She asked, pointing to a picture on the chart.

"No, that one." Jack corrected. "See, you can just make out the spiny dorsal fin there." Ross was suddenly overwhelmed by affection for this man. She looked at his strong jaw line, covered in stubbly hairs. The same face she had been looking at for over a week, day in and day out. Now she was finding out he had an inner scientist. He had even developed his own method for tracking the different species.

"I love you too." Ross said. The words were out of her mouth before she thought about it, and she was more than a little surprised to find she had actually said them out loud. For a moment, Ross thought she had gotten lucky and he hadn't heard her. He didn't react, but then he turned his head slowly to look at her.

"What?" Busted! Ross thought to herself.

"At the hospital, you said you loved me. I love you too." The sideways grin she loved looked directly at her.

"I didn't think you heard that."

"Why do you think I fainted?"

"Seriously?" The smile disappeared.

"Of course not." Jack wrapped an arm around her waist and pulled her close.

"So here we are. In love." Jack said.

"See, it sounds really strange when you say it like that." Jack decided to say it another way. Ross was once again reminded what a fantastic kisser Jack was when he wanted to be. Right now, he was giving it all he had. When they separated, Ross felt a little faint again.

"You okay?"

"Just need some fresh air." Ross stumbled back on deck.

# 42

Night fell on another day on the boat. Not able to sleep, Ross had gotten up to get some water and realized Si was still in the wheelhouse. Neither gentleman had said anything, but it hadn't escaped Ross's notice that one of them was always in the wheelhouse, which had a three hundred and sixty degree view. She had seen Si several times throughout the day scanning the horizon with binoculars. The fellas were quietly doing what they had promised. Guarding her.

Ross went to sit with Si who was enjoying a Scotch while driving a boat. She thought about saying something to him about drinking and driving, but decided against it. Ross said nothing but looked out the window. It was amazing. This far out in the water, it was hard to tell where the ocean ended and the stars began.

"Amazing." Ross said. She sat down next to Si who offered her his glass. She declined. Si grabbed her hand and held it. "How ya doing, girl?"

"All right. All things considered."

"You look good. Really. I didn't know what to expect." Whether it was the late hour or the scotch, Si was unusually fatherly and concerned. It wasn't the side of him he often showed. "You gave me a hellova scare. If it had been a lesser woman, I would have really been worried."

Si was a fan of Ross. Ross wasn't sure what she had done to deserve it, but she knew it was an honor bestowed to few.

"I was a bit worried there myself if I'm honest. I thought Ikan Hui was the most scared I had ever been. I was wrong."

'Hmm...Jack could hear how scared you were. Said it was in your voice."

"It got worse." Ross said, thinking to herself of that evening. When she had dropped the phone with Jack on the other end, it had really just been the beginning. "He followed us through the boat. Lillian, the other scientist I was found with, thought she had a hiding spot. She hid me and then stayed where the Spartan could see her, thinking that if he found her, he wouldn't go looking for me. They knew how many of us there were though."

"You must have been terrified, Love." Si said, squeezing her hand.

"Si."

"Hmm."

"I went wherever it was you went. When you weren't dead, but not really alive either." Si lowered his scotch glass and looked Ross in the eye. He had revealed his otherworldly experience when he had been slightly concussed. Si had not spoken of it since. Jack didn't even know, but the previous year when they had barely escaped the resort, Si had almost joined Davy Jones in his locker. His deceased wife Bev had been there and talked him out of staying. As usual, Bev had won.

"Was Bev there?" Si had not wanted to come back to the land of the living. Having found where Bev had gone when she left him, he had wanted to stay there.

"No. Nils was."

"Nils? Who the bloody hell is Nils?"

"He was the one who organized the trip. Another

scientist. He was sitting in my lab back in the states. The lab was beautiful. Pristine. No one around to bother me. Even the trash cans were empty."

"Sounds like you enjoyed being there."

"I did, not sure I would have wanted to stay there forever though."

"What made you come back?"

"I had to tell them it was a Spartan. I knew I was the only one who knew. I saw his eyes just before. I had to tell them."

"Do you regret it?" Si was serious. He had wanted nothing more than to stay floating there in the water with Bev. He hadn't regretted his decision yet, but he asked himself the question almost every day.

"No. No I don't. The relief in Jack's eyes when I woke up. The relief in Sam's voice when I called. My mother's had a hell of a year as well. Last thing she needed was me leaving." Si nodded.

"He loves you, you know that don't you?" Ross looked out at the ocean and let out a deep breath.

"Yeah, I know." Ross said, sadly. Si laughed.

"Don't sound so happy about it." Si said.

"I don't know what to do with it, Si. I'm not normal when it comes to that sort of thing. I want Jack to stay.

I want to be around him all the time, but then I don't want to hurt him. Or for him to find out what a weirdo I really am and have him leave." Si laughed. Si laughed out loud. Si laughed to the point he was crying. Ross sat in horor.

"Oh dear. That's love." Si said, wiping away the tears. "That's what love is Ross."

"Fear? I've watched several romantic comedies and none of them showed fear like this."

"Well they wouldn't. No one would want to watch the truth. When I was dating Bev, things were getting serious. I knew she was the one, I was scared to death. How could you love another person that much? What was I gonna do if she didn't love me? I could deal with her not loving me as much as I loved her, but if she didn't love me at all….I would have been crushed." Ross paid attention. Si was hitting some key points. "When we were out on a date, I was Mr. Charming, cleaned up, smelled nice, wore a suit and tie. I was scared to death she was going to find out I was really a slob who worked in overalls and smelled of fish all the time. How could a woman like that ever love a scrubber like me?"

"But she did."

"Said she did.  Every morning and every night for twenty-five years.  We had been married a few years, Jack had been born, and she said she had been worried as well once we were engaged.  She was afraid I was going to see her first thing in the morning, hair all a mess, morning breath and be horrified."

"And you weren't?"

"Loved it too.  She was adorable first thing in the morning.  Breath was pretty bad, but as soon as she brushed her teeth it was fine."  Ross smiled.

"How will I know if Jack is my Si?"

"That's where the leap of faith comes into it, darlin."

"See, I'm not good at that. I like proof."

"Listen here girl.  In the short time I've known you, you have escaped death twice.  Compared to that, what is the worst that can happen?" Si had a point.  Pain of the heart was a different pain, but she had survived worse.

As if summoned by his name, a sleepy Jack emerged from below.

"What's going on?"

"Just having a chat." Si said.

"Can't you sleep?" Jack asked Ross.

"No, time change I think."

"Come out here and let me show you something." Jack was wearing nothing but a pair of shorts. He took her hand and led her out to the deck. "Look over the side."

"This is a prank isn't it?" Ross said, holding back. Jack rolled his eyes.

"I'll look over with you." They both leaned over the side and looked.

"Jesus, what the hell is that?" Ross immediately said. Jack was smiling ear to ear.

"Bioluminescence."

"It's amazing."

"Tiny little creatures in the water. They get turned up when the water is disturbed and light up like this." Where the boat was going through the water, a gentle blue glow was coming up in the water. "You can see when fish jump at night because the water will light up in the spot they come out and go back in the water."

"Could you see them with a microscope? Do you have a microscope?"

"I have an old one I keep for my own amusement. We'll take a water sample tomorrow and you can try and find them."

"I can't believe there is something so amazing and

mother nature came up with it." Ross was still leaning over the side. She looked up and found Jack staring at her, looking surprisingly serious. The moon was hanging high in the sky and reflecting off the water. "What's the matter?" Ross asked.

"Just thinking of the night we first met. I took you to the aquarium, you had much the same look on your face." Jack took her hand and pulled her into him. "It feels really good to have you here." He said into her ear. Ross let herself relax into his warmth. He smelled like sleep, his skin warm. Ross nuzzled into his neck.

"It's good to be here." It was true. She had thought it would be strange being on a boat with two men, but it wasn't. It even felt comfortable.

"I never want to find myself in the situation I was in at that hospital." Jack said.

"Hopefully, you'll never have to. I am going to try really hard to not get shot again. I promise."

"Ross, I want to be next to you no matter where life takes you. I don't ever want to be that far away from you again. Marry me?" Ross shot backwards out of his arms, her eyes wide.

"What?"

"Marry me? Please." Jack repeated, keeping his voice

calm so as not to frighten her further. The panic was clear in her eyes. "Ross, you are the most incredible woman. When I'm with you it's like I feel complete, and all I know is after the last week, I never want to let you go." For a while Ross said nothing. Jack was keeping a sharp eye on her. He was pretty sure she was smart enough to not jump out of the boat, but she was pretty freaked at the moment.

"Jack...."

"I can't help it, Ross. I keep trying to imagine my life without you, and I just don't like what I see."

"But you don't want me."

"What?" It was Jack's turn to be confused.

"You are too good for a woman like me, you want some New Zealand supermodel named Ivy who is six feet tall and perfect."

"What the hell are you talking about?"

"You may think you want me right now. We've been through a lot together, we obviously have feelings for one another, but eventually you are going to find Ivy and then you are going to look at me and look at her, and it will all be over." Jack leaned against the boat and crossed his arms over his chest, listening. "So I think it's best if we do what it is we are doing now, so there are no strings attached when that time comes."

"So you are saying, let's not get married because I will eventually find my true love, Ivy. A supermodel from New Zealand, and will want to run off with her?" Ross thought about it for a moment. She could picture Ivy in her head. Long, lean and perfect.

"Yeah."

"Ross, completely ignoring how insulting this is...my first wife was an Ivy. Super hot, still is. I've seen puddles with more depth. I don't know how you've gotten this far in life without knowing how attractive you are, but one of the reasons you are so attractive is how extremely intelligent you are. Now why in the world would I leave you for an Ivy when I could have both brains and looks?"

"I don't know." Ross shrugged.

"I know you don't know. Ross, I love you. I love you in a way that I don't think I have ever loved anyone or anything. For God's sake woman, I'm willing to leave the water for ya." Jack held out his hand and approached slowly. Ross stayed where she was, though the wide-eyed expression stayed. "I don't even care where we live anymore. It's true I hope you love the boat and we can stay here for a while, but if you want to go back to Boston, I'm all for it." Ross couldn't ignore the fact that the man loved her. He was saying it, all the evidence was there. She just couldn't figure out why. "I don't even care if we actually get married. We can just stay engaged if that would make it easier for you." Ross locked eyes with him.

"Really?"

"Yeah, if that's what you want."

"Okay. I can do that." It was Jack's turn to look shocked.

"Is that a yes?"

"Yes." Jack reached in his pocket and pulled out a ring box, got down on one knee, and opened it. Taking the ring out of the box, he put it on Ross's finger.

"Why didn't you do this to begin with?" Ross asked. "You've got a ring in the pocket of your pajamas?"

"I wasn't sure how you would react. I've been carrying around in my pocket since I left a week ago. I didn't want to lead with it, and I didn't want you to throw the ring into the water. It was my mother's." There was a sharp intake of air.

"JACK." Ross jumped back again like she was trying to run from her hand. Jack smiled.

"She would be thrilled for you to have it."

"Does Si know I have it?"

"He gave it with his blessing." Ross didn't think until later that Jack's first wife Marta didn't have the ring. She had never met the woman, but from what Ross had heard, Marta didn't seem like the type to give back a family heirloom. Turned out Bev hadn't liked Marta very much. Si hadn't offered the ring and Jack had known better than to ask. Ross was something she never thought she would be, a fiance.

Jack approached slowly, so as not to make her jump. He managed to get his arms around her, and Ross relaxed and returned the embrace. "I love you babe." Jack said.

"I love you too." It felt really strange to say it. Ross thought. But not entirely in a bad way.

"What's the answer? Can I open the booze?" Si asked, from the wheel house.

"Open her up. She said yes." Jack said.

"Thank god for that." Si said, disappearing into the ship.

"Thank god for that." Jack tucked his hand behind Ross's head and brought it towards him. They stood out there kissing until Si came back with the drinks.

# 43

Ross had FaceTimed her Mom to let her know she was engaged. Her mother took the phone over so that she could tell her Dad who was pleased. He liked Jack. "Maybe he can keep you out of trouble." Her father had said, his speech still slightly slurred from the stroke. Her mother instantly started talking about grandchildren. Leaving her mother to go call the rest of the eastern seaboard, Ross immediately Facetimed Sam. She placed the hand with the ring against her face.

"Hey doll. How's living on a boat with two guys going?" To Ross's disappointment, Sam wasn't looking at her. She was changing Ruby.

"So far so good. It's actually interesting. I'm not as cramped as I thought I would be." Ross said, moving her hand around so the diamond would sparkle.

"So you think you are going to....is that a FUCKING RING?" Sam said, finally looking up. Ross smiled.

"What happened to not cussing?"

"Is that a FUDGING RING?"

"Maybe."

"ROSS! Did he really ask you?" Ross felt like a dumb teenager, but she was loving it.

"He did. Said he wanted to be legally allowed to sit next to my hospital bed."

"That's kind of weird and romantic all at the same time. Fits the two of you though. I can't believe this Ross. This is huge. Have you picked a date yet? I'm going to assume I'm the matron of honor. I've waited a long time for this."

"We have agreed to just be engaged for a while." Ross said, trying to calm her down. Sam smiled.

"You flipped your shit didn't you?"

"Almost ran off the boat."

"How did Jack keep you from going overboard? That would have been the second coast guard trip this month."

"He didn't give me the ring until I had calmed down, he was worried I would throw it into the ocean."

"He isn't wrong."

"It's his mother's ring Sam."

"DAAAAAMN. Is Si okay with that?"

"It was given with his blessing."

"Ross, I don't know how you did it, but those men both love you."

"I'm not sure how it happened either."

"Maybe you have just been dating in the wrong country. Before you actually marry Jack, you should probably go to Australia. You might be hot shit over there."

"I think I've found my Aussie. He sat next to my bed and gave me his blood."

"You're right. He's probably the best one anyway. I can't imagine there being a hotter one. Ross, you have a hot husband."

"He's not my husband. He's my fiance."

"Either way, he's hot and he's yours. Did you ever think you would be able to say that?"

"No, I thought if it ever happened, he would be average looking. Really smart, and average looking."

"Oh honey, I wish I could hug you. I'm glad you're there, you look really well, but I wish I could hug you. It's a bitchin ring too."

"It is. Beverly had good taste." Ross and Sam signed

off. It was late in the morning. Jack and Si were up in the wheelhouse toasting one another. Jack came downstairs looking rather drunk.

"Hello my lovely fiance. How are you?" He said, pulling Ross to her feet.

"Feeling dumb and in love."

"You couldn't be dumb if you tried, love." He kissed her and then picked her up and carried her to his room.

The following days were some of the best Ross could remember. She was more relaxed than she could ever remember being. A few years ago, if you had told Ross she would be happy and content on a boat in the middle of nowhere, with nothing to research, no contact with her lab, no immediate plans, and a hot Australian fiance, she would have laughed. But she was content. More settled than she could ever remember being. With Si steering the boat and Jack operating the equipment, Ross spent her days counting fish, and enjoying every moment of it.

"Hot damn." Ross said. She turned around and made another tally mark.

"What did you find?"

"Another Coelacanth." Ross said. "Sydney is going

to love that."

"Who's he when he's at home?" Si said.

"They are an endangered species. We have now seen three of them. Someone is going to find this very interesting."

After a month, Ross sat down and looked at the data from the arctic trip. She hadn't touched it since she got on the boat. Ross hadn't decided whether she was going to write the paper yet, but since everything before the attack had turned into a blur, she thought she should at least see if there was anything to write about. It was late at night when she did it. Ross wasn't sure why, but she had been thinking about the trip more and more and what Nils had told her in her dream before she woke up. Ross knew the information would be useful, and before all of this, she would have argued vehemently that it should be published at all costs.

Looking it over, the data was all there. Lillian had done a wonderful job on her end, even making notes. It would be no trouble to write up the data without her help. That being said, if the Spartans and whoever had hired them had forgotten about her, she didn't want to remind them she was still around.

"Couldn't sleep?" Jack said, from the door of the

kitchen. Ross slowly lowered the top of the laptop.

"No, my phone keeps buzzing. Mom has been sending me wedding dresses again. I keep telling her about the time change, but frankly, I don't think she cares." Ross may have had the Ph.D., but Jack wasn't dumb. He recognized the thumb drive sticking out of the computer as the one Lillian had given Ross.

"Thinking about writing the paper?" Ross was both annoyed and relieved that he wasn't fooled.

"Only just. Hate to kick up the water if there isn't a need to."

"Is there a need to protect the place?" That was the thought that kept turning over in Ross's mind. Ross had the data to show what was happening. As far as she knew, she was the only person with such data.

"In a word...yeah. They are drilling. Not only does it seem unfair, it's destroying the unknown. Whatever is up there has been frozen in ice for millions of years. Millions. Humans have never seen it. Some of it may be good, some of it may be bad. Either way, I think we need to know about it before destroying it all for a few more gallons of oil." Ross said. Jack shrugged.

"Sounds like you have a paper to write."

"We haven't heard if there has been any progress on

the case yet. Seems stupid to put a target on my back again."

"So you write the paper. No one knows you are writing it. Say you finish the paper. Can't you just send it to whoever this Nils guy was working for? Do you have to publish it under your name?" Ross wanted to yell 'yes'. Who ever heard of writing a breakthrough scientific paper and not putting your name on it?

"It would still be peer reviewed. They would have to know it was one of us....right?"

"Or Nils sent some of the info before it all went down. It may piss them off, but it doesn't point the finger directly at you."

"Lillian said she kept asking herself if this work was worth dying for. I think I am trying to figure out if it's worth the risk."

"Did Darwin know the importance of what he was writing when he wrote *Origin of Species*?"

"Um, yeah. By all accounts he knew it was going to send shock waves. His own wife didn't want him to publish."

"Okay, bad example. My point is if you write the paper, the area gets protection and something miraculous is found, then it will all be worth it. You aren't going to know that though if they bulldoze the place before anyone gets a look."

"You're pretty smart for a salty sea dog." Ross said.

"Not just a pretty face." Jack kissed her on the head and went back to bed. Ross wrote two pages and made some notes before she joined him. She would write it and then see if it was worth anything.

The evenings on the boat were her favorite. Si and Jack would pull everything on the boat and secure it and then they would come down for dinner. Ross usually cooked, but not always. Si was pretty good in the kitchen as well. The three of them would eat while they watched the news. A reminder that there was a world out there. A world Ross was surprised she didn't miss. Okay, she wasn't all that surprised she didn't miss it, but she thought she would miss it more than she did.

Ross was just putting the plates on the table when Jack and Si came stomping down the stairs. "The weather is moving in. Might be a rough night." Si was saying.

"Nothing much showing up on the radar." Jack said.

"Don't care what the radar says. The seas are rough, there's a storm out there somewhere." Si answered.

"I'll go back up after dinner and double check everything." Jack said, knowing better than to question Si and the sea.

They were eating in silence and watching the news when Lillian's picture appeared on TV.

"Turn it up, it's Lillian." Ross said. She at first was pleased to see Lillian even though it was an old photo probably from ten years ago. Ross was hoping it was something to do with the case. Maybe it was over at last.

"Who's Lillian?" Si asked. Jack was answering him but stopped. Lillian's picture was replaced by a picture of a house with a blue gate.

*"Dr. Lillian Petrov and her father were found struggling to breathe in a park near Cambridge this morning. Passersby tried to assist but the pair died shortly after arriving at the hospital."*

Ross inhaled sharply.

*"Hospital staff said they immediately alerted the authorities as it was clear both patients had come in contact with a toxin or poison. The good samaritans that had assisted them in the park also fell ill shortly after coming into contact, and are being treated at local hospitals. In addition, a police officer who was first on the scene is being treated for*

*milder but similar symptoms. At this time, they are expected to make a full recovery. After a brief search of Dr. Lillian Petrov's house, a woman assumed to be her mother was found dead in the kitchen. She too had been exposed to a similar toxin or poison. As we speak, the park and the house in Cambridge have been sectioned off while authorities try to determine the source. "* The camera showed a park with a huge white tent in the middle of it and people in white suits searching the area. *"Traces of Novichok have been found on the surface of the garden gate and on the door handle going into the house. Dr. Petrov had recently returned home to recover after surviving a near lethal attack on the research vessel 'The Hunter'. It is not clear at this time if the two incidents are related. Dr. Petrov was teaching at the University and has lived in the United Kingdom for some years coming to study from Russia, she had made Cambridge her home. In other news..."* Jack turned off the TV.

They sat there in stunned silence for a moment.

"I'm going to get some air." Ross said, and she headed up to the deck. Jack gave her a moment to herself.

"She was on the boat with Ross?" Si asked. Jack nodded.

"Yeah, she had just been reunited with her parents after not having seen them for ten years."

"Poor girl." Si said, with a great amount of sympathy.

The sun was setting on the horizon and the wind was blowing strongly out of the north, which Ross was glad about because she knew if the guys heard her doing the ugly cry, they would come up and try to make her feel better, and she didn't want to feel better. Ross let the tears fall. She had just about cried herself out when Jack came up behind her. He said nothing, which Ross appreciated. There was nothing to say. Jack simply folded her into him and let her cry into his shoulder for a bit.

"That poor woman had just found happiness, and they took it from her." Ross finally said, sounding more angry than sad. "Her wounds hadn't healed from the last time they tried to kill her." She added. Jack still said nothing, but his jaw was clenched, he stared out at the horizon.

"I'm glad she got to see her parents. It would have been more tragic if they had managed to kill her before she had a chance to see them again." Jack said.

"She just seemed so happy, so hopeful, knowing her parents were going to be there waiting for her when she got home. It was all so short lived."

"Ross, you have to write that paper now." Jack said, quietly. Ross looked at him. She nodded in response.

"You have Lillian's legacy, and Nils. If you don't publish that paper in time for it to be of any use to anyone, then the bastards win. Right now you can still give them a voice, and I think you have to do that. We will deal with whatever happens."

"Life is so short, isn't it?" This was something Ross had been thinking about a lot since being shot. "I don't want to be scared anymore, when I stop and think about it, I have been worried most of my life. Stupid things mainly, like why I feel the need to spurt out scientific facts when the room goes strangely quiet."

"Why you can't stop correcting someone when they are wrong." Jack offered.

"How are you going to learn if I don't correct you? I'm not going to waste time worrying anymore. I mean look at you. You have been everything to me since I woke up in that hospital and I was still nervous as hell coming out here with you. And why?"

"You were scared stiff when I proposed."

"I still think you are going to come to your senses about that."

"I might.  In fifty years or so."

"I'm not going to waste any more energy on worrying so much.  What will be will be."

"Does that mean you are actually going to marry me?"

"Abso-damn-lutely."